SIMPSONS
COMICS
CHAOS

HARPER

NEW YORK · LONDON · TORONTO · SYDNEY

SIMPSONS COMICS CHAOS

Simpsons Comics #112, 113, 114, 115,
and Simpsons Summer Shindig #6

Copyright © 2015 by
Bongo Entertainment, Inc. All rights reserved.
No part of this book may be used or reproduced in any manner whatsoever
without written permission except in the case of brief quotations
embodied in critical articles and reviews. For information address
HarperCollins Publishers,
195 Broadway, New York, New York 10007.

FIRST EDITION

ISBN 978-0-06-241947-7

15 16 17 18 19 TC 10 9 8 7 6 5 4 3 2 1

Publisher: Matt Groening
Creative Director: Nathan Kane
Managing Editor: Terry Delegeane
Director of Operations: Robert Zaugh
Art Director: Jason Ho
Art Director Special Projects: Serban Cristescu
Assistant Art Director: Mike Rote
Production Manager: Christopher Ungar
Assistant Editor: Karen Bates
Production: Art Villanueva
Administration: Ruth Waytz
Legal Guardian: Susan A. Grode

Printed by TC Transcontinental, Beauceville, QC, Canada. 11/23/2015

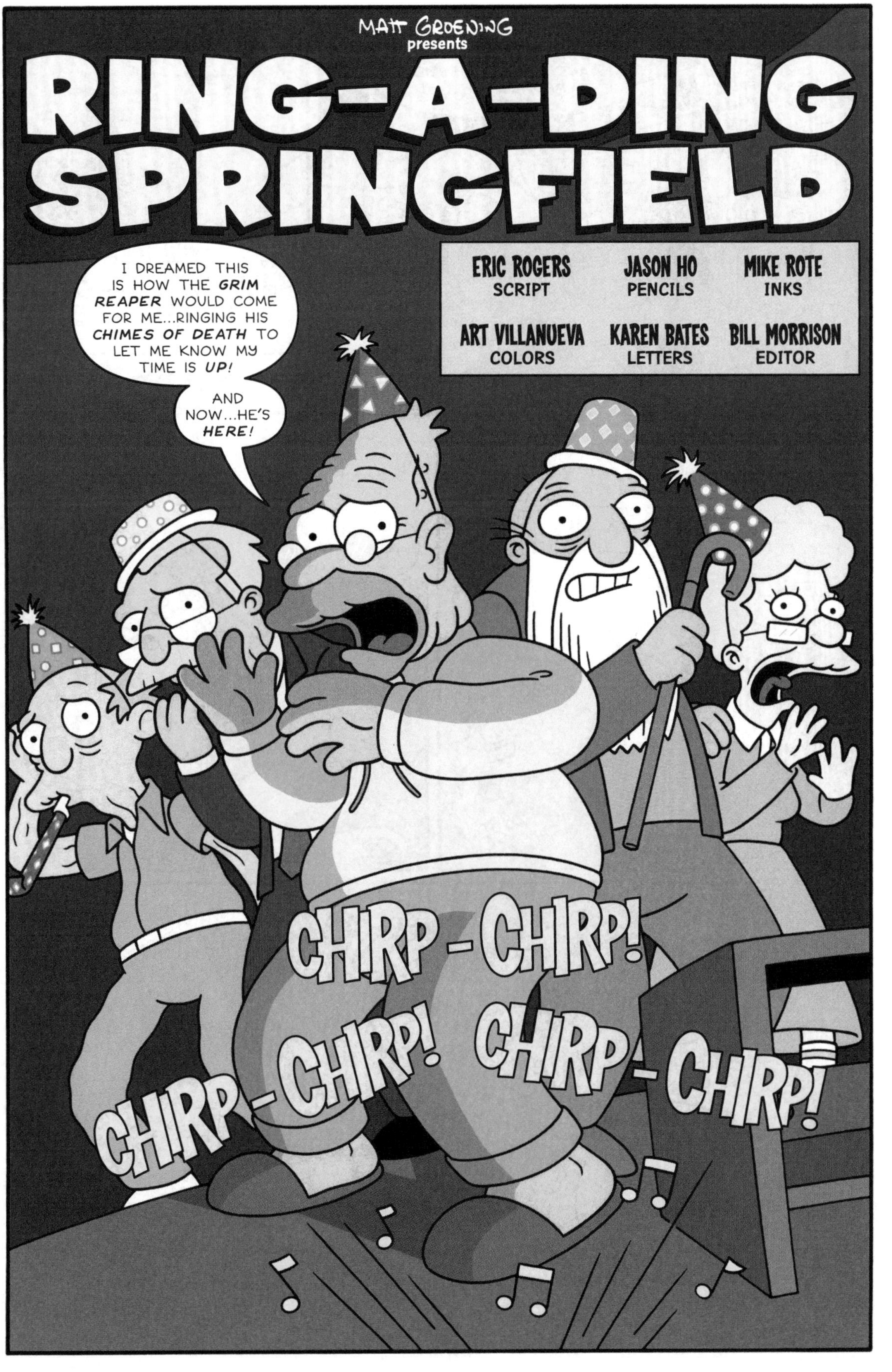
MATT GROENING presents
RING-A-DING SPRINGFIELD
ERIC ROGERS SCRIPT
JASON HO PENCILS
MIKE ROTE INKS
ART VILLANUEVA COLORS
KAREN BATES LETTERS
BILL MORRISON EDITOR
I DREAMED THIS IS HOW THE GRIM REAPER WOULD COME FOR ME...RINGING HIS CHIMES OF DEATH TO LET ME KNOW MY TIME IS UP!
AND NOW...HE'S HERE!
CHIRP-CHIRP!
CHIRP-CHIRP! CHIRP-CHIRP!

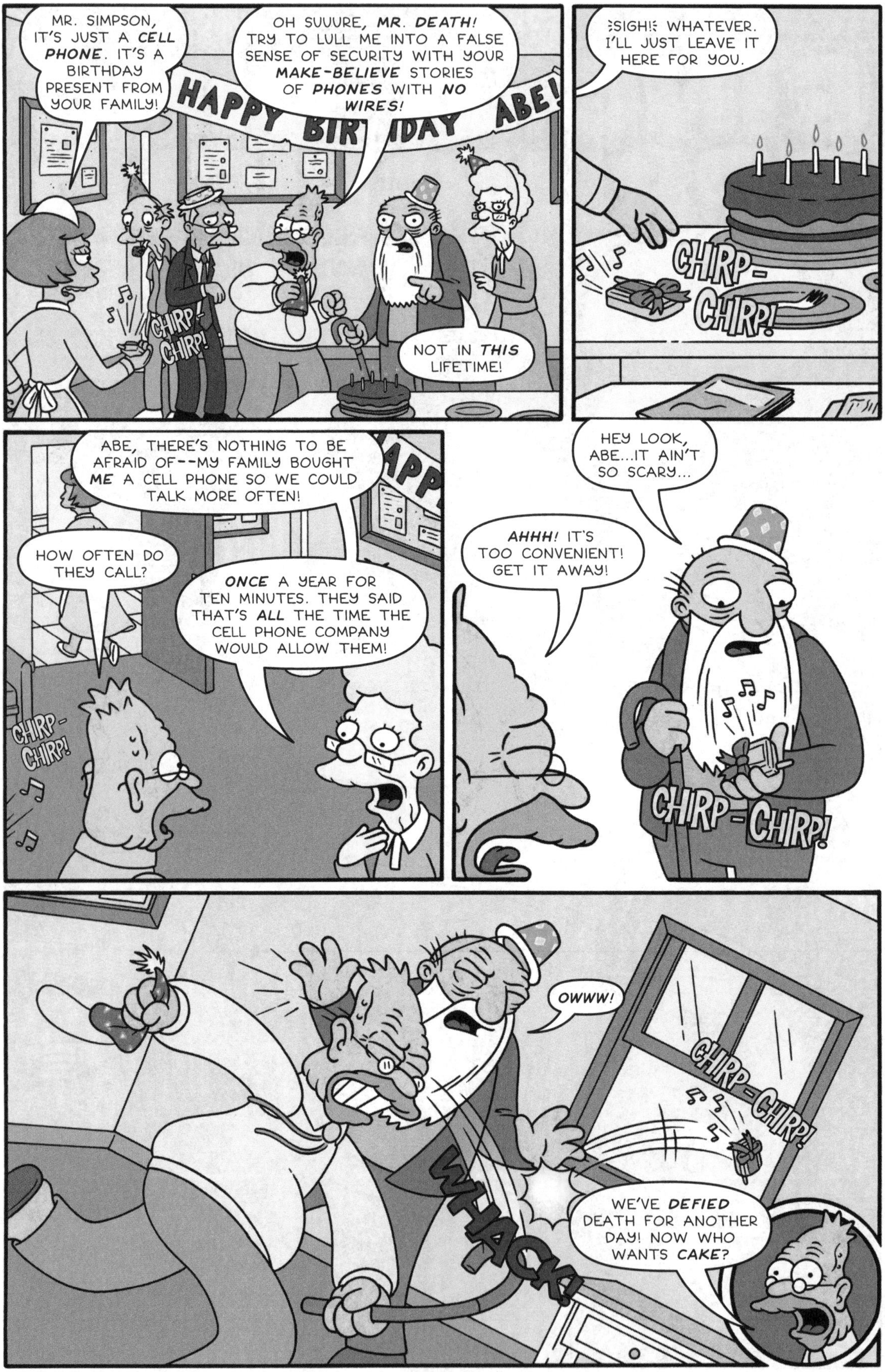
MR. SIMPSON, IT'S JUST A CELL PHONE. IT'S A BIRTHDAY PRESENT FROM YOUR FAMILY!
OH SUUURE, MR. DEATH! TRY TO LULL ME INTO A FALSE SENSE OF SECURITY WITH YOUR MAKE-BELIEVE STORIES OF PHONES WITH NO WIRES!
HAPPY BIRTHDAY ABE!
CHIRP-CHIRP!
NOT IN THIS LIFETIME!
SIGH! WHATEVER. I'LL JUST LEAVE IT HERE FOR YOU.
CHIRP-CHIRP!
ABE, THERE'S NOTHING TO BE AFRAID OF--MY FAMILY BOUGHT ME A CELL PHONE SO WE COULD TALK MORE OFTEN!
HOW OFTEN DO THEY CALL?
ONCE A YEAR FOR TEN MINUTES. THEY SAID THAT'S ALL THE TIME THE CELL PHONE COMPANY WOULD ALLOW THEM!
CHIRP-CHIRP!
HEY LOOK, ABE...IT AIN'T SO SCARY...
AHHH! IT'S TOO CONVENIENT! GET IT AWAY!
CHIRP-CHIRP!
OWWW!
CHIRP-CHIRP!
WHACK!
WE'VE DEFIED DEATH FOR ANOTHER DAY! NOW WHO WANTS CAKE?

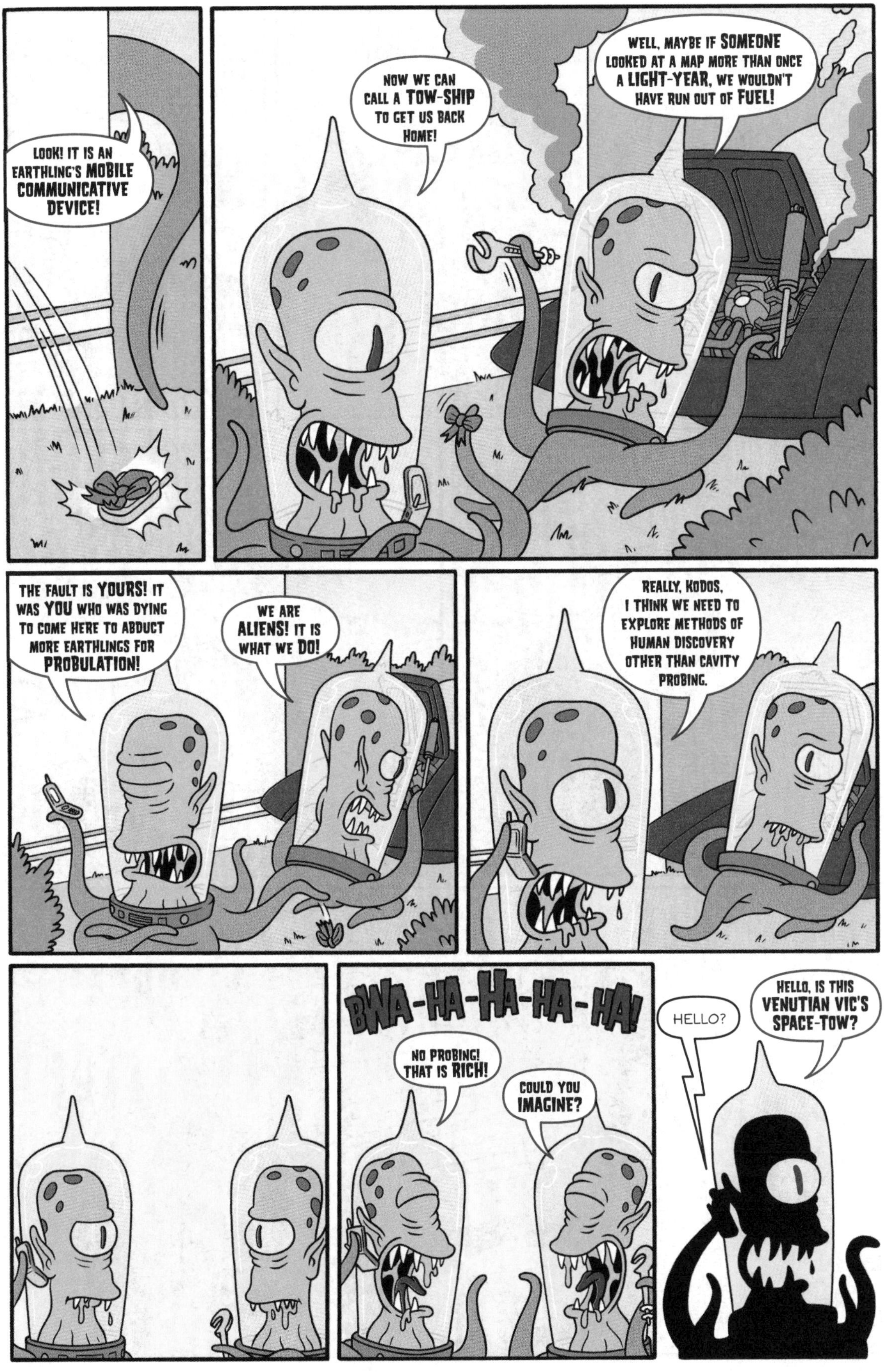
LOOK! IT IS AN EARTHLING'S MOBILE COMMUNICATIVE DEVICE!
NOW WE CAN CALL A TOW-SHIP TO GET US BACK HOME!
WELL, MAYBE IF SOMEONE LOOKED AT A MAP MORE THAN ONCE A LIGHT-YEAR, WE WOULDN'T HAVE RUN OUT OF FUEL!
THE FAULT IS YOURS! IT WAS YOU WHO WAS DYING TO COME HERE TO ABDUCT MORE EARTHLINGS FOR PROBULATION!
WE ARE ALIENS! IT IS WHAT WE DO!
REALLY, KODOS, I THINK WE NEED TO EXPLORE METHODS OF HUMAN DISCOVERY OTHER THAN CAVITY PROBING.
BWA-HA-HA-HA-HA!
NO PROBING! THAT IS RICH!
COULD YOU IMAGINE?
HELLO?
HELLO, IS THIS VENUTIAN VIC'S SPACE-TOW?

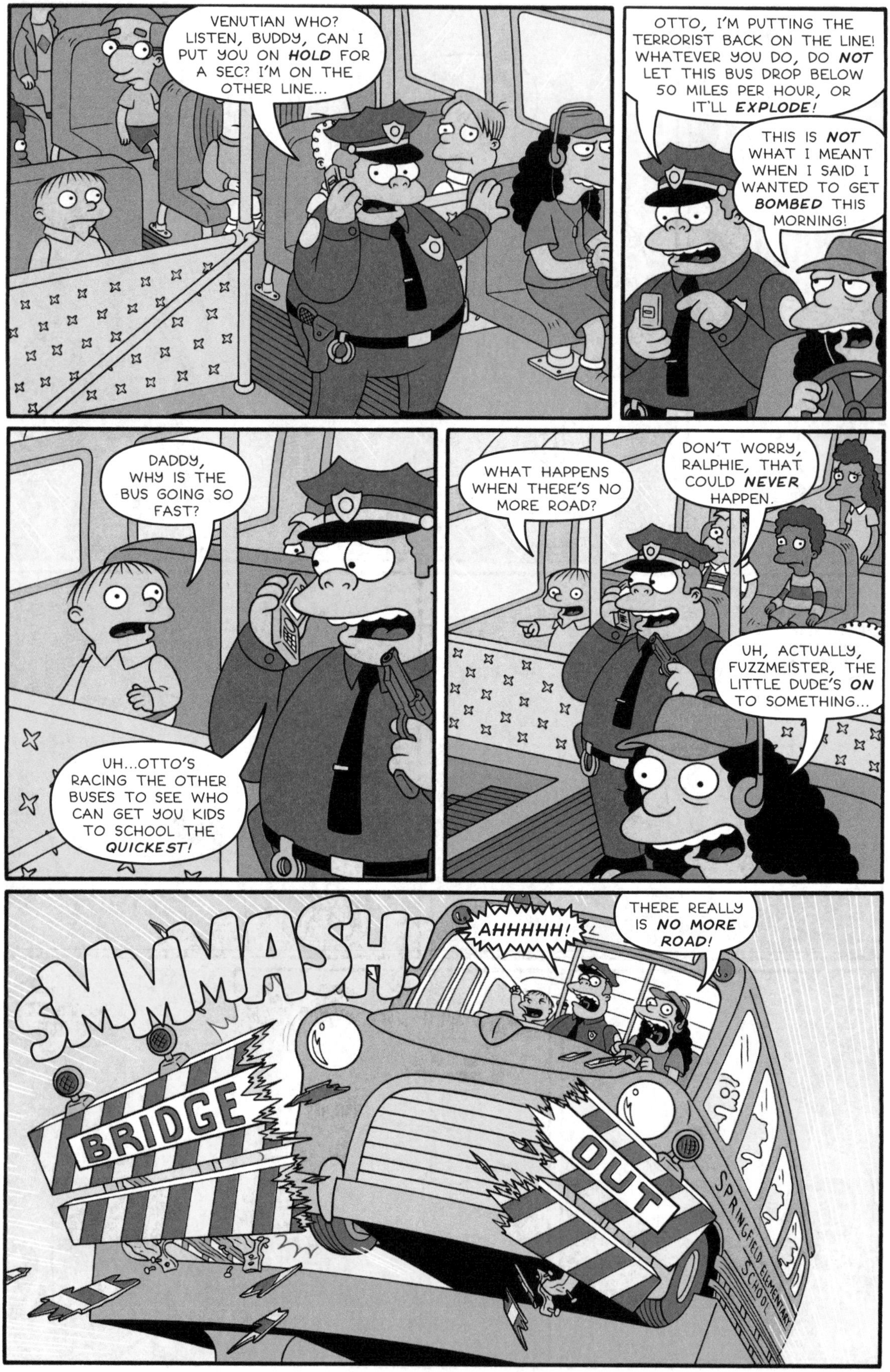
VENUTIAN WHO? LISTEN, BUDDY, CAN I PUT YOU ON **HOLD** FOR A SEC? I'M ON THE OTHER LINE...
OTTO, I'M PUTTING THE TERRORIST BACK ON THE LINE! WHATEVER YOU DO, DO **NOT** LET THIS BUS DROP BELOW 50 MILES PER HOUR, OR IT'LL **EXPLODE**!
THIS IS **NOT** WHAT I MEANT WHEN I SAID I WANTED TO GET **BOMBED** THIS MORNING!
DADDY, WHY IS THE BUS GOING SO FAST?
UH...OTTO'S RACING THE OTHER BUSES TO SEE WHO CAN GET YOU KIDS TO SCHOOL THE **QUICKEST**!
WHAT HAPPENS WHEN THERE'S NO MORE ROAD?
DON'T WORRY, RALPHIE, THAT COULD **NEVER** HAPPEN.
UH, ACTUALLY, FUZZMEISTER, THE LITTLE DUDE'S **ON** TO SOMETHING...
SMMMASH!
AHHHHH!
THERE REALLY IS **NO MORE ROAD**!
BRIDGE
OUT
SPRINGFIELD ELEMENTARY SCHOOL

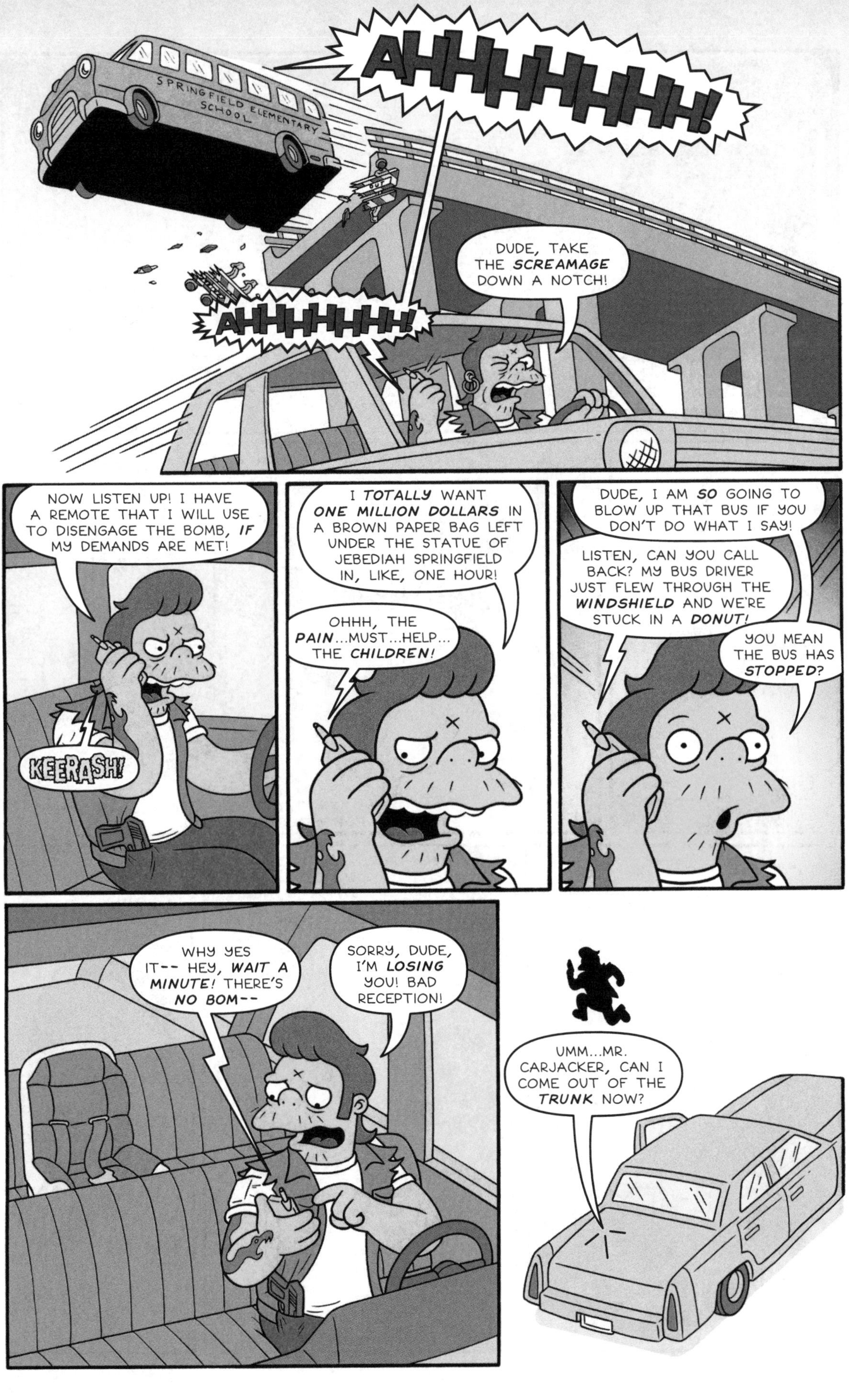
SPRINGFIELD ELEMENTARY SCHOOL
AHHHHHHHH!
DUDE, TAKE THE SCREAMAGE DOWN A NOTCH!
AHHHHHHHH!
NOW LISTEN UP! I HAVE A REMOTE THAT I WILL USE TO DISENGAGE THE BOMB, IF MY DEMANDS ARE MET!
KEERASH!
I TOTALLY WANT ONE MILLION DOLLARS IN A BROWN PAPER BAG LEFT UNDER THE STATUE OF JEBEDIAH SPRINGFIELD IN, LIKE, ONE HOUR!
OHHH, THE PAIN...MUST...HELP... THE CHILDREN!
DUDE, I AM SO GOING TO BLOW UP THAT BUS IF YOU DON'T DO WHAT I SAY!
LISTEN, CAN YOU CALL BACK? MY BUS DRIVER JUST FLEW THROUGH THE WINDSHIELD AND WE'RE STUCK IN A DONUT!
YOU MEAN THE BUS HAS STOPPED?
WHY YES IT-- HEY, WAIT A MINUTE! THERE'S NO BOM--
SORRY, DUDE, I'M LOSING YOU! BAD RECEPTION!
UMM...MR. CARJACKER, CAN I COME OUT OF THE TRUNK NOW?

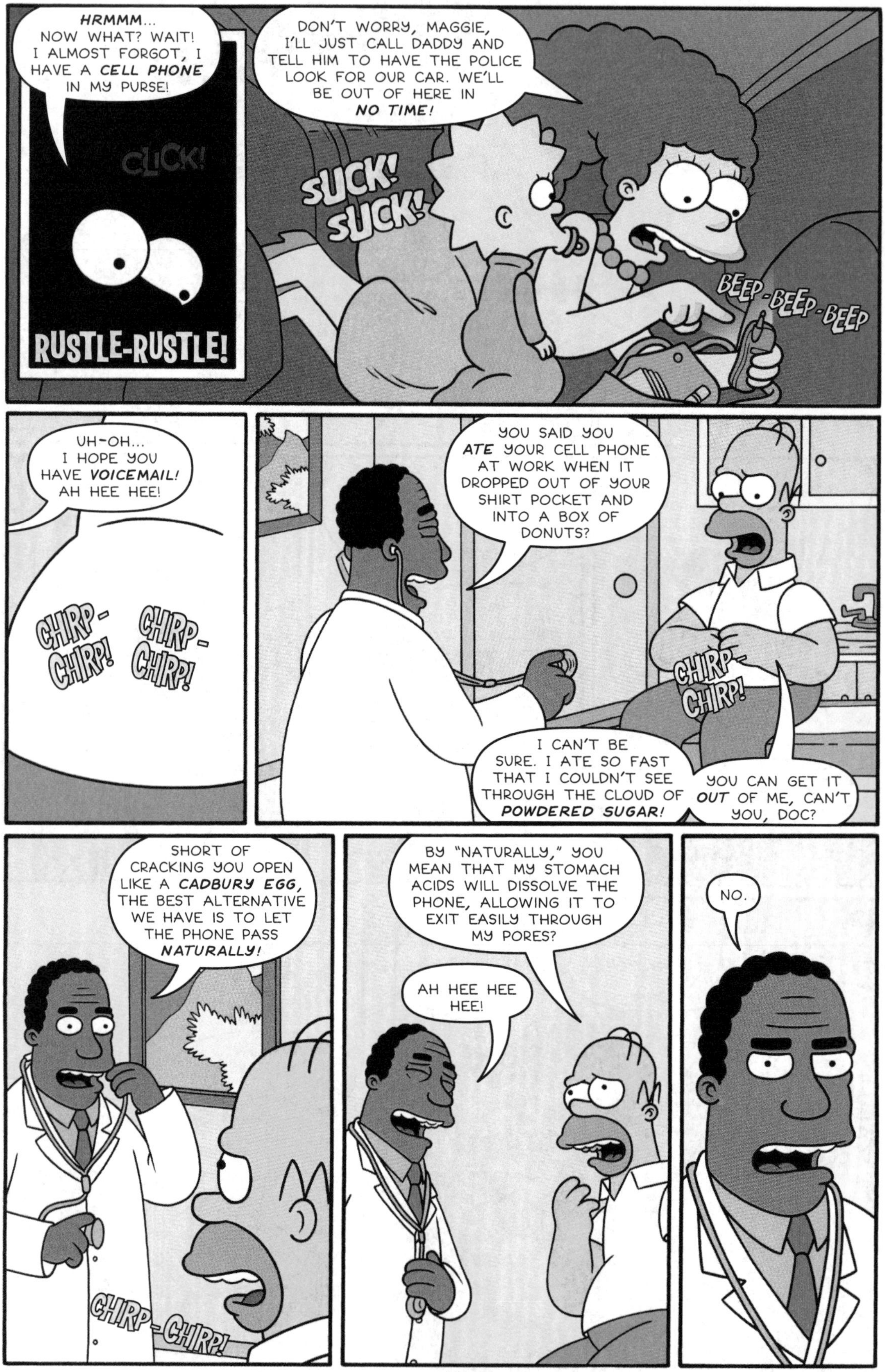
HRMMM... NOW WHAT? WAIT! I ALMOST FORGOT, I HAVE A CELL PHONE IN MY PURSE!
CLICK!
RUSTLE-RUSTLE!
DON'T WORRY, MAGGIE, I'LL JUST CALL DADDY AND TELL HIM TO HAVE THE POLICE LOOK FOR OUR CAR. WE'LL BE OUT OF HERE IN NO TIME!
SUCK! SUCK!
BEEP-BEEP-BEEP
UH-OH... I HOPE YOU HAVE VOICEMAIL! AH HEE HEE!
CHIRP-CHIRP! CHIRP-CHIRP!
YOU SAID YOU ATE YOUR CELL PHONE AT WORK WHEN IT DROPPED OUT OF YOUR SHIRT POCKET AND INTO A BOX OF DONUTS?
CHIRP-CHIRP!
I CAN'T BE SURE. I ATE SO FAST THAT I COULDN'T SEE THROUGH THE CLOUD OF POWDERED SUGAR!
YOU CAN GET IT OUT OF ME, CAN'T YOU, DOC?
SHORT OF CRACKING YOU OPEN LIKE A CADBURY EGG, THE BEST ALTERNATIVE WE HAVE IS TO LET THE PHONE PASS NATURALLY!
CHIRP-CHIRP!
BY "NATURALLY," YOU MEAN THAT MY STOMACH ACIDS WILL DISSOLVE THE PHONE, ALLOWING IT TO EXIT EASILY THROUGH MY PORES?
AH HEE HEE HEE!
NO.

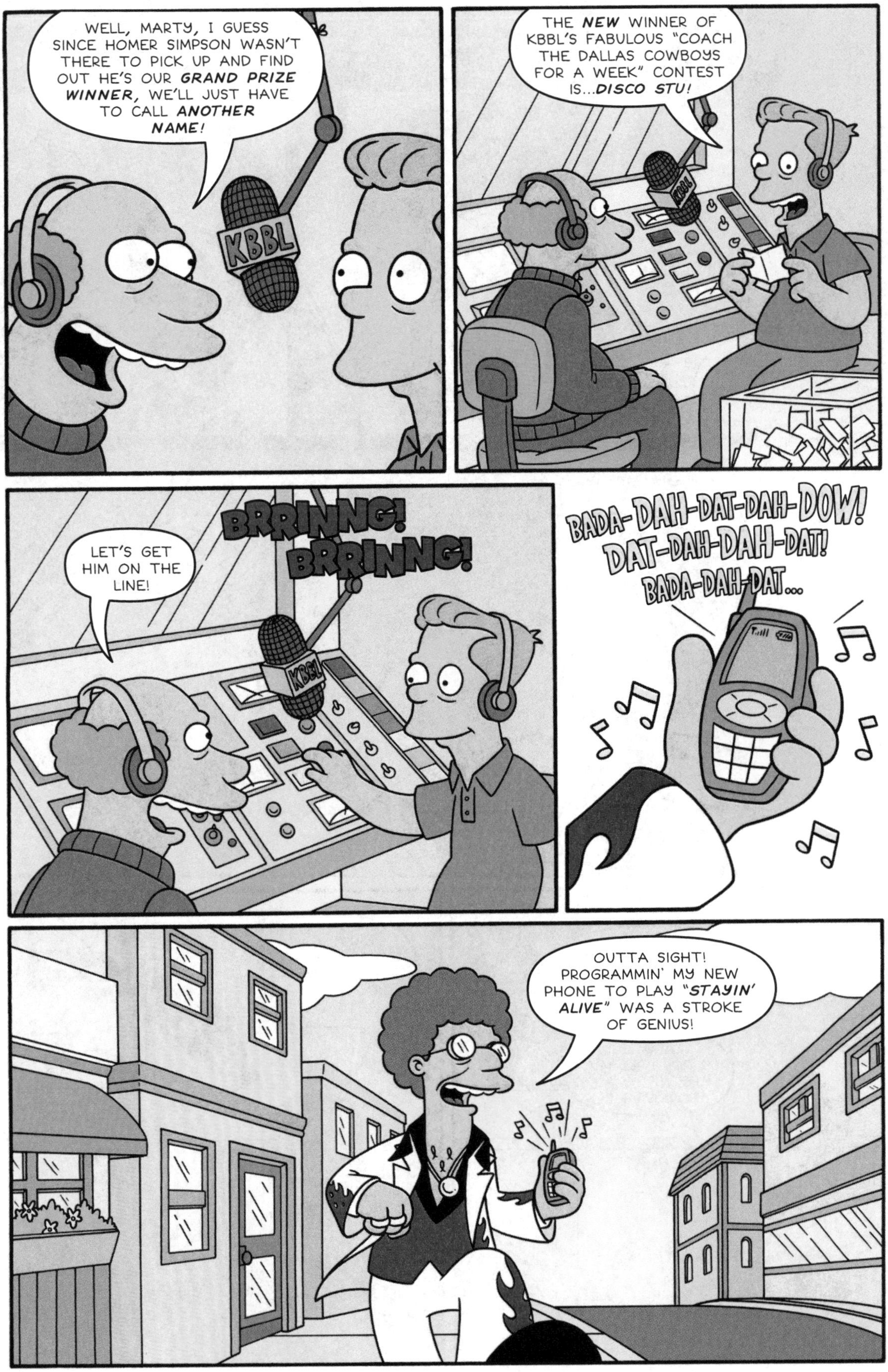
WELL, MARTY, I GUESS SINCE HOMER SIMPSON WASN'T THERE TO PICK UP AND FIND OUT HE'S OUR GRAND PRIZE WINNER, WE'LL JUST HAVE TO CALL ANOTHER NAME!
KBBL
THE NEW WINNER OF KBBL'S FABULOUS "COACH THE DALLAS COWBOYS FOR A WEEK" CONTEST IS...DISCO STU!
BRRINNG! BRRINNG!
LET'S GET HIM ON THE LINE!
KBBL
BADA-DAH-DAT-DAH-DOW! DAT-DAH-DAH-DAT! BADA-DAH-DAT...
OUTTA SIGHT! PROGRAMMIN' MY NEW PHONE TO PLAY "STAYIN' ALIVE" WAS A STROKE OF GENIUS!

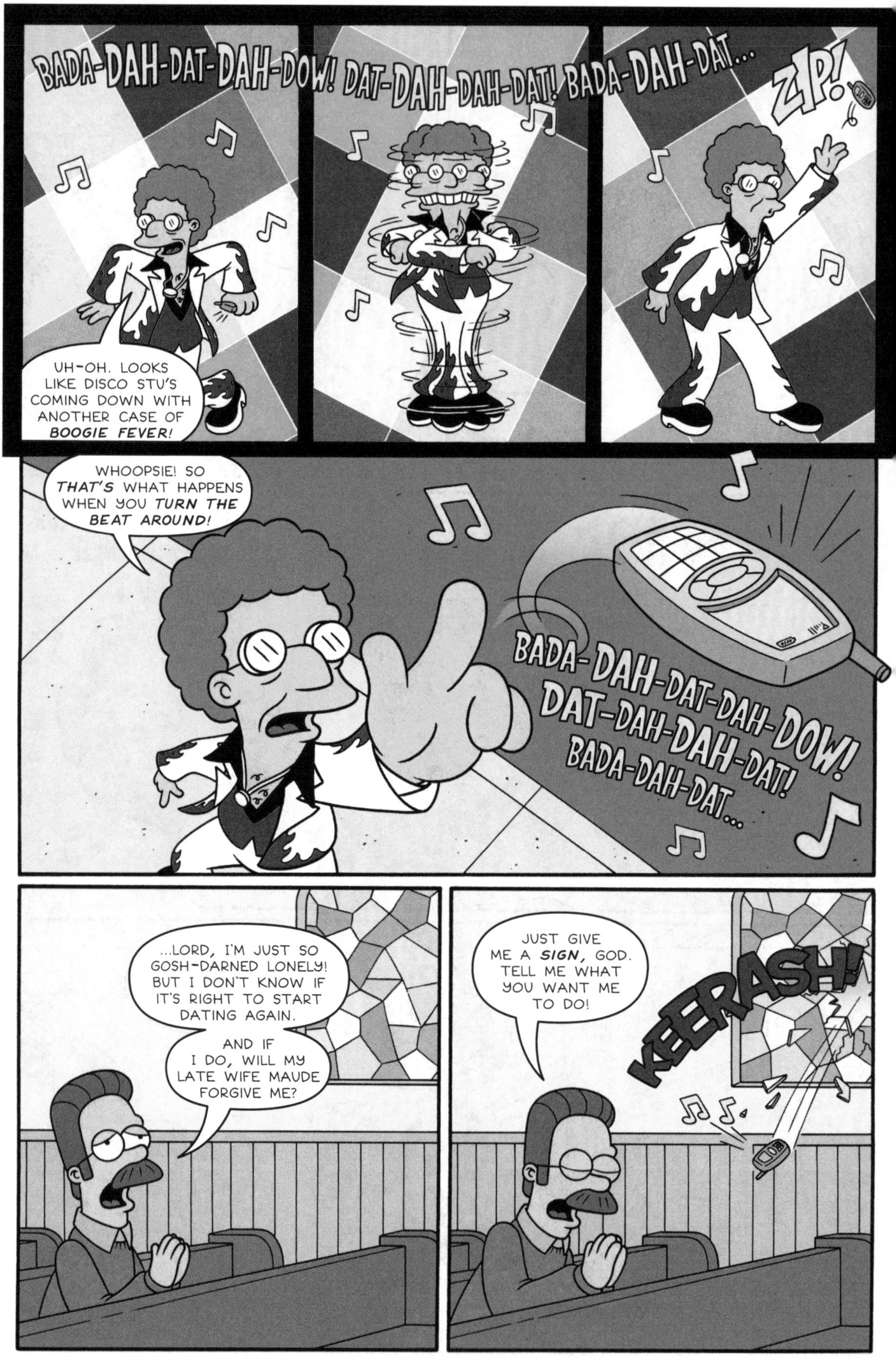

BADA-DAH-DAT-DAH-DOW! DAT-DAH-DAH-DAT! BADA-DAH-DAT...
UH-OH. LOOKS LIKE DISCO STU'S COMING DOWN WITH ANOTHER CASE OF BOOGIE FEVER!
ZIP!
WHOOPSIE! SO THAT'S WHAT HAPPENS WHEN YOU TURN THE BEAT AROUND!
BADA-DAH-DAT-DAH-DOW! DAT-DAH-DAH-DAT! BADA-DAH-DAT...
...LORD, I'M JUST SO GOSH-DARNED LONELY! BUT I DON'T KNOW IF IT'S RIGHT TO START DATING AGAIN.
AND IF I DO, WILL MY LATE WIFE MAUDE FORGIVE ME?
JUST GIVE ME A SIGN, GOD. TELL ME WHAT YOU WANT ME TO DO!
KEERASH!

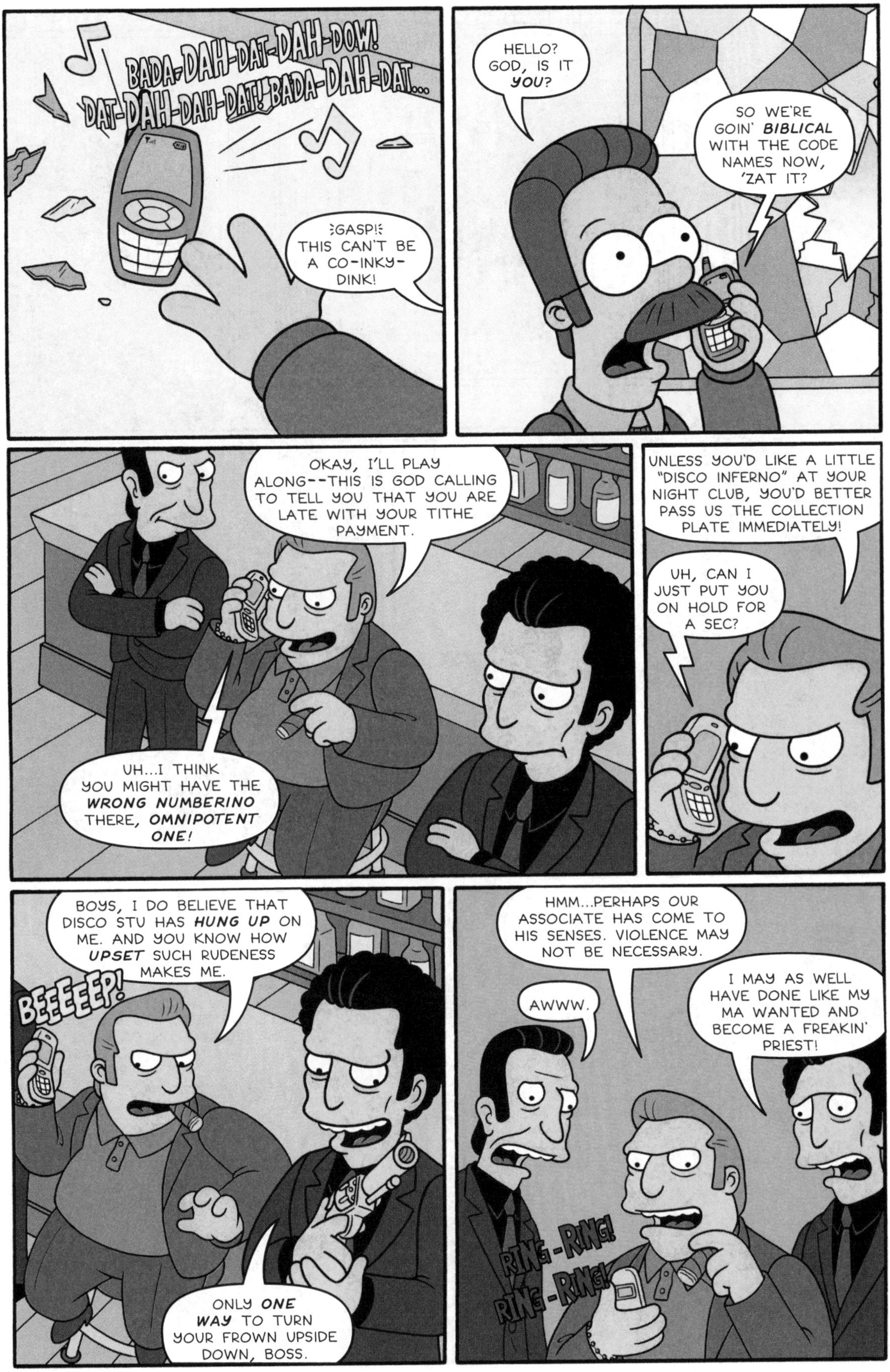
BADA-DAH-DAT-DAH-DOW!
DAT-DAH-DAH-DAT! BADA-DAH-DAT...
GASP! THIS CAN'T BE A CO-INKY-DINK!
HELLO? GOD, IS IT YOU?
SO WE'RE GOIN' BIBLICAL WITH THE CODE NAMES NOW, 'ZAT IT?
OKAY, I'LL PLAY ALONG--THIS IS GOD CALLING TO TELL YOU THAT YOU ARE LATE WITH YOUR TITHE PAYMENT.
UH...I THINK YOU MIGHT HAVE THE WRONG NUMBERINO THERE, OMNIPOTENT ONE!
UNLESS YOU'D LIKE A LITTLE "DISCO INFERNO" AT YOUR NIGHT CLUB, YOU'D BETTER PASS US THE COLLECTION PLATE IMMEDIATELY!
UH, CAN I JUST PUT YOU ON HOLD FOR A SEC?
BOYS, I DO BELIEVE THAT DISCO STU HAS HUNG UP ON ME. AND YOU KNOW HOW UPSET SUCH RUDENESS MAKES ME.
BEEEEEP!
ONLY ONE WAY TO TURN YOUR FROWN UPSIDE DOWN, BOSS.
HMM...PERHAPS OUR ASSOCIATE HAS COME TO HIS SENSES. VIOLENCE MAY NOT BE NECESSARY.
AWWW.
I MAY AS WELL HAVE DONE LIKE MY MA WANTED AND BECOME A FREAKIN' PRIEST!
RING-RING!
RING-RING!

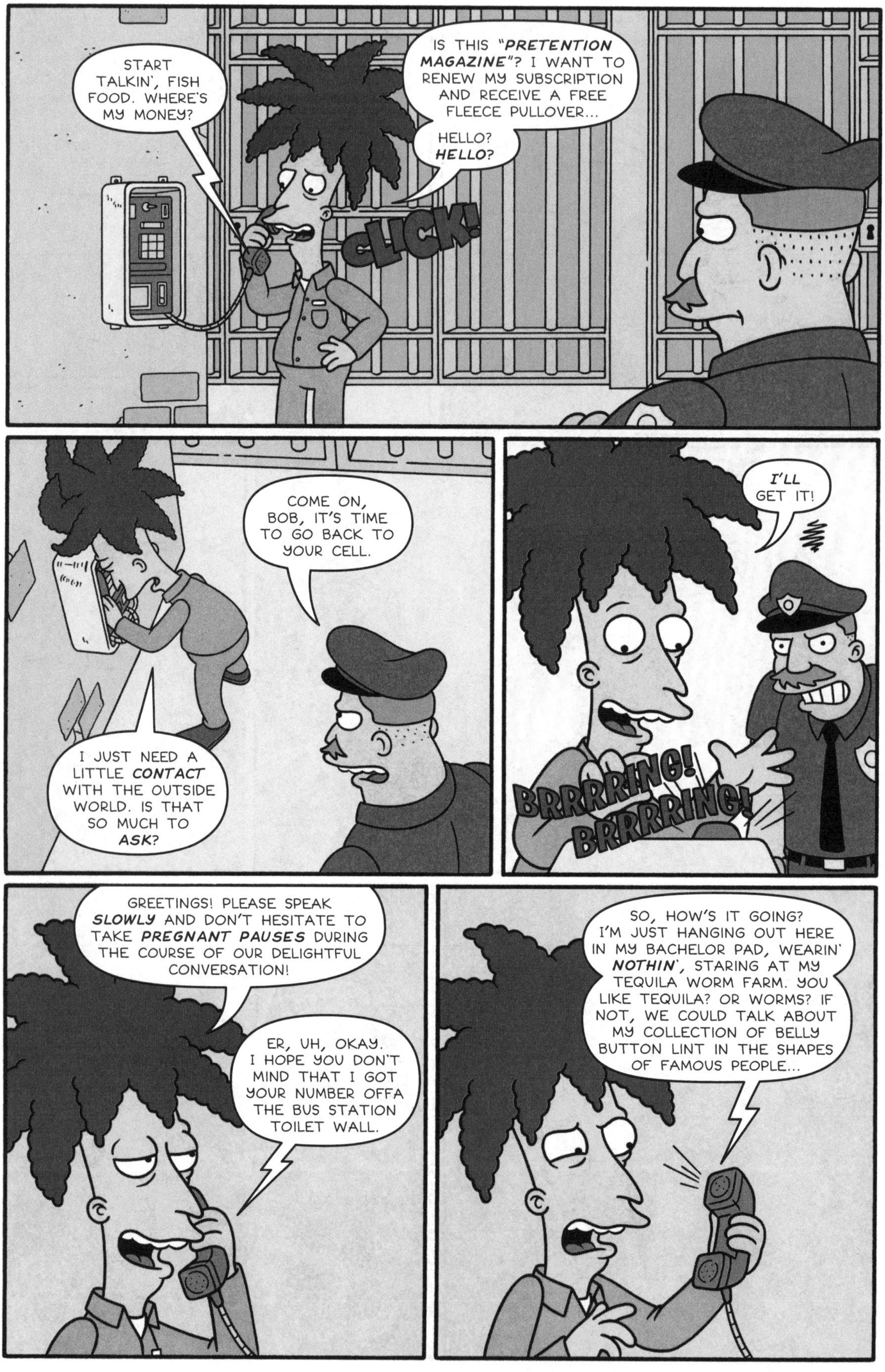
START TALKIN', FISH FOOD. WHERE'S MY MONEY?
IS THIS "PRETENTION MAGAZINE"? I WANT TO RENEW MY SUBSCRIPTION AND RECEIVE A FREE FLEECE PULLOVER...
HELLO? HELLO?
CLICK!
COME ON, BOB, IT'S TIME TO GO BACK TO YOUR CELL.
I JUST NEED A LITTLE CONTACT WITH THE OUTSIDE WORLD. IS THAT SO MUCH TO ASK?
I'LL GET IT!
BRRRRING! BRRRRING!
GREETINGS! PLEASE SPEAK SLOWLY AND DON'T HESITATE TO TAKE PREGNANT PAUSES DURING THE COURSE OF OUR DELIGHTFUL CONVERSATION!
ER, UH, OKAY. I HOPE YOU DON'T MIND THAT I GOT YOUR NUMBER OFFA THE BUS STATION TOILET WALL.
SO, HOW'S IT GOING? I'M JUST HANGING OUT HERE IN MY BACHELOR PAD, WEARIN' NOTHIN', STARING AT MY TEQUILA WORM FARM. YOU LIKE TEQUILA? OR WORMS? IF NOT, WE COULD TALK ABOUT MY COLLECTION OF BELLY BUTTON LINT IN THE SHAPES OF FAMOUS PEOPLE...

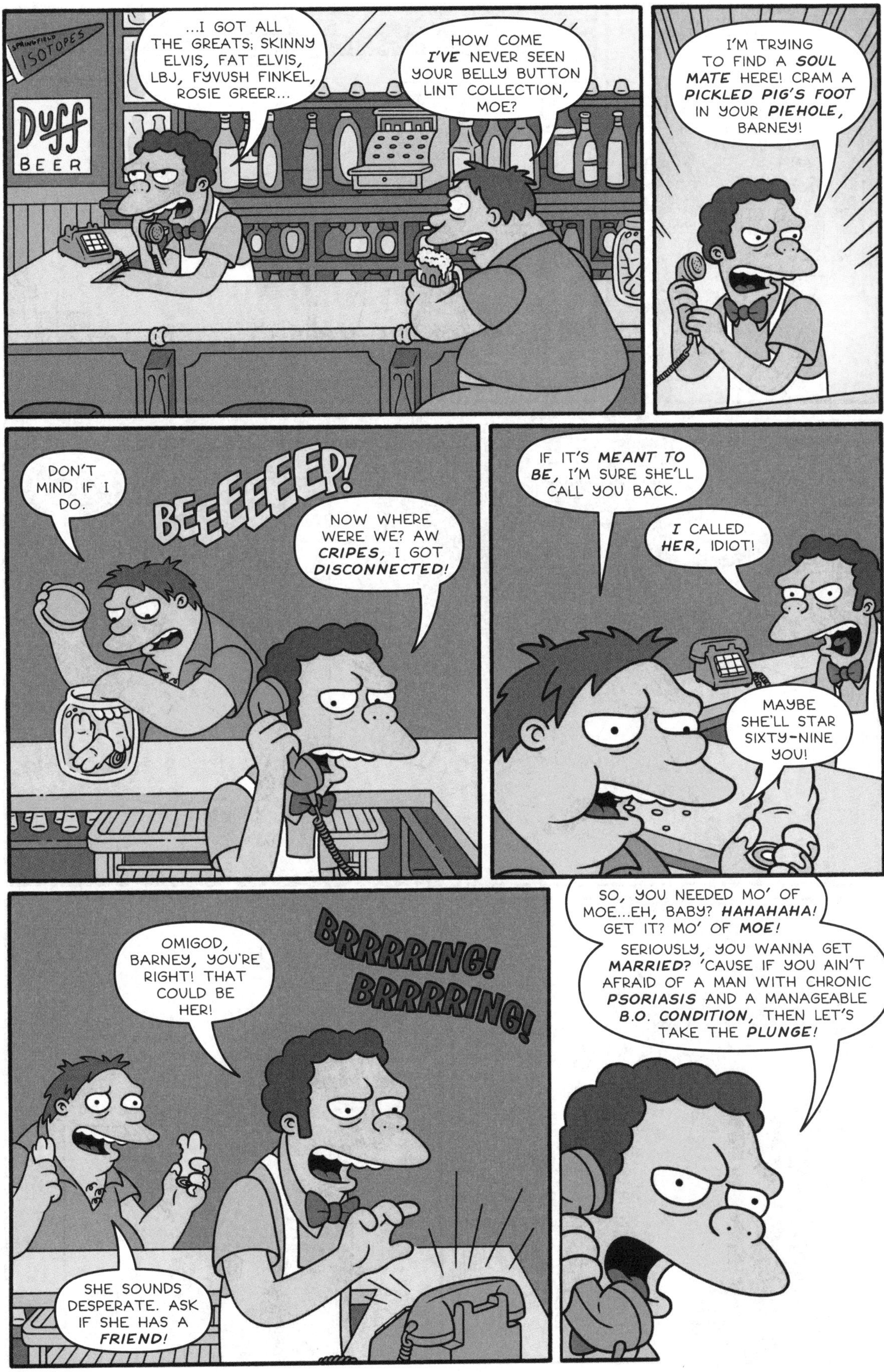
SPRINGFIELD ISOTOPES
Duff BEER
...I GOT ALL THE GREATS; SKINNY ELVIS, FAT ELVIS, LBJ, FYVUSH FINKEL, ROSIE GREER...
HOW COME *I'VE* NEVER SEEN YOUR BELLY BUTTON LINT COLLECTION, MOE?
I'M TRYING TO FIND A **SOUL MATE** HERE! CRAM A ***PICKLED PIG'S FOOT*** IN YOUR ***PIEHOLE,*** BARNEY!
DON'T MIND IF I DO.
BEEEEEEP!
NOW WHERE WERE WE? AW ***CRIPES,*** I GOT ***DISCONNECTED!***
IF IT'S ***MEANT TO BE,*** I'M SURE SHE'LL CALL YOU BACK.
I CALLED ***HER,*** IDIOT!
MAYBE SHE'LL STAR SIXTY-NINE YOU!
BRRRRING! BRRRRING!
OMIGOD, BARNEY, YOU'RE RIGHT! THAT COULD BE HER!
SHE SOUNDS DESPERATE. ASK IF SHE HAS A ***FRIEND!***
SO, YOU NEEDED MO' OF MOE...EH, BABY? ***HAHAHAHA!*** GET IT? MO' OF ***MOE!***
SERIOUSLY, YOU WANNA GET ***MARRIED?*** 'CAUSE IF YOU AIN'T AFRAID OF A MAN WITH CHRONIC ***PSORIASIS*** AND A MANAGEABLE ***B.O. CONDITION,*** THEN LET'S TAKE THE ***PLUNGE!***

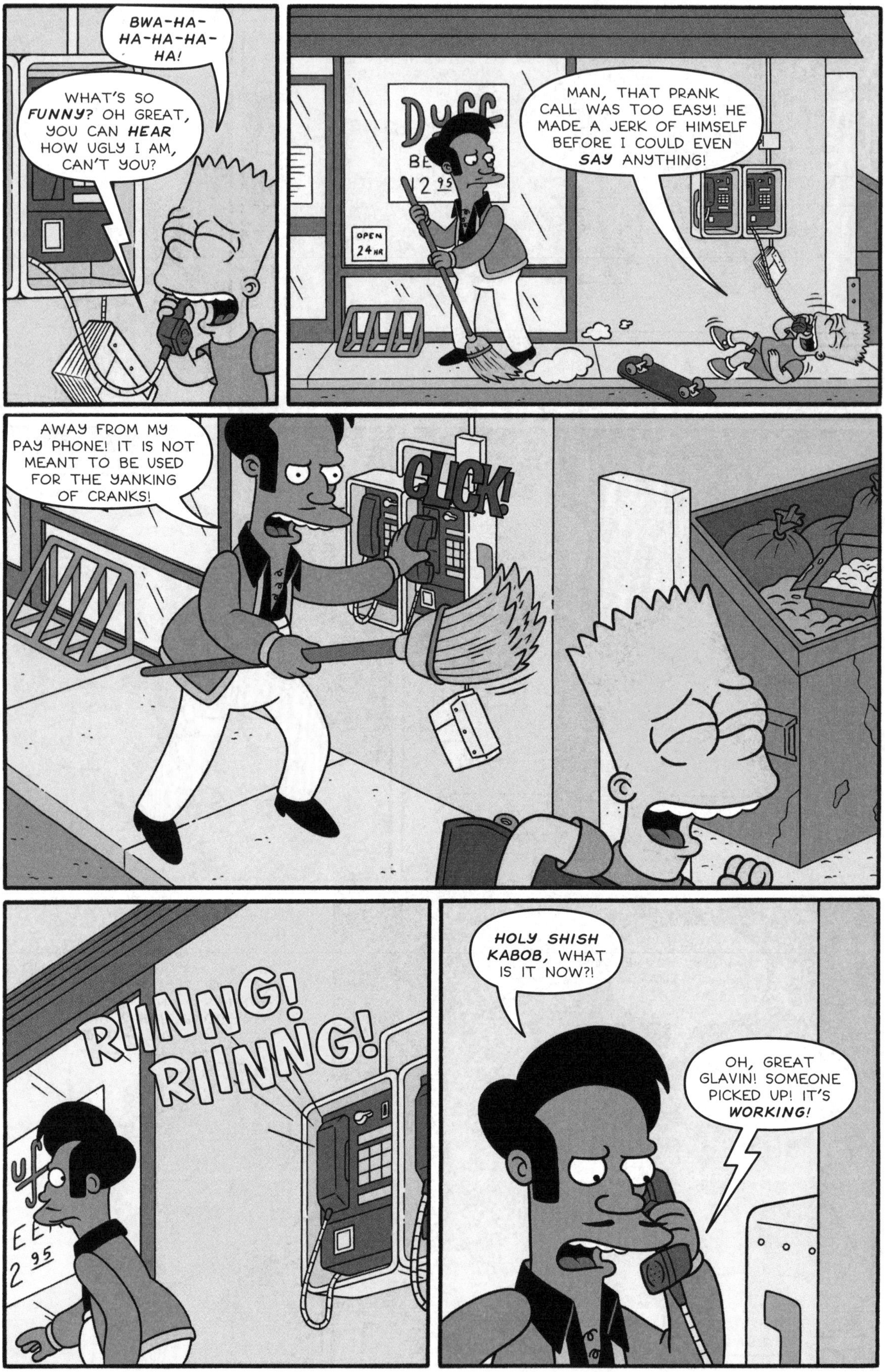
BWA-HA-HA-HA-HA-HA!
WHAT'S SO FUNNY? OH GREAT, YOU CAN HEAR HOW UGLY I AM, CAN'T YOU?
Duff
OPEN 24 HR
MAN, THAT PRANK CALL WAS TOO EASY! HE MADE A JERK OF HIMSELF BEFORE I COULD EVEN SAY ANYTHING!
AWAY FROM MY PAY PHONE! IT IS NOT MEANT TO BE USED FOR THE YANKING OF CRANKS!
CLICK!
RIINNG! RIINNG!
HOLY SHISH KABOB, WHAT IS IT NOW?!
OH, GREAT GLAVIN! SOMEONE PICKED UP! IT'S WORKING!

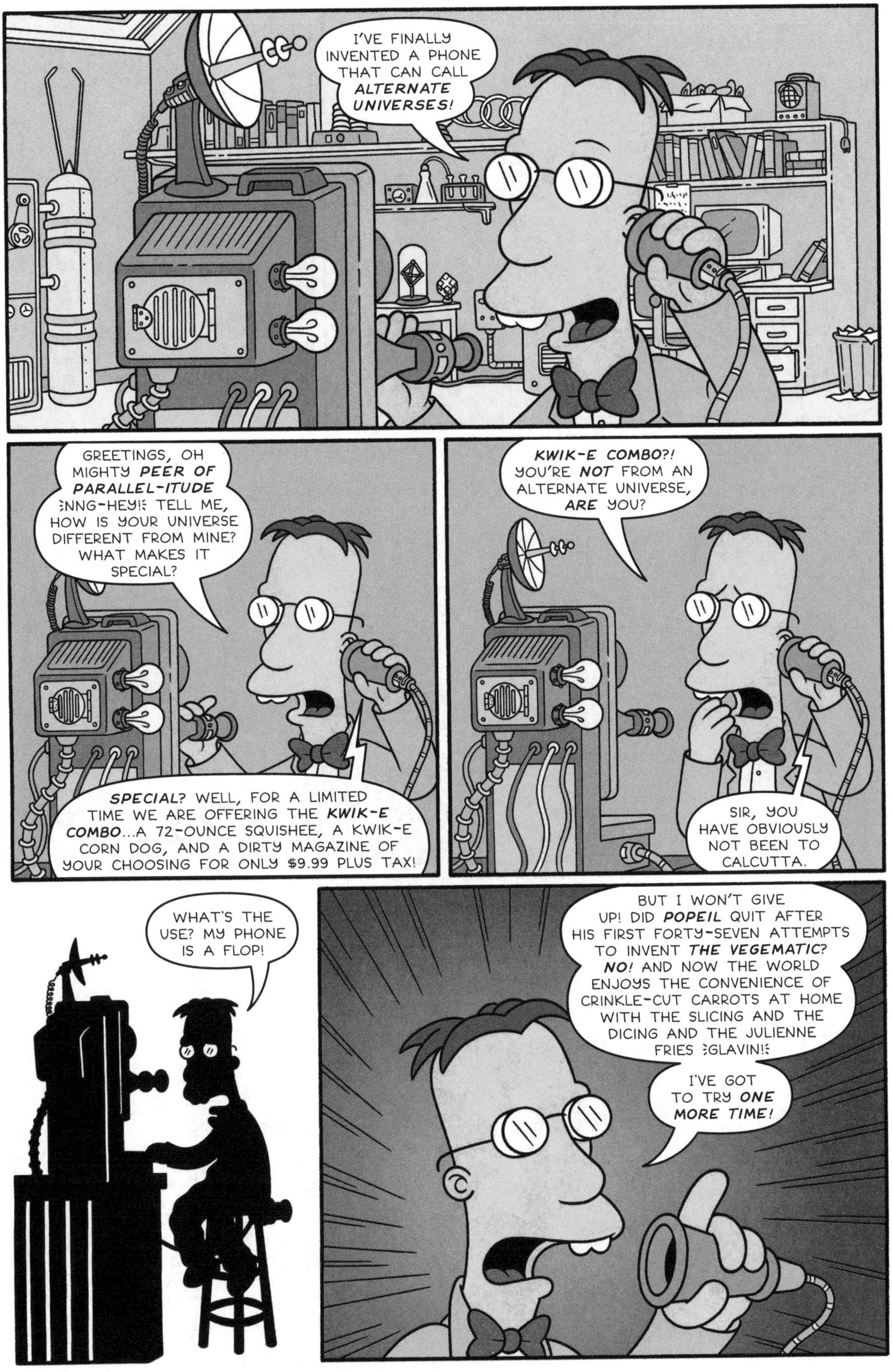
I'VE FINALLY INVENTED A PHONE THAT CAN CALL *ALTERNATE UNIVERSES!*
GREETINGS, OH MIGHTY *PEER OF PARALLEL-ITUDE* ⁝NNG-HEY!⁝ TELL ME, HOW IS YOUR UNIVERSE DIFFERENT FROM MINE? WHAT MAKES IT SPECIAL?
SPECIAL? WELL, FOR A LIMITED TIME WE ARE OFFERING THE *KWIK-E COMBO*...A 72-OUNCE SQUISHEE, A KWIK-E CORN DOG, AND A DIRTY MAGAZINE OF YOUR CHOOSING FOR ONLY $9.99 PLUS TAX!
KWIK-E COMBO?! YOU'RE *NOT* FROM AN ALTERNATE UNIVERSE, *ARE* YOU?
SIR, YOU HAVE OBVIOUSLY NOT BEEN TO CALCUTTA.
WHAT'S THE USE? MY PHONE IS A FLOP!
BUT I WON'T GIVE UP! DID *POPEIL* QUIT AFTER HIS FIRST FORTY-SEVEN ATTEMPTS TO INVENT *THE VEGEMATIC?* *NO!* AND NOW THE WORLD ENJOYS THE CONVENIENCE OF CRINKLE-CUT CARROTS AT HOME WITH THE SLICING AND THE DICING AND THE JULIENNE FRIES ⁝GLAVIN!⁝
I'VE GOT TO TRY *ONE MORE TIME!*

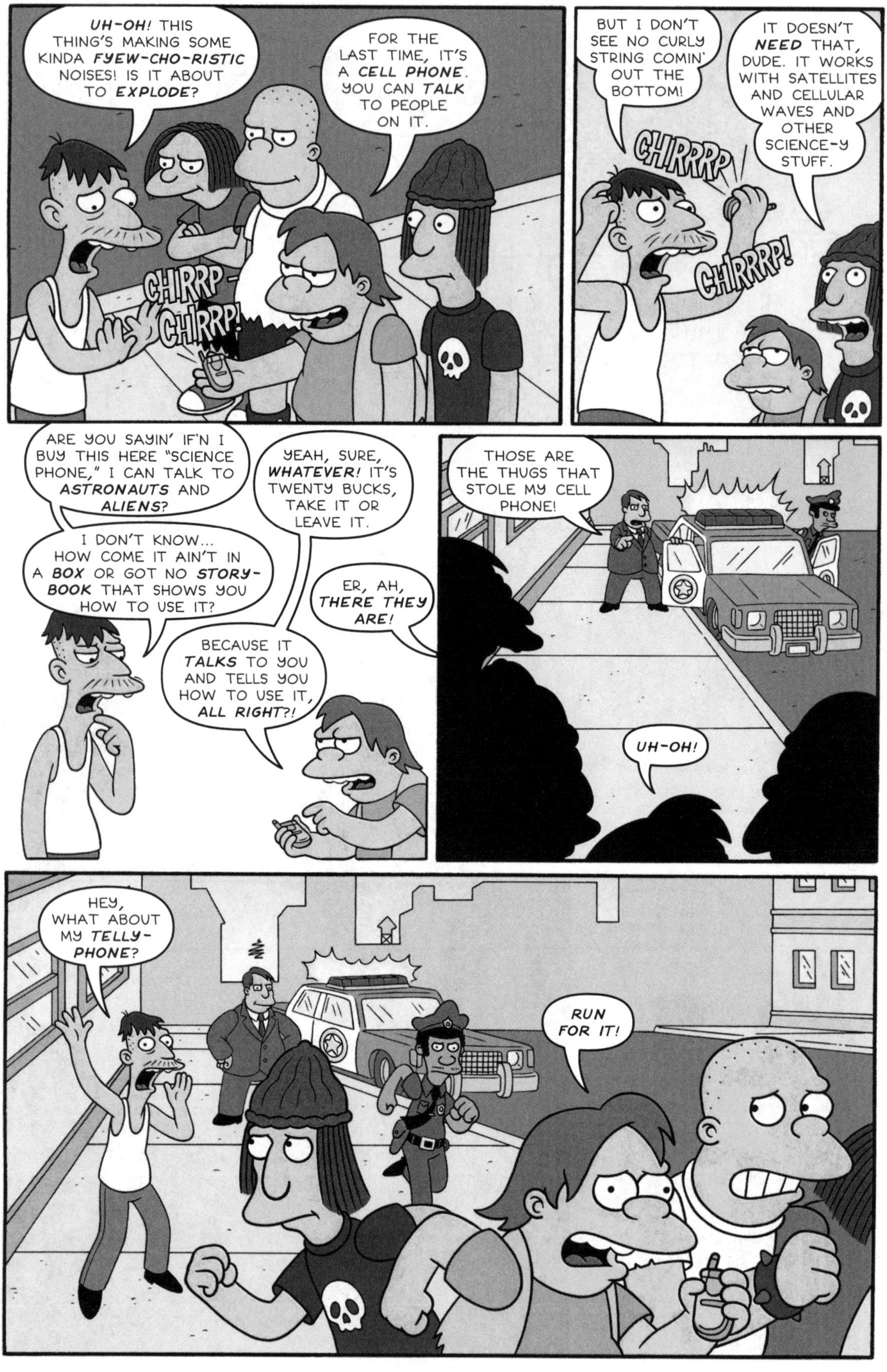
UH-OH! THIS THING'S MAKING SOME KINDA FYEW-CHO-RISTIC NOISES! IS IT ABOUT TO EXPLODE?
FOR THE LAST TIME, IT'S A CELL PHONE. YOU CAN TALK TO PEOPLE ON IT.
CHIRRP-
CHIRRP!
BUT I DON'T SEE NO CURLY STRING COMIN' OUT THE BOTTOM!
IT DOESN'T NEED THAT, DUDE. IT WORKS WITH SATELLITES AND CELLULAR WAVES AND OTHER SCIENCE-Y STUFF.
CHIRRRP
CHIRRRP!
ARE YOU SAYIN' IF'N I BUY THIS HERE "SCIENCE PHONE," I CAN TALK TO ASTRONAUTS AND ALIENS?
YEAH, SURE, WHATEVER! IT'S TWENTY BUCKS, TAKE IT OR LEAVE IT.
I DON'T KNOW... HOW COME IT AIN'T IN A BOX OR GOT NO STORY-BOOK THAT SHOWS YOU HOW TO USE IT?
BECAUSE IT TALKS TO YOU AND TELLS YOU HOW TO USE IT, ALL RIGHT?!
ER, AH, THERE THEY ARE!
THOSE ARE THE THUGS THAT STOLE MY CELL PHONE!
UH-OH!
HEY, WHAT ABOUT MY TELLY-PHONE?
RUN FOR IT!

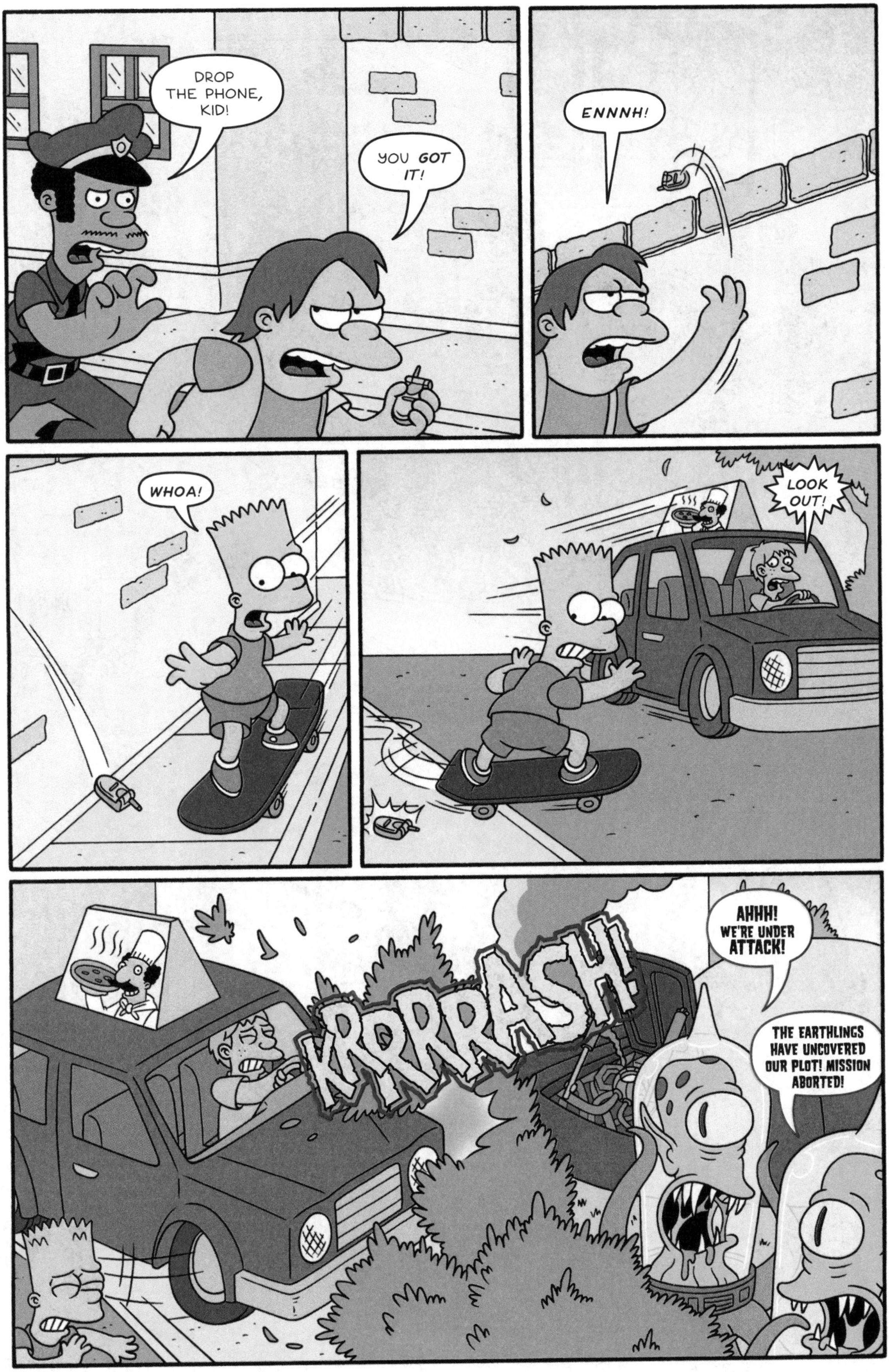
DROP THE PHONE, KID!
YOU GOT IT!
ENNNH!
WHOA!
LOOK OUT!
KRRRRASH!
AHHH! WE'RE UNDER ATTACK!
THE EARTHLINGS HAVE UNCOVERED OUR PLOT! MISSION ABORTED!

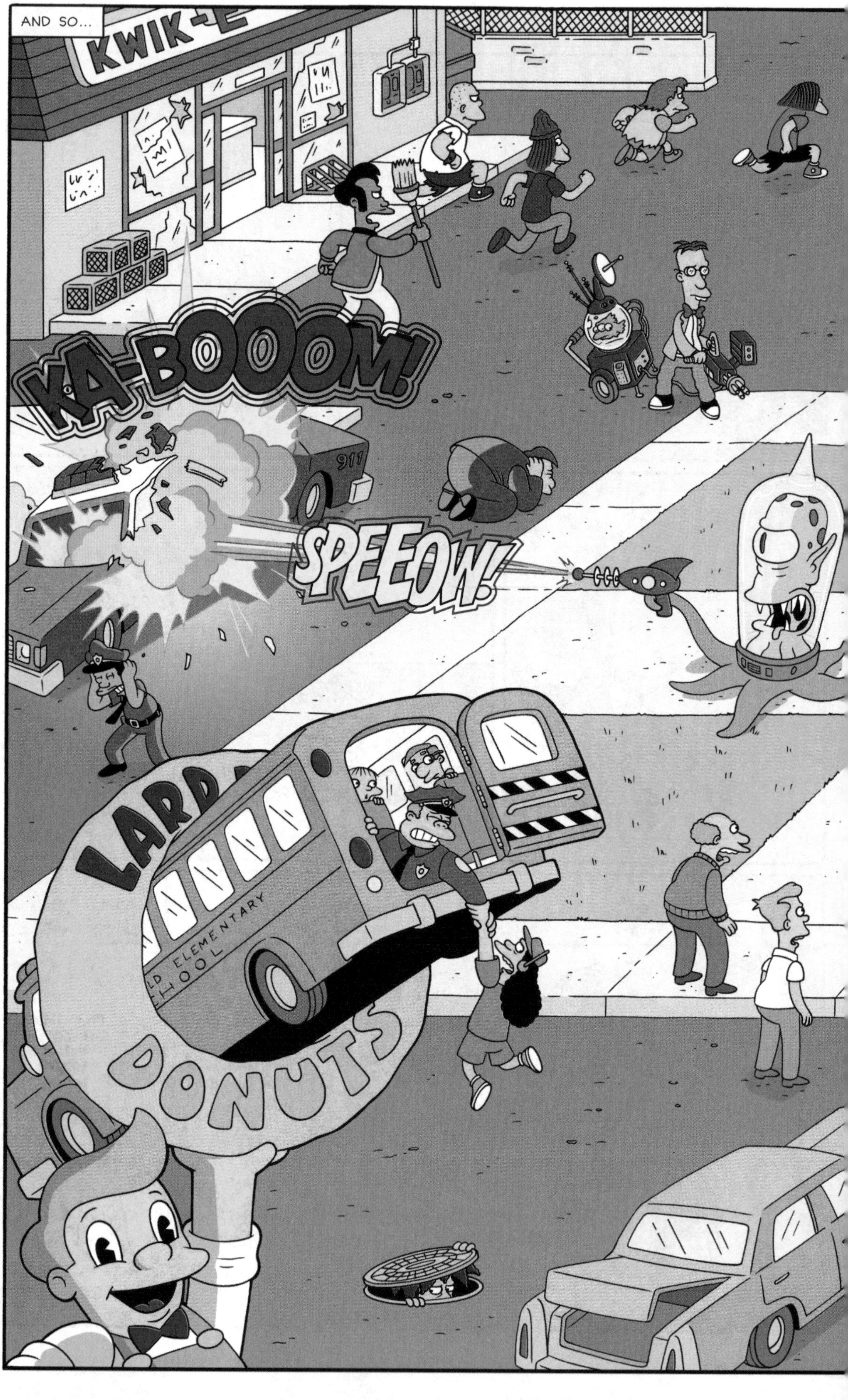

AND SO...
KWIK-E
KA-BOOOM!
911
SPEEOW!
DONUTS

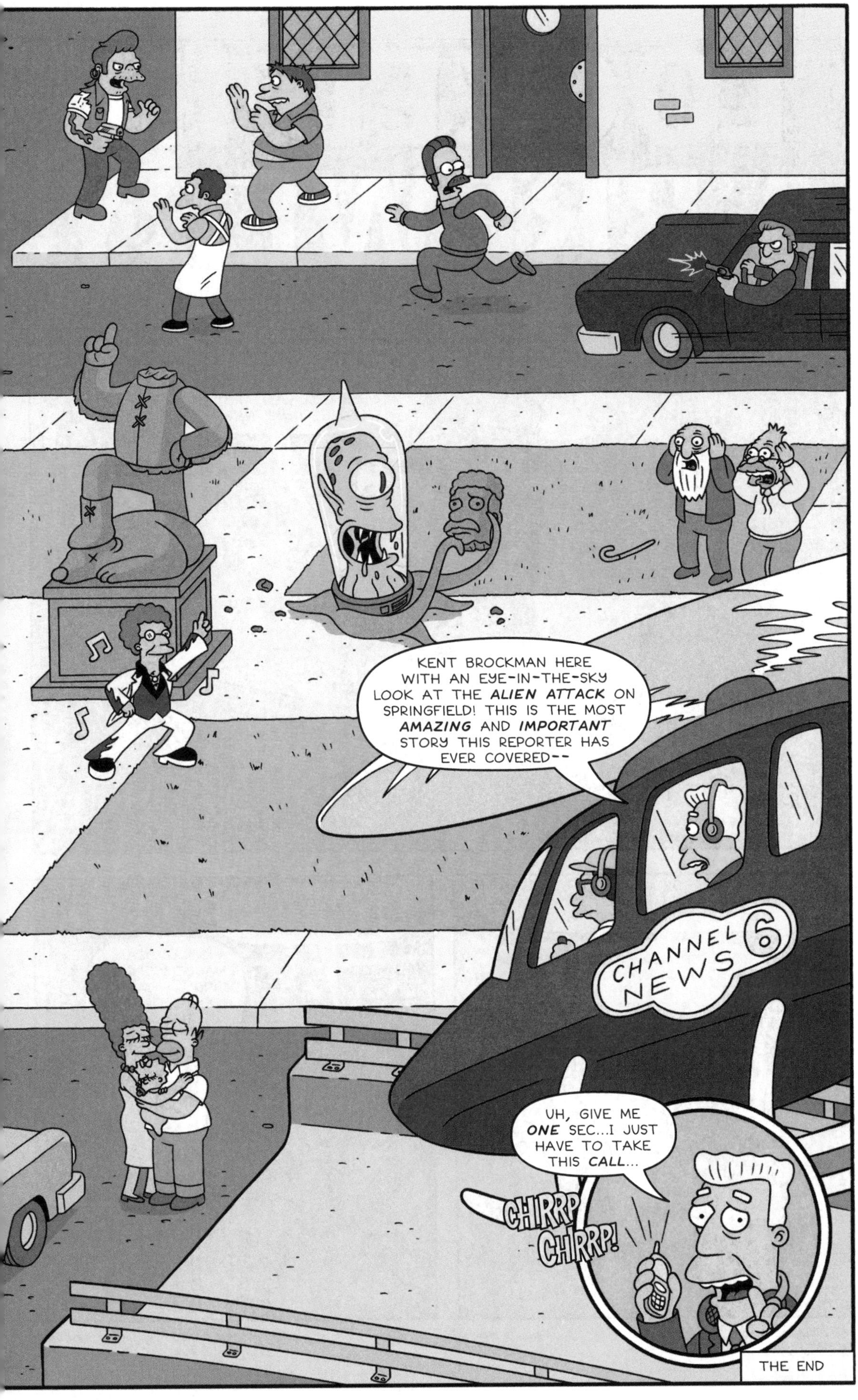
KENT BROCKMAN HERE WITH AN EYE-IN-THE-SKY LOOK AT THE ALIEN ATTACK ON SPRINGFIELD! THIS IS THE MOST AMAZING AND IMPORTANT STORY THIS REPORTER HAS EVER COVERED--
CHANNEL 6 NEWS
CHIRRP CHIRRP!
UH, GIVE ME ONE SEC...I JUST HAVE TO TAKE THIS CALL...
THE END

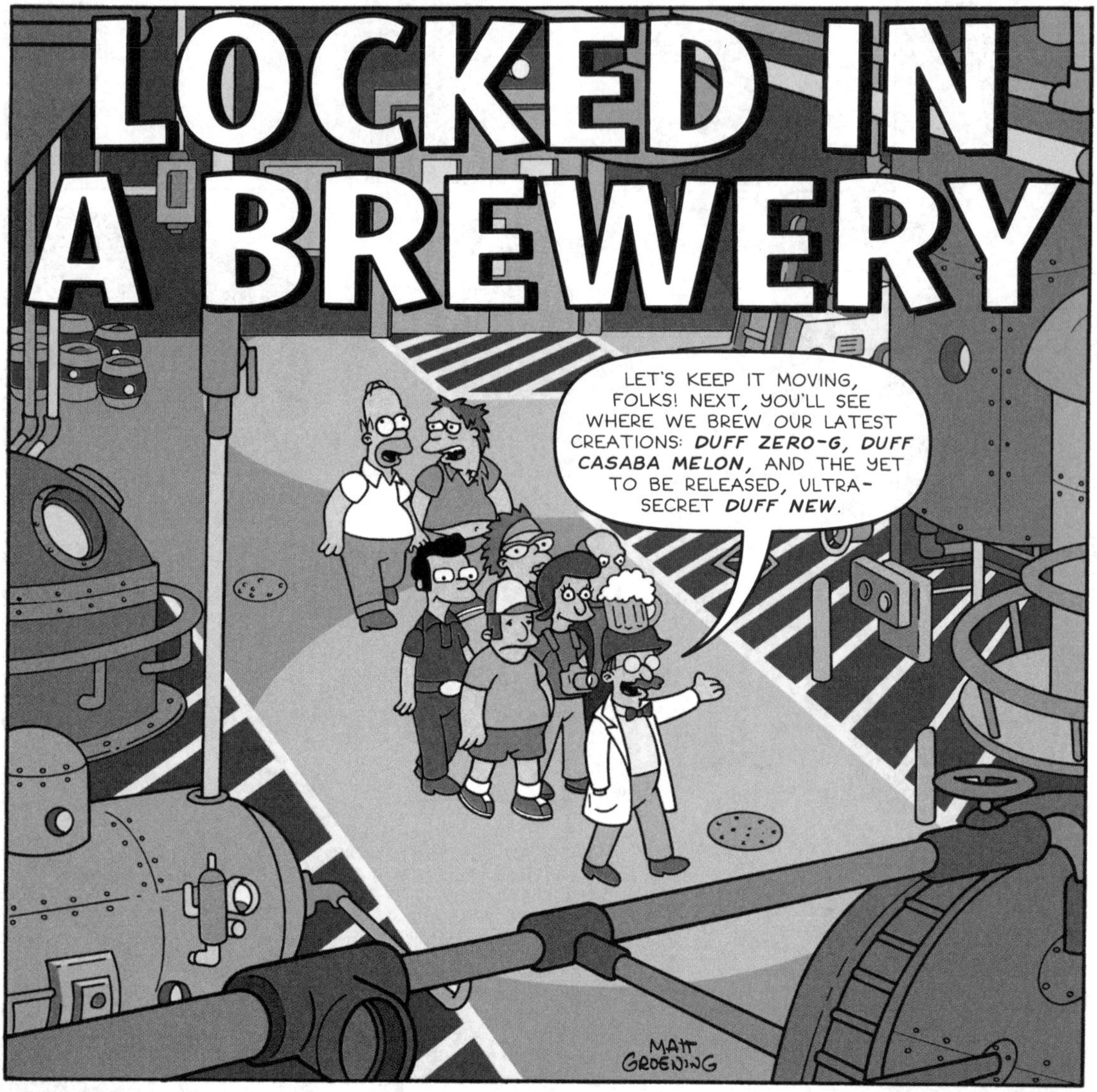
LOCKED IN A BREWERY
LET'S KEEP IT MOVING, FOLKS! NEXT, YOU'LL SEE WHERE WE BREW OUR LATEST CREATIONS: ***DUFF ZERO-G, DUFF CASABA MELON,*** AND THE YET TO BE RELEASED, ULTRA-SECRET ***DUFF NEW***.
MATT GROENING

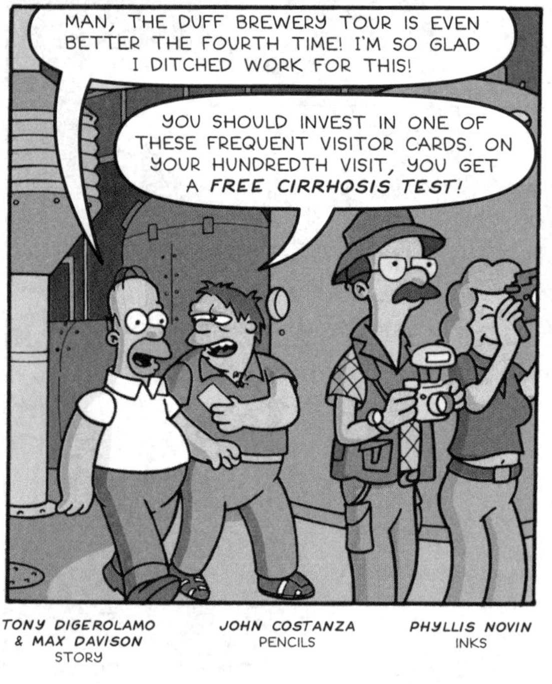
MAN, THE DUFF BREWERY TOUR IS EVEN BETTER THE FOURTH TIME! I'M SO GLAD I DITCHED WORK FOR THIS!
YOU SHOULD INVEST IN ONE OF THESE FREQUENT VISITOR CARDS. ON YOUR HUNDREDTH VISIT, YOU GET A ***FREE CIRRHOSIS TEST***!

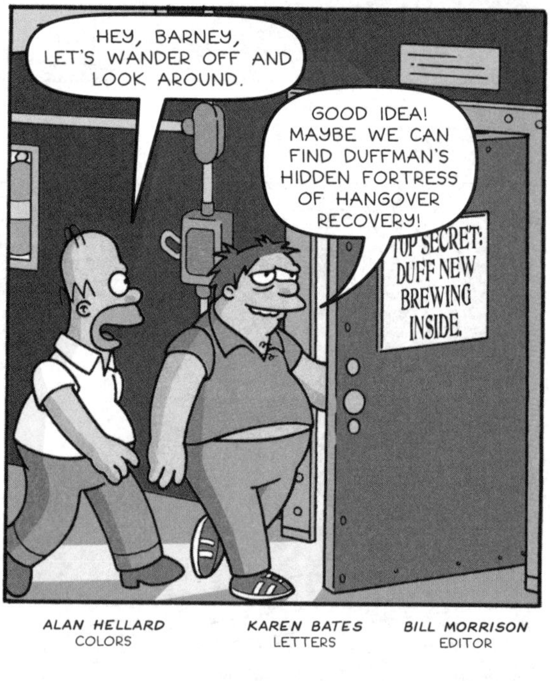
HEY, BARNEY, LET'S WANDER OFF AND LOOK AROUND.
GOOD IDEA! MAYBE WE CAN FIND DUFFMAN'S HIDDEN FORTRESS OF HANGOVER RECOVERY!
TOP SECRET: DUFF NEW BREWING INSIDE.

TONY DIGEROLAMO & MAX DAVISON STORY

JOHN COSTANZA PENCILS

PHYLLIS NOVIN INKS

ALAN HELLARD COLORS

KAREN BATES LETTERS

BILL MORRISON EDITOR

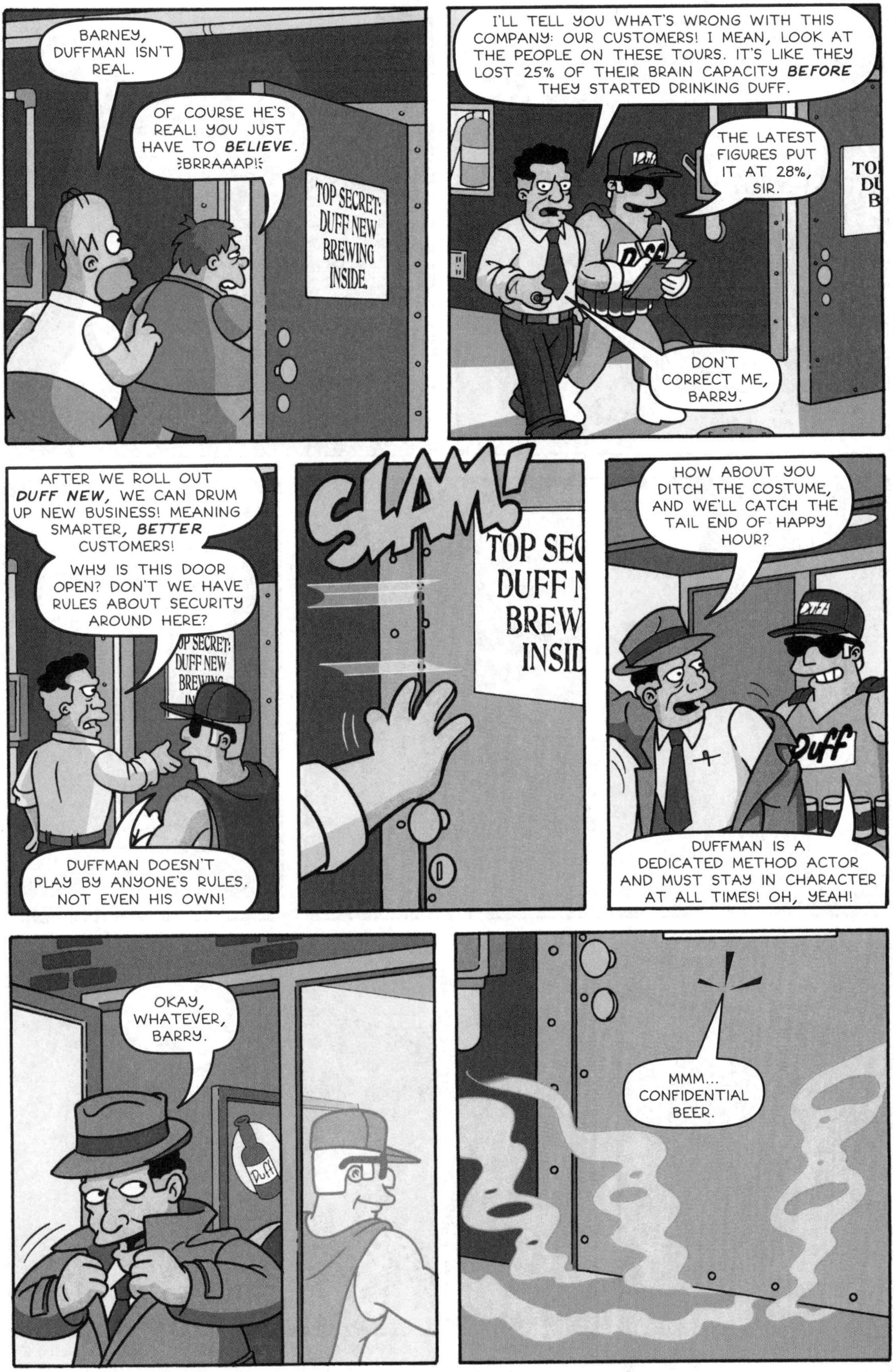
BARNEY, DUFFMAN ISN'T REAL.
OF COURSE HE'S REAL! YOU JUST HAVE TO **BELIEVE**. BRRAAAP!
TOP SECRET: DUFF NEW BREWING INSIDE.
I'LL TELL YOU WHAT'S WRONG WITH THIS COMPANY: OUR CUSTOMERS! I MEAN, LOOK AT THE PEOPLE ON THESE TOURS. IT'S LIKE THEY LOST 25% OF THEIR BRAIN CAPACITY **BEFORE** THEY STARTED DRINKING DUFF.
THE LATEST FIGURES PUT IT AT 28%, SIR.
DON'T CORRECT ME, BARRY.
AFTER WE ROLL OUT **DUFF NEW,** WE CAN DRUM UP NEW BUSINESS! MEANING SMARTER, **BETTER** CUSTOMERS!
WHY IS THIS DOOR OPEN? DON'T WE HAVE RULES ABOUT SECURITY AROUND HERE?
DUFFMAN DOESN'T PLAY BY ANYONE'S RULES. NOT EVEN HIS OWN!
SLAM!
HOW ABOUT YOU DITCH THE COSTUME, AND WE'LL CATCH THE TAIL END OF HAPPY HOUR?
DUFFMAN IS A DEDICATED METHOD ACTOR AND MUST STAY IN CHARACTER AT ALL TIMES! OH, YEAH!
OKAY, WHATEVER, BARRY.
MMM... CONFIDENTIAL BEER.

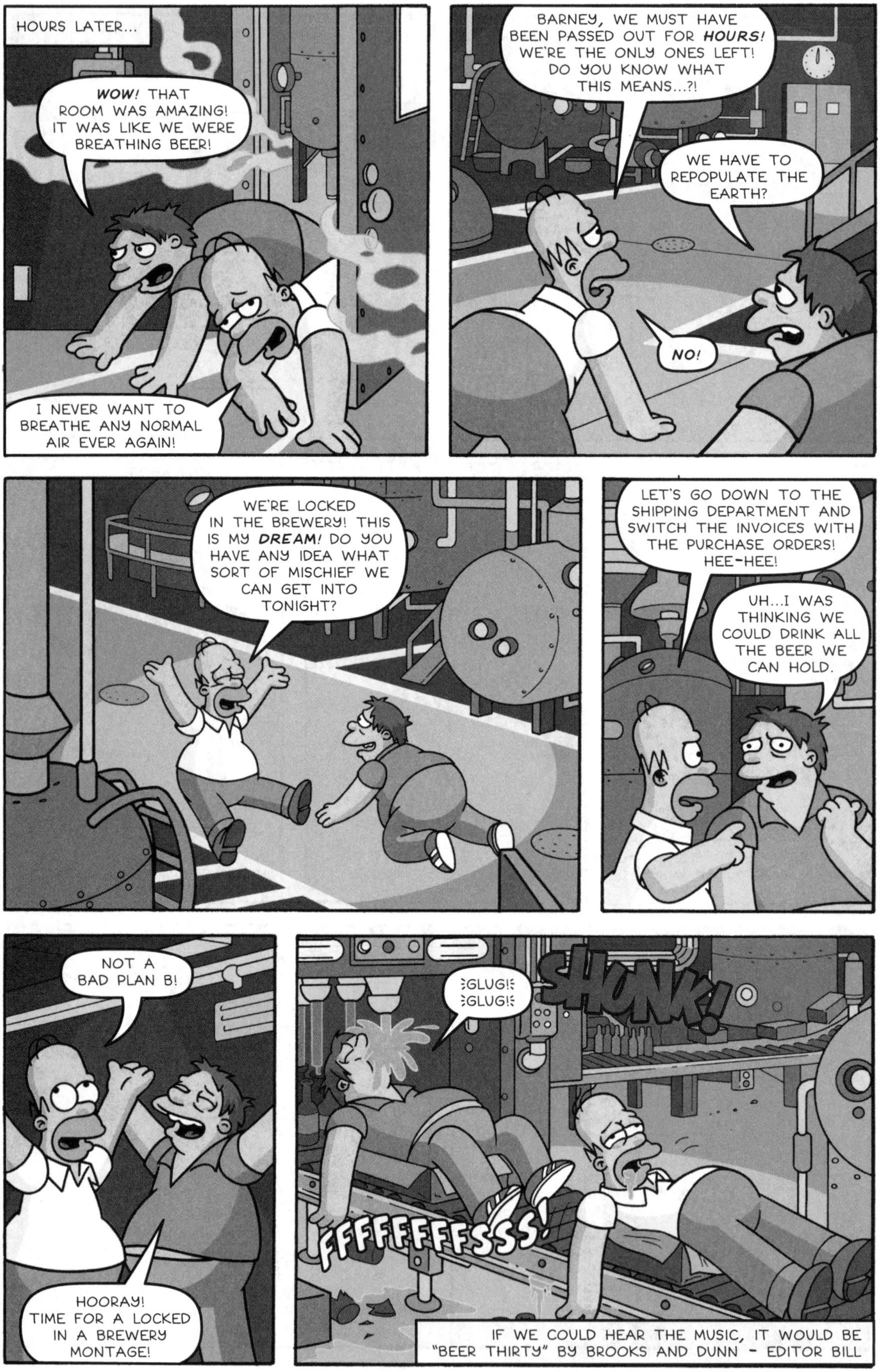
HOURS LATER...
WOW! THAT ROOM WAS AMAZING! IT WAS LIKE WE WERE BREATHING BEER!
I NEVER WANT TO BREATHE ANY NORMAL AIR EVER AGAIN!
BARNEY, WE MUST HAVE BEEN PASSED OUT FOR *HOURS!* WE'RE THE ONLY ONES LEFT! DO YOU KNOW WHAT THIS MEANS...?!
WE HAVE TO REPOPULATE THE EARTH?
NO!
WE'RE LOCKED IN THE BREWERY! THIS IS MY *DREAM!* DO YOU HAVE ANY IDEA WHAT SORT OF MISCHIEF WE CAN GET INTO TONIGHT?
LET'S GO DOWN TO THE SHIPPING DEPARTMENT AND SWITCH THE INVOICES WITH THE PURCHASE ORDERS! HEE-HEE!
UH...I WAS THINKING WE COULD DRINK ALL THE BEER WE CAN HOLD.
NOT A BAD PLAN B!
HOORAY! TIME FOR A LOCKED IN A BREWERY MONTAGE!
GLUG! GLUG!
SHUNK!
FFFFFFFFSSS!
IF WE COULD HEAR THE MUSIC, IT WOULD BE "BEER THIRTY" BY BROOKS AND DUNN - EDITOR BILL

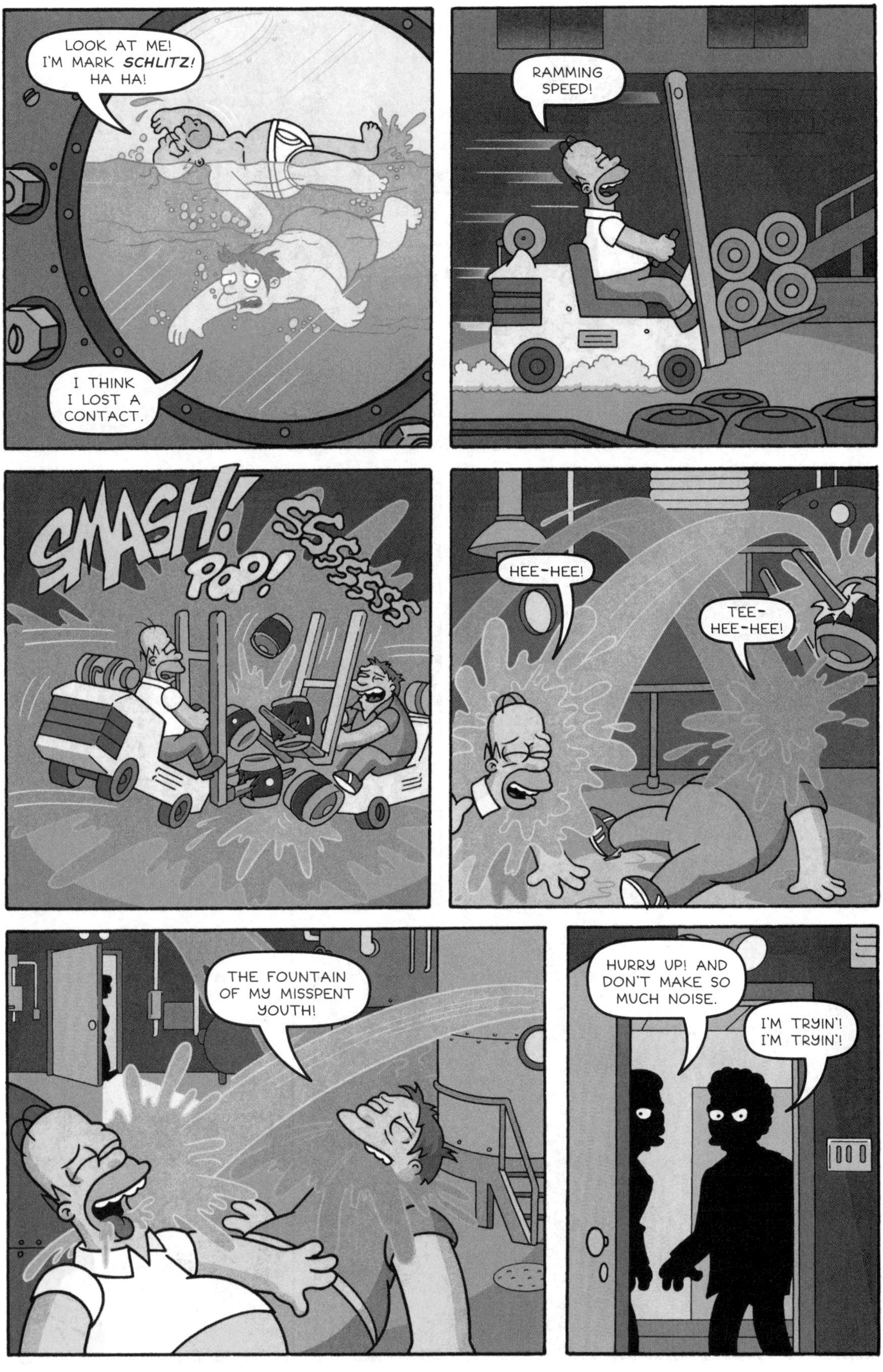
LOOK AT ME! I'M MARK SCHLITZ! HA HA!
I THINK I LOST A CONTACT.
RAMMING SPEED!
SMASH!
POP!
SSSSSSS
HEE-HEE!
TEE-HEE-HEE!
THE FOUNTAIN OF MY MISSPENT YOUTH!
HURRY UP! AND DON'T MAKE SO MUCH NOISE.
I'M TRYIN'! I'M TRYIN'!

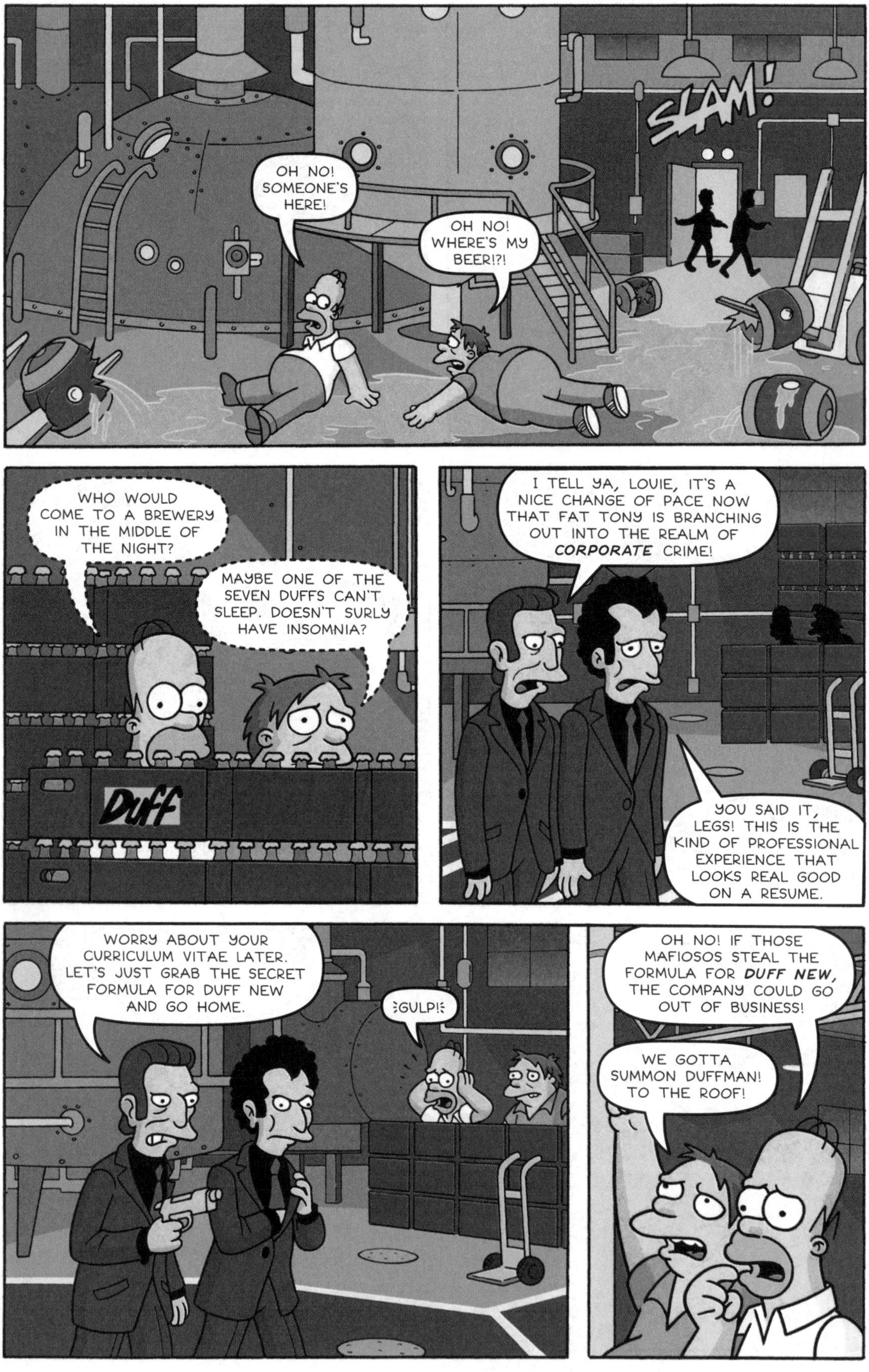
SLAM!
OH NO! SOMEONE'S HERE!
OH NO! WHERE'S MY BEER!?!
WHO WOULD COME TO A BREWERY IN THE MIDDLE OF THE NIGHT?
MAYBE ONE OF THE SEVEN DUFFS CAN'T SLEEP. DOESN'T SURLY HAVE INSOMNIA?
Duff
I TELL YA, LOUIE, IT'S A NICE CHANGE OF PACE NOW THAT FAT TONY IS BRANCHING OUT INTO THE REALM OF *CORPORATE* CRIME!
YOU SAID IT, LEGS! THIS IS THE KIND OF PROFESSIONAL EXPERIENCE THAT LOOKS REAL GOOD ON A RESUME.
WORRY ABOUT YOUR CURRICULUM VITAE LATER. LET'S JUST GRAB THE SECRET FORMULA FOR DUFF NEW AND GO HOME.
GULP!
OH NO! IF THOSE MAFIOSOS STEAL THE FORMULA FOR ***DUFF NEW,*** THE COMPANY COULD GO OUT OF BUSINESS!
WE GOTTA SUMMON DUFFMAN! TO THE ROOF!

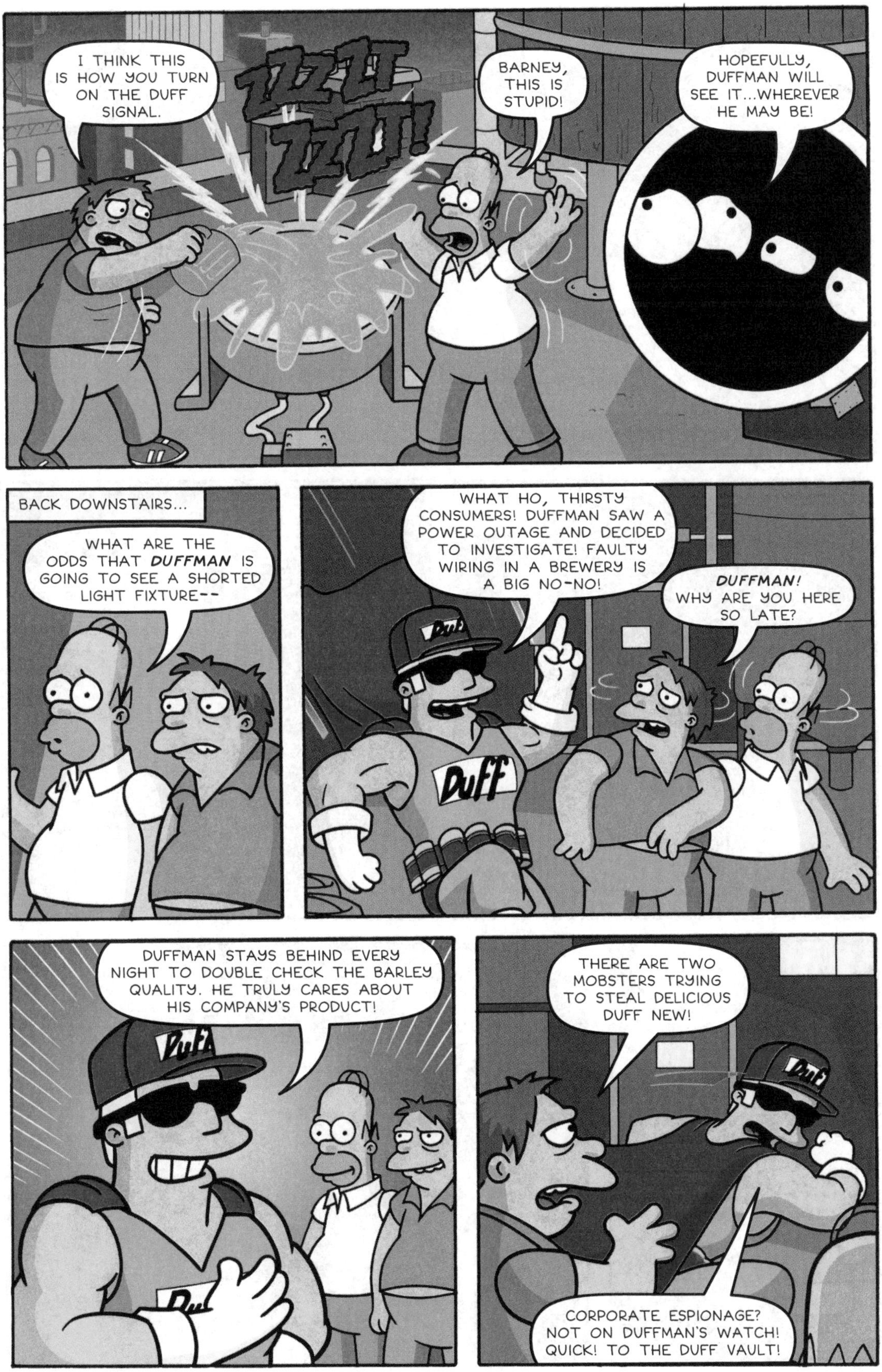

I THINK THIS IS HOW YOU TURN ON THE DUFF SIGNAL.
ZZZZZT ZZZZT!
BARNEY, THIS IS STUPID!
HOPEFULLY, DUFFMAN WILL SEE IT...WHEREVER HE MAY BE!
BACK DOWNSTAIRS...
WHAT ARE THE ODDS THAT *DUFFMAN* IS GOING TO SEE A SHORTED LIGHT FIXTURE--
WHAT HO, THIRSTY CONSUMERS! DUFFMAN SAW A POWER OUTAGE AND DECIDED TO INVESTIGATE! FAULTY WIRING IN A BREWERY IS A BIG NO-NO!
DUFFMAN! WHY ARE YOU HERE SO LATE?
DUFFMAN STAYS BEHIND EVERY NIGHT TO DOUBLE CHECK THE BARLEY QUALITY. HE TRULY CARES ABOUT HIS COMPANY'S PRODUCT!
THERE ARE TWO MOBSTERS TRYING TO STEAL DELICIOUS DUFF NEW!
CORPORATE ESPIONAGE? NOT ON DUFFMAN'S WATCH! QUICK! TO THE DUFF VAULT!

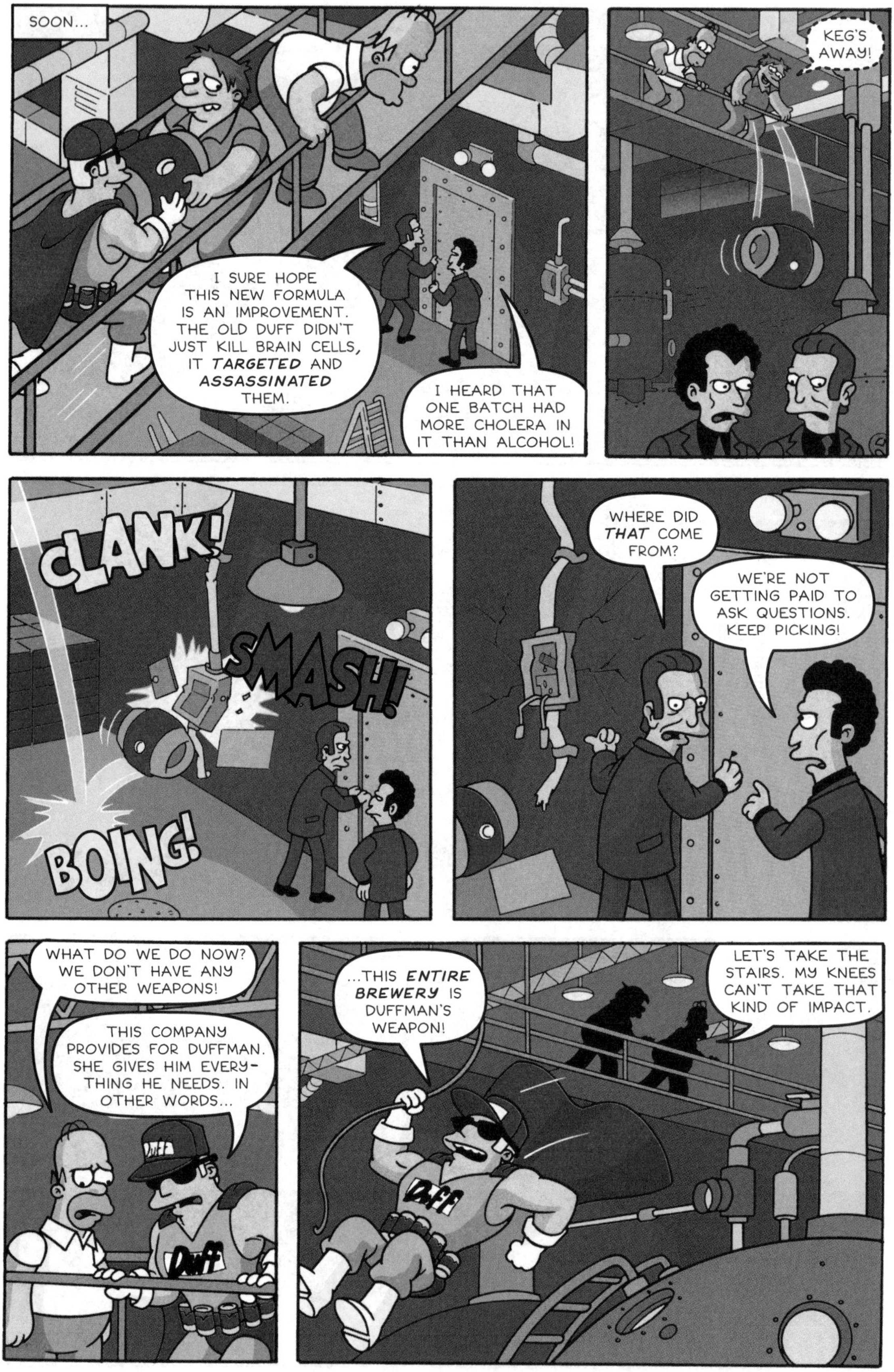
SOON...
I SURE HOPE THIS NEW FORMULA IS AN IMPROVEMENT. THE OLD DUFF DIDN'T JUST KILL BRAIN CELLS, IT *TARGETED* AND *ASSASSINATED* THEM.
I HEARD THAT ONE BATCH HAD MORE CHOLERA IN IT THAN ALCOHOL!
KEG'S AWAY!
CLANK!
SMASH!
BOING!
WHERE DID *THAT* COME FROM?
WE'RE NOT GETTING PAID TO ASK QUESTIONS. KEEP PICKING!
WHAT DO WE DO NOW? WE DON'T HAVE ANY OTHER WEAPONS!
THIS COMPANY PROVIDES FOR DUFFMAN. SHE GIVES HIM EVERY-THING HE NEEDS. IN OTHER WORDS...
...THIS *ENTIRE BREWERY* IS DUFFMAN'S WEAPON!
LET'S TAKE THE STAIRS. MY KNEES CAN'T TAKE THAT KIND OF IMPACT.

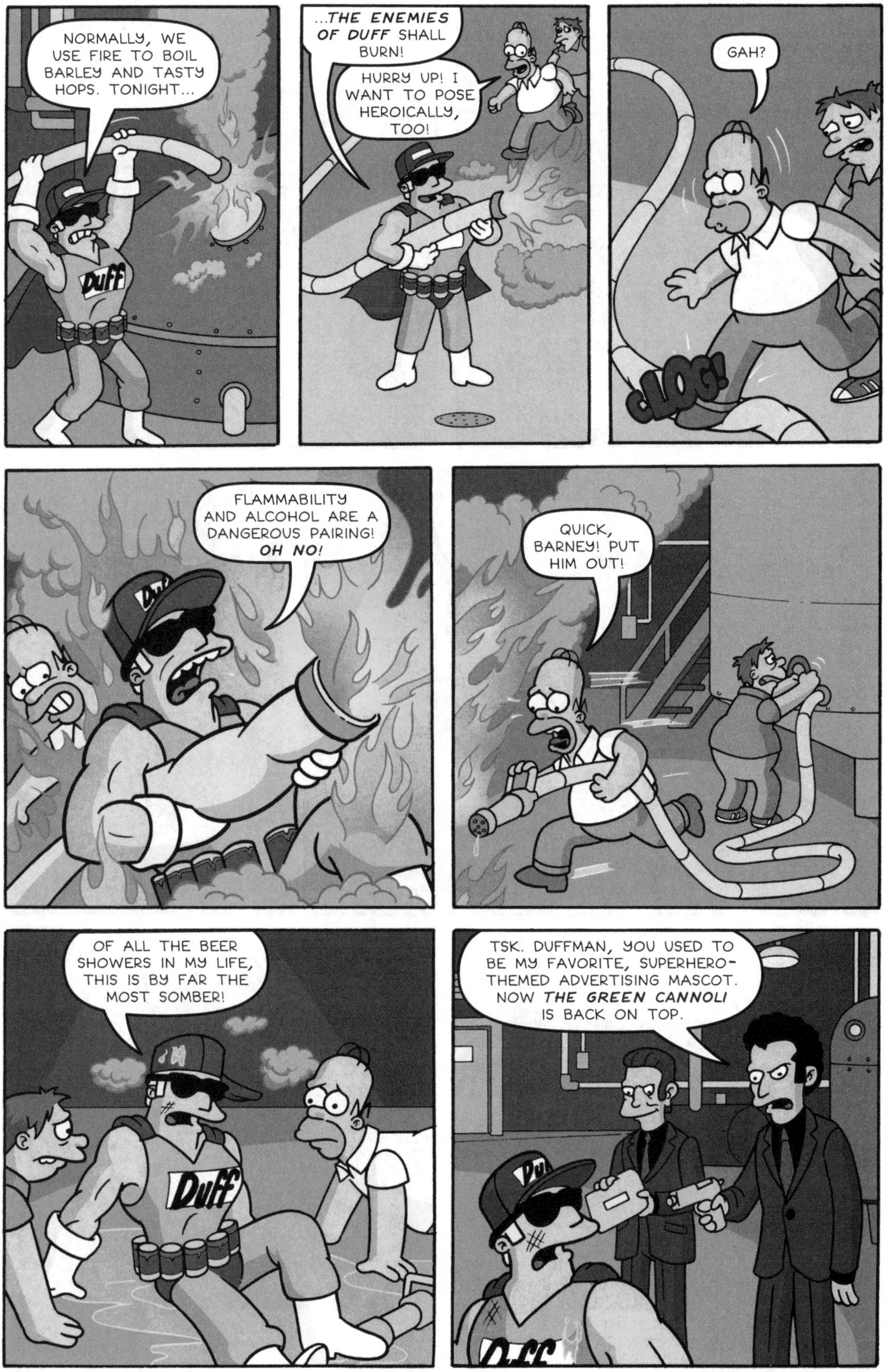
NORMALLY, WE USE FIRE TO BOIL BARLEY AND TASTY HOPS. TONIGHT...
...*THE ENEMIES OF DUFF* SHALL BURN!
HURRY UP! I WANT TO POSE HEROICALLY, TOO!
GAH?
CLOG!
FLAMMABILITY AND ALCOHOL ARE A DANGEROUS PAIRING! *OH NO!*
QUICK, BARNEY! PUT HIM OUT!
OF ALL THE BEER SHOWERS IN MY LIFE, THIS IS BY FAR THE MOST SOMBER!
TSK. DUFFMAN, YOU USED TO BE MY FAVORITE, SUPERHERO-THEMED ADVERTISING MASCOT. NOW *THE GREEN CANNOLI* IS BACK ON TOP.

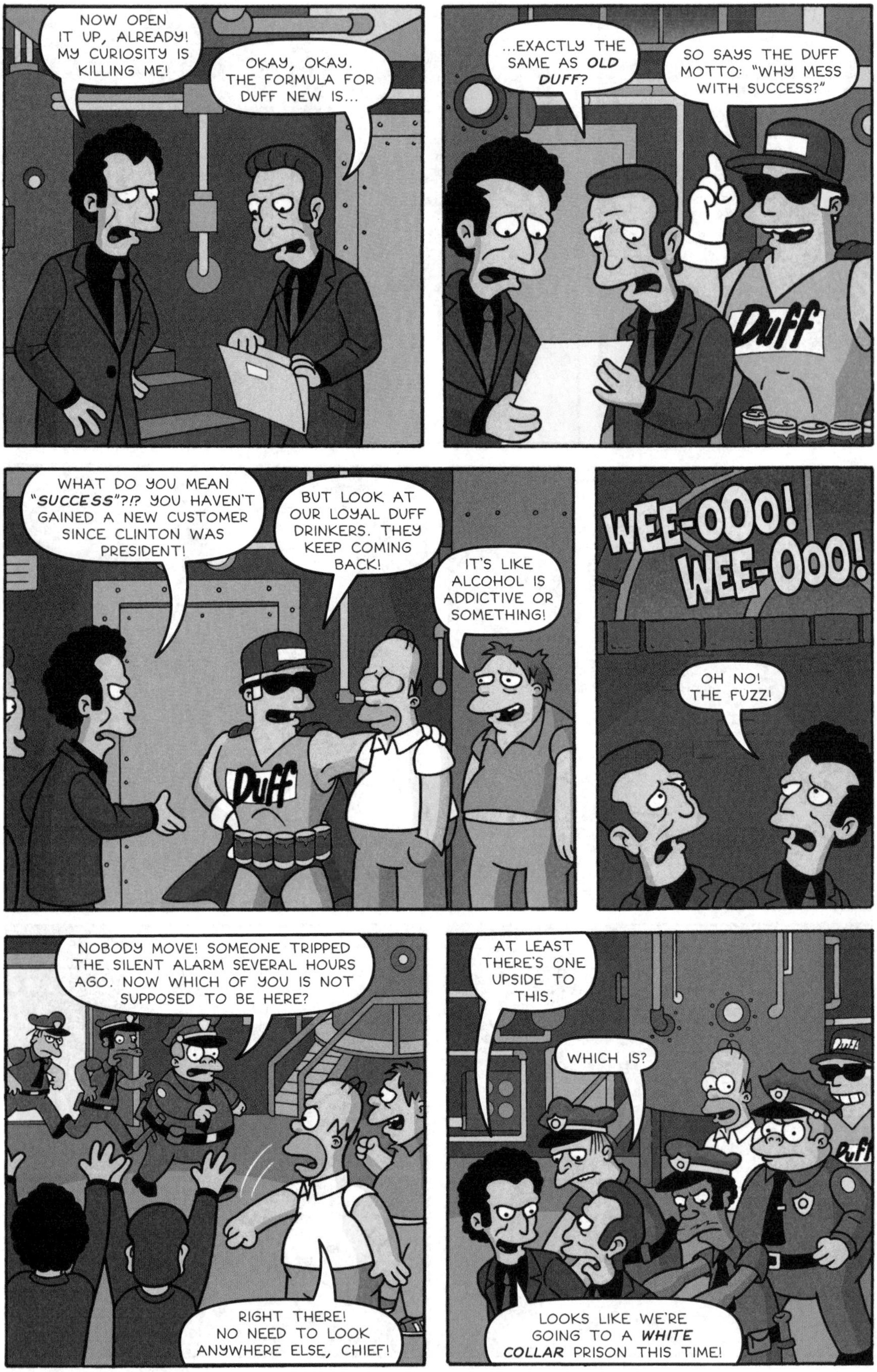
NOW OPEN IT UP, ALREADY! MY CURIOSITY IS KILLING ME!
OKAY, OKAY. THE FORMULA FOR DUFF NEW IS...
...EXACTLY THE SAME AS OLD DUFF?
SO SAYS THE DUFF MOTTO: "WHY MESS WITH SUCCESS?"
Duff
WHAT DO YOU MEAN "SUCCESS"?!? YOU HAVEN'T GAINED A NEW CUSTOMER SINCE CLINTON WAS PRESIDENT!
BUT LOOK AT OUR LOYAL DUFF DRINKERS. THEY KEEP COMING BACK!
IT'S LIKE ALCOHOL IS ADDICTIVE OR SOMETHING!
Duff
WEE-OOO! WEE-OOO!
OH NO! THE FUZZ!
NOBODY MOVE! SOMEONE TRIPPED THE SILENT ALARM SEVERAL HOURS AGO. NOW WHICH OF YOU IS NOT SUPPOSED TO BE HERE?
RIGHT THERE! NO NEED TO LOOK ANYWHERE ELSE, CHIEF!
AT LEAST THERE'S ONE UPSIDE TO THIS.
WHICH IS?
LOOKS LIKE WE'RE GOING TO A WHITE COLLAR PRISON THIS TIME!

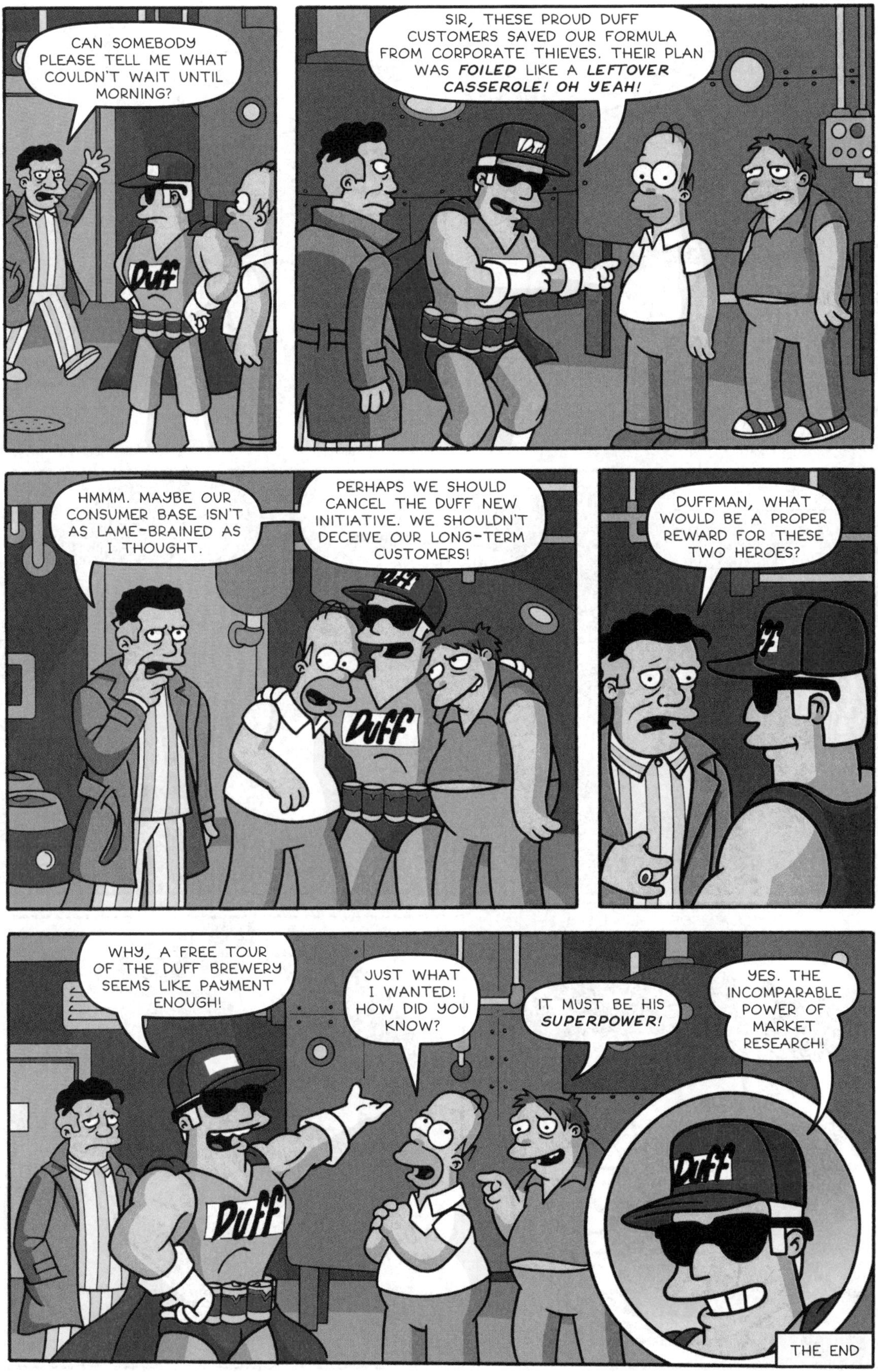
CAN SOMEBODY PLEASE TELL ME WHAT COULDN'T WAIT UNTIL MORNING?
SIR, THESE PROUD DUFF CUSTOMERS SAVED OUR FORMULA FROM CORPORATE THIEVES. THEIR PLAN WAS *FOILED* LIKE A *LEFTOVER CASSEROLE! OH YEAH!*
HMMM. MAYBE OUR CONSUMER BASE ISN'T AS LAME-BRAINED AS I THOUGHT.
PERHAPS WE SHOULD CANCEL THE DUFF NEW INITIATIVE. WE SHOULDN'T DECEIVE OUR LONG-TERM CUSTOMERS!
DUFFMAN, WHAT WOULD BE A PROPER REWARD FOR THESE TWO HEROES?
WHY, A FREE TOUR OF THE DUFF BREWERY SEEMS LIKE PAYMENT ENOUGH!
JUST WHAT I WANTED! HOW DID YOU KNOW?
IT MUST BE HIS *SUPERPOWER!*
YES. THE INCOMPARABLE POWER OF MARKET RESEARCH!
THE END

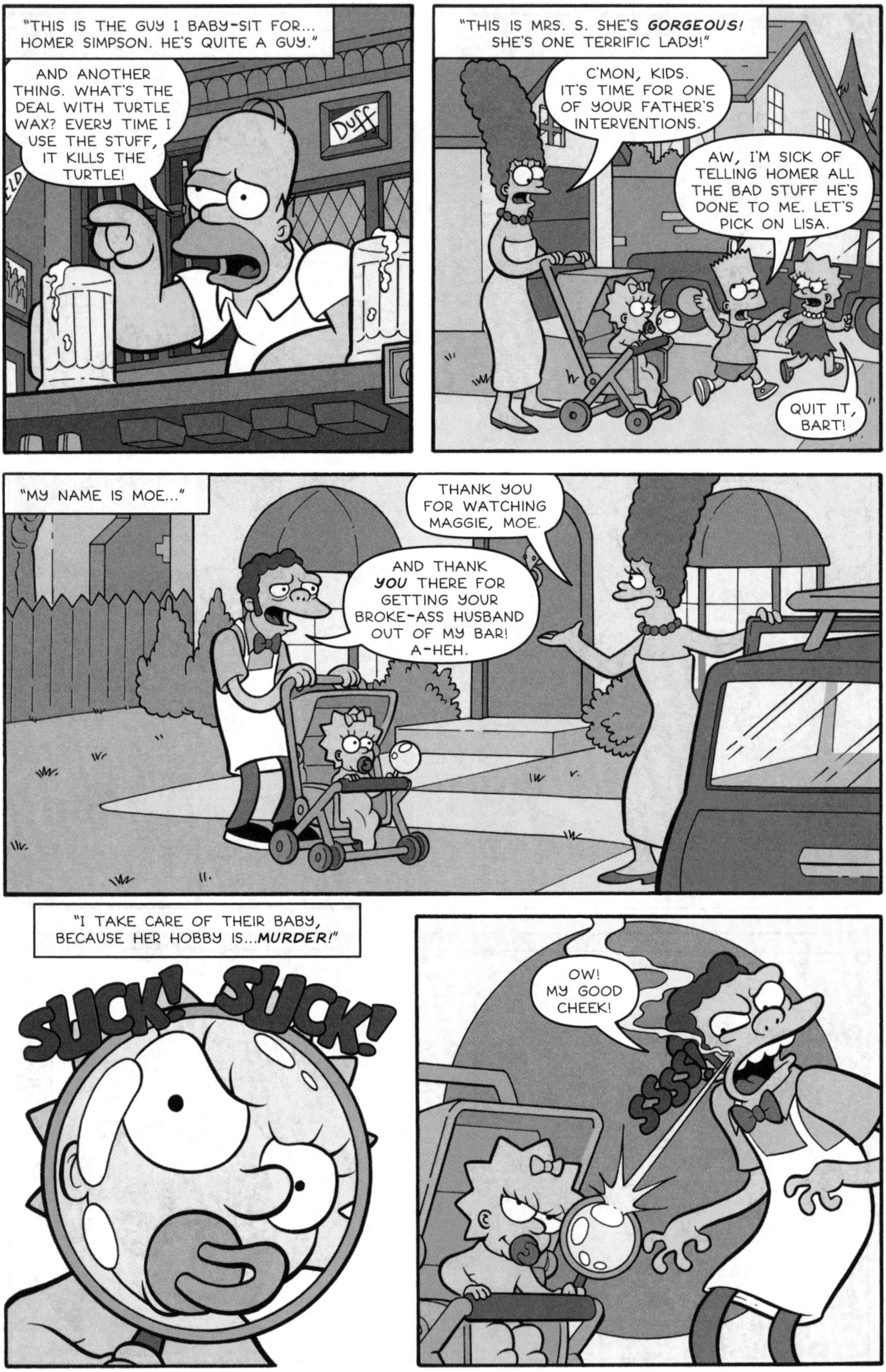
"THIS IS THE GUY I BABY-SIT FOR... HOMER SIMPSON. HE'S QUITE A GUY."
AND ANOTHER THING. WHAT'S THE DEAL WITH TURTLE WAX? EVERY TIME I USE THE STUFF, IT KILLS THE TURTLE!
Duff
"THIS IS MRS. S. SHE'S **GORGEOUS!** SHE'S ONE TERRIFIC LADY!"
C'MON, KIDS. IT'S TIME FOR ONE OF YOUR FATHER'S INTERVENTIONS.
AW, I'M SICK OF TELLING HOMER ALL THE BAD STUFF HE'S DONE TO ME. LET'S PICK ON LISA.
QUIT IT, BART!
"MY NAME IS MOE..."
THANK YOU FOR WATCHING MAGGIE, MOE.
AND THANK **YOU** THERE FOR GETTING YOUR BROKE-ASS HUSBAND OUT OF MY BAR! A-HEH.
"I TAKE CARE OF THEIR BABY, BECAUSE HER HOBBY IS...**MURDER!**"
SUCK! SUCK!
OW! MY GOOD CHEEK!
SSSS!

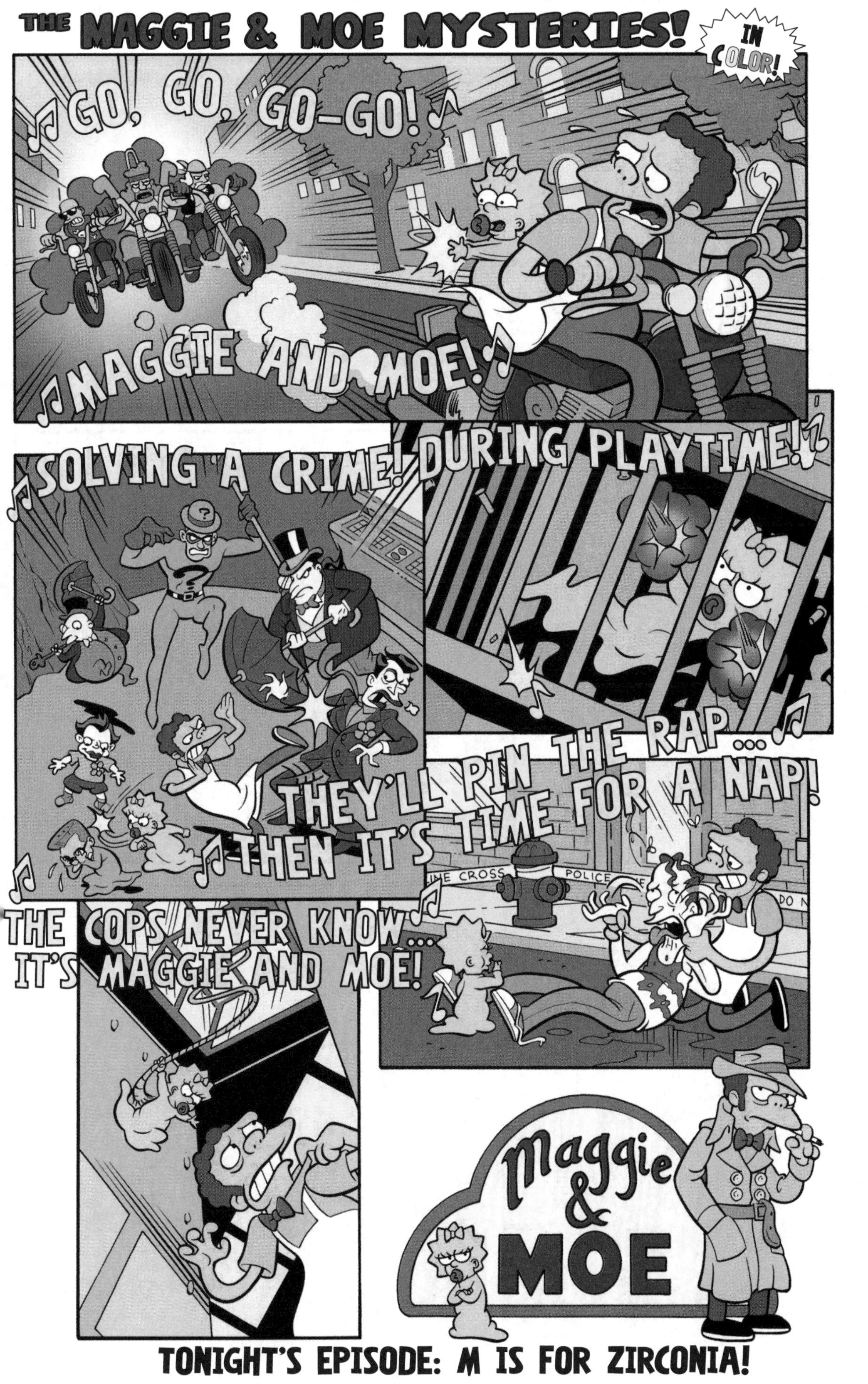
THE MAGGIE & MOE MYSTERIES!
IN COLOR!
GO, GO, GO-GO!
MAGGIE AND MOE!
SOLVING A CRIME! DURING PLAYTIME!
THEY'LL PIN THE RAP...
THEN IT'S TIME FOR A NAP!
POLICE
THE COPS NEVER KNOW...
IT'S MAGGIE AND MOE!
Maggie & MOE
TONIGHT'S EPISODE: M IS FOR ZIRCONIA!

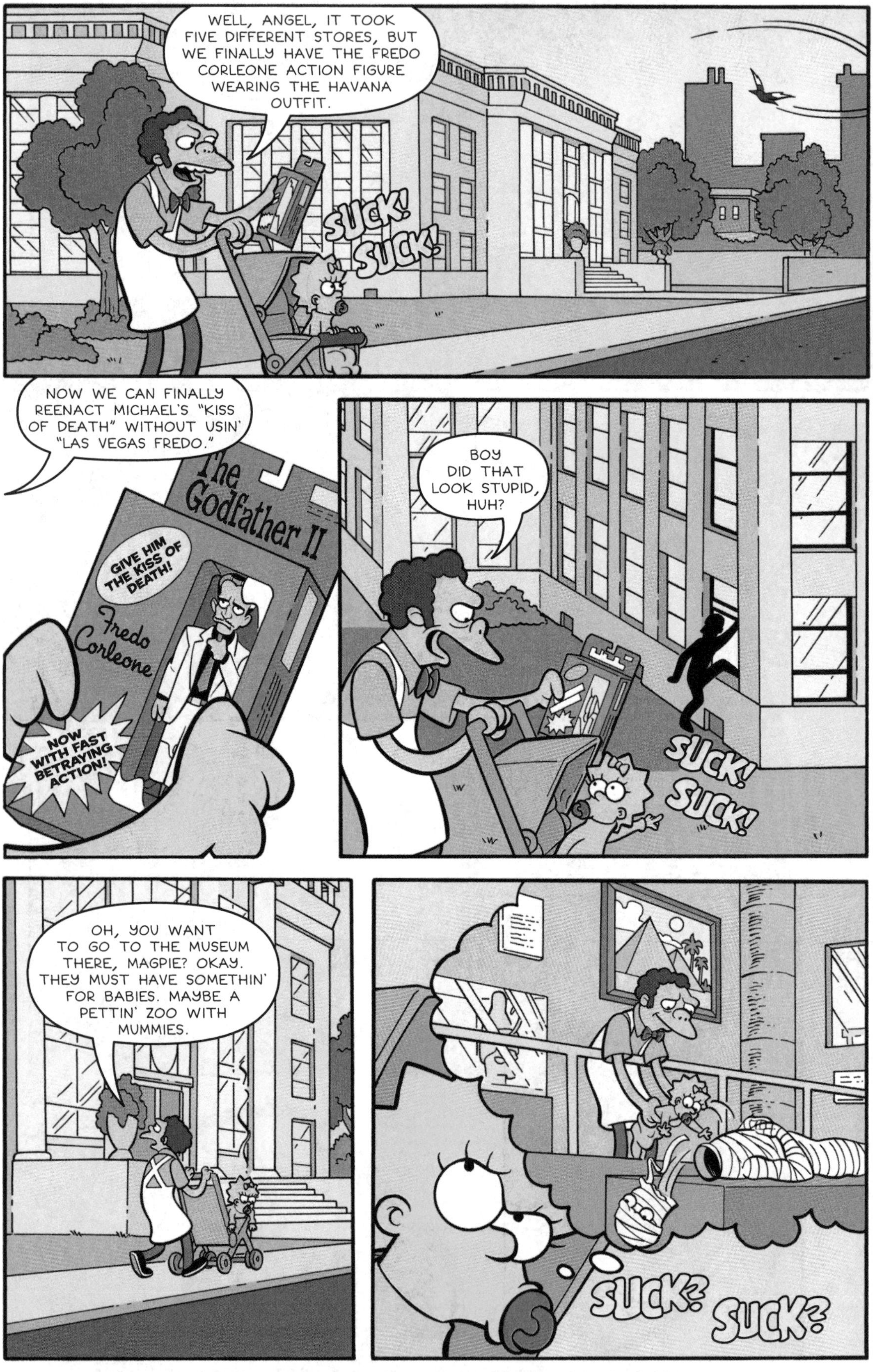
WELL, ANGEL, IT TOOK FIVE DIFFERENT STORES, BUT WE FINALLY HAVE THE FREDO CORLEONE ACTION FIGURE WEARING THE HAVANA OUTFIT.
SUCK! SUCK!
NOW WE CAN FINALLY REENACT MICHAEL'S "KISS OF DEATH" WITHOUT USIN' "LAS VEGAS FREDO."
The Godfather II
GIVE HIM THE KISS OF DEATH!
Fredo Corleone
NOW WITH FAST BETRAYING ACTION!
BOY DID THAT LOOK STUPID, HUH?
SUCK! SUCK!
OH, YOU WANT TO GO TO THE MUSEUM THERE, MAGPIE? OKAY. THEY MUST HAVE SOMETHIN' FOR BABIES. MAYBE A PETTIN' ZOO WITH MUMMIES.
SUCK? SUCK?

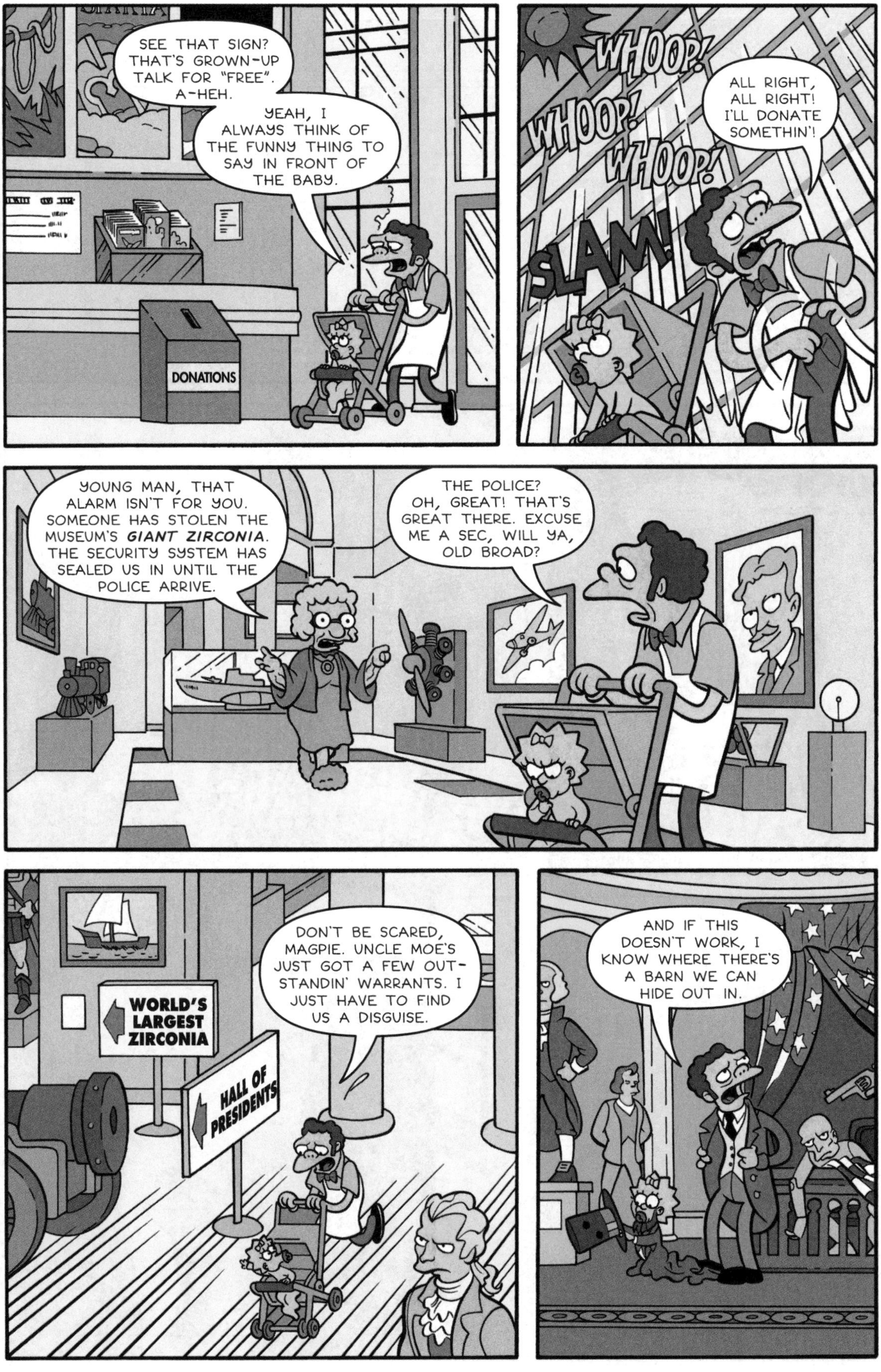
SEE THAT SIGN? THAT'S GROWN-UP TALK FOR "FREE". A-HEH.
YEAH, I ALWAYS THINK OF THE FUNNY THING TO SAY IN FRONT OF THE BABY.
DONATIONS
WHOOP! WHOOP! WHOOP!
SLAM!
ALL RIGHT, ALL RIGHT! I'LL DONATE SOMETHIN'!
YOUNG MAN, THAT ALARM ISN'T FOR YOU. SOMEONE HAS STOLEN THE MUSEUM'S GIANT ZIRCONIA. THE SECURITY SYSTEM HAS SEALED US IN UNTIL THE POLICE ARRIVE.
THE POLICE? OH, GREAT! THAT'S GREAT THERE. EXCUSE ME A SEC, WILL YA, OLD BROAD?
WORLD'S LARGEST ZIRCONIA
HALL OF PRESIDENTS
DON'T BE SCARED, MAGPIE. UNCLE MOE'S JUST GOT A FEW OUT-STANDIN' WARRANTS. I JUST HAVE TO FIND US A DISGUISE.
AND IF THIS DOESN'T WORK, I KNOW WHERE THERE'S A BARN WE CAN HIDE OUT IN.

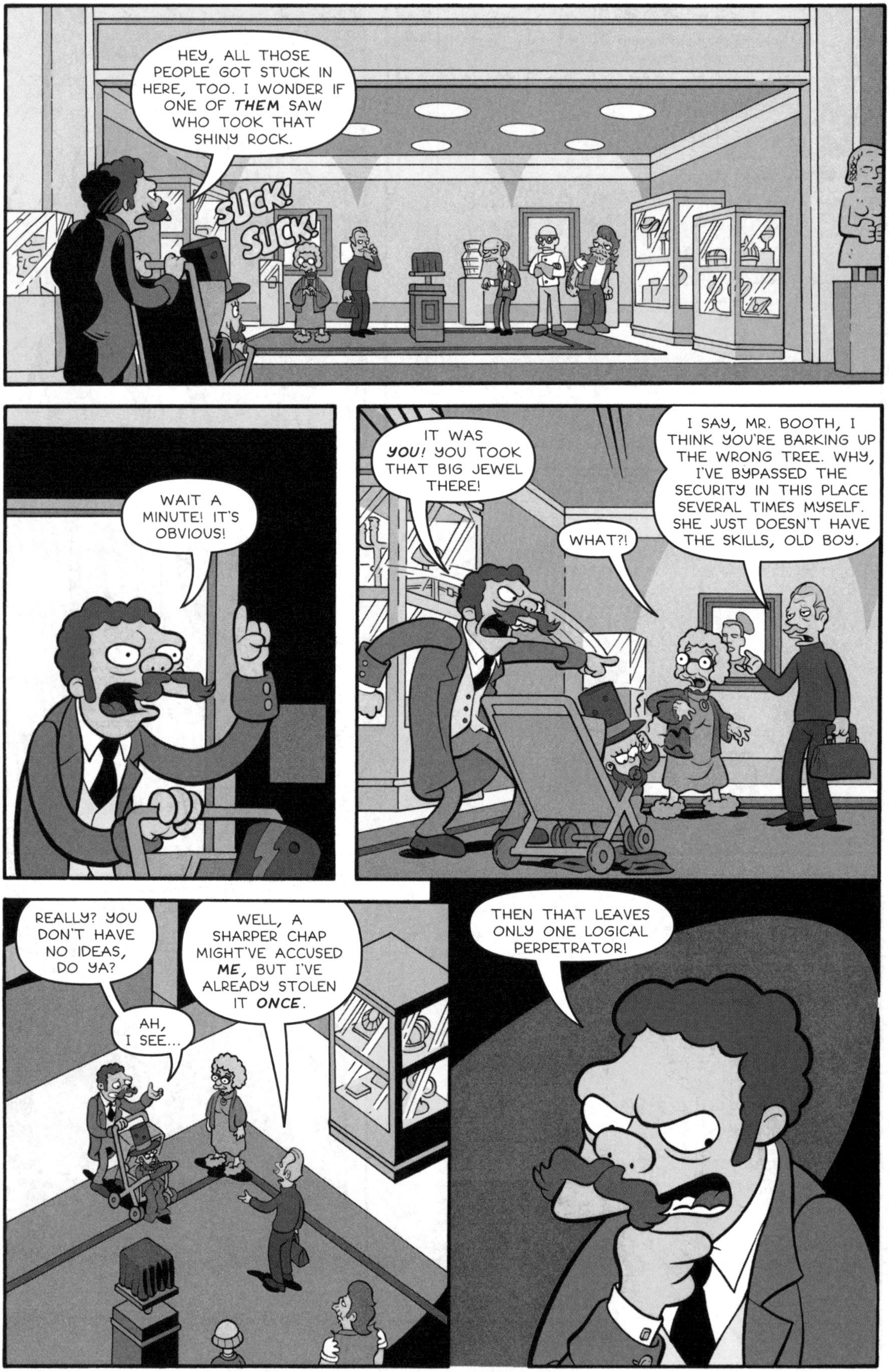
HEY, ALL THOSE PEOPLE GOT STUCK IN HERE, TOO. I WONDER IF ONE OF *THEM* SAW WHO TOOK THAT SHINY ROCK.
SUCK! SUCK!
WAIT A MINUTE! IT'S OBVIOUS!
IT WAS *YOU!* YOU TOOK THAT BIG JEWEL THERE!
WHAT?!
I SAY, MR. BOOTH, I THINK YOU'RE BARKING UP THE WRONG TREE. WHY, I'VE BYPASSED THE SECURITY IN THIS PLACE SEVERAL TIMES MYSELF. SHE JUST DOESN'T HAVE THE SKILLS, OLD BOY.
REALLY? YOU DON'T HAVE NO IDEAS, DO YA?
AH, I SEE...
WELL, A SHARPER CHAP MIGHT'VE ACCUSED *ME*, BUT I'VE ALREADY STOLEN IT *ONCE*.
THEN THAT LEAVES ONLY ONE LOGICAL PERPETRATOR!

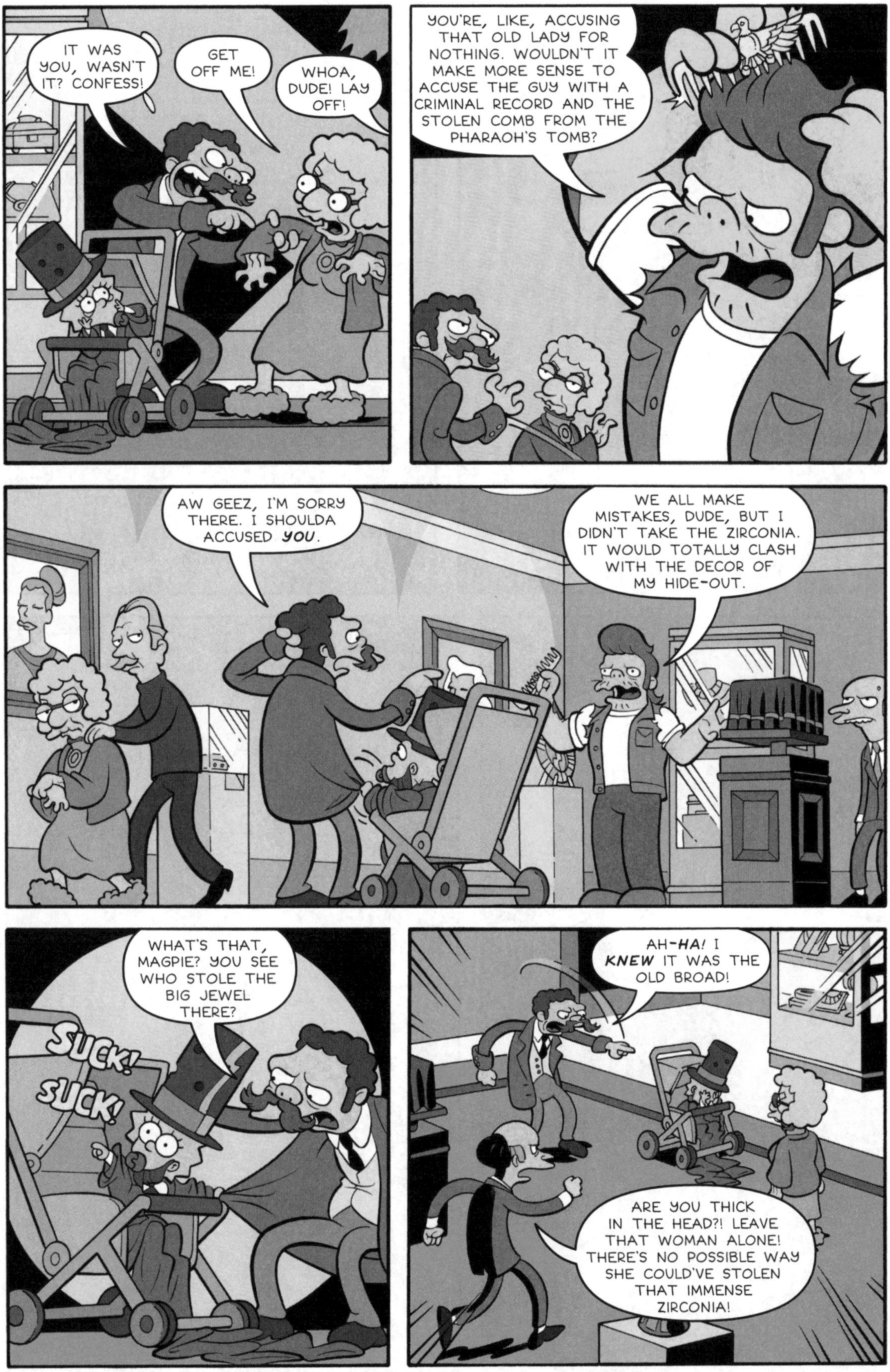

IT WAS YOU, WASN'T IT? CONFESS!
GET OFF ME!
WHOA, DUDE! LAY OFF!
YOU'RE, LIKE, ACCUSING THAT OLD LADY FOR NOTHING. WOULDN'T IT MAKE MORE SENSE TO ACCUSE THE GUY WITH A CRIMINAL RECORD AND THE STOLEN COMB FROM THE PHARAOH'S TOMB?
AW GEEZ, I'M SORRY THERE. I SHOULDA ACCUSED ***YOU***.
WE ALL MAKE MISTAKES, DUDE, BUT I DIDN'T TAKE THE ZIRCONIA. IT WOULD TOTALLY CLASH WITH THE DECOR OF MY HIDE-OUT.
WHAT'S THAT, MAGPIE? YOU SEE WHO STOLE THE BIG JEWEL THERE?
SUCK! SUCK!
AH-***HA!*** I ***KNEW*** IT WAS THE OLD BROAD!
ARE YOU THICK IN THE HEAD?! LEAVE THAT WOMAN ALONE! THERE'S NO POSSIBLE WAY SHE COULD'VE STOLEN THAT IMMENSE ZIRCONIA!

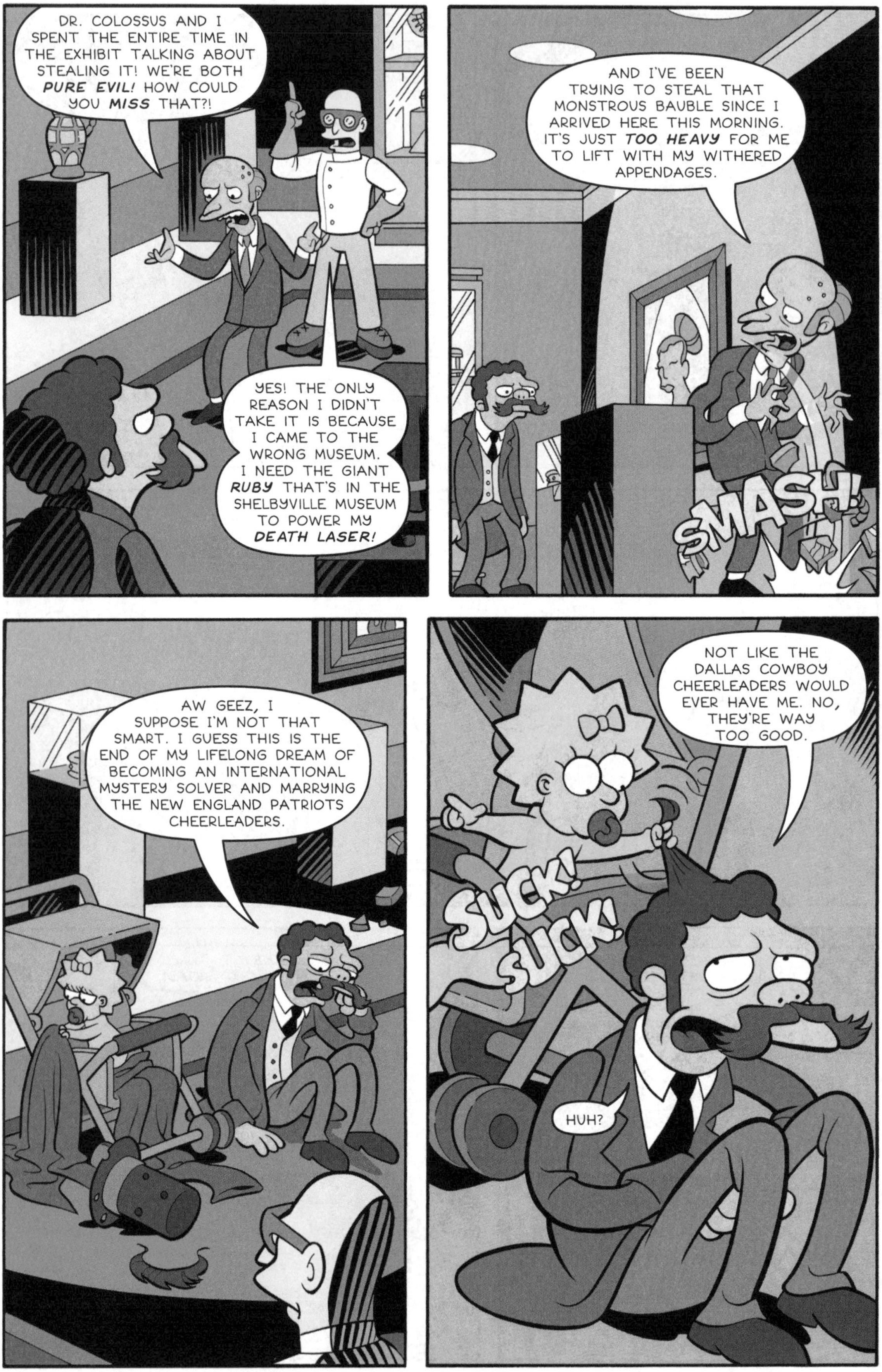
DR. COLOSSUS AND I SPENT THE ENTIRE TIME IN THE EXHIBIT TALKING ABOUT STEALING IT! WE'RE BOTH PURE EVIL! HOW COULD YOU MISS THAT?!
YES! THE ONLY REASON I DIDN'T TAKE IT IS BECAUSE I CAME TO THE WRONG MUSEUM. I NEED THE GIANT RUBY THAT'S IN THE SHELBYVILLE MUSEUM TO POWER MY DEATH LASER!
AND I'VE BEEN TRYING TO STEAL THAT MONSTROUS BAUBLE SINCE I ARRIVED HERE THIS MORNING. IT'S JUST TOO HEAVY FOR ME TO LIFT WITH MY WITHERED APPENDAGES.
SMASH!
AW GEEZ, I SUPPOSE I'M NOT THAT SMART. I GUESS THIS IS THE END OF MY LIFELONG DREAM OF BECOMING AN INTERNATIONAL MYSTERY SOLVER AND MARRYING THE NEW ENGLAND PATRIOTS CHEERLEADERS.
NOT LIKE THE DALLAS COWBOY CHEERLEADERS WOULD EVER HAVE ME. NO, THEY'RE WAY TOO GOOD.
SUCK! SUCK!
HUH?

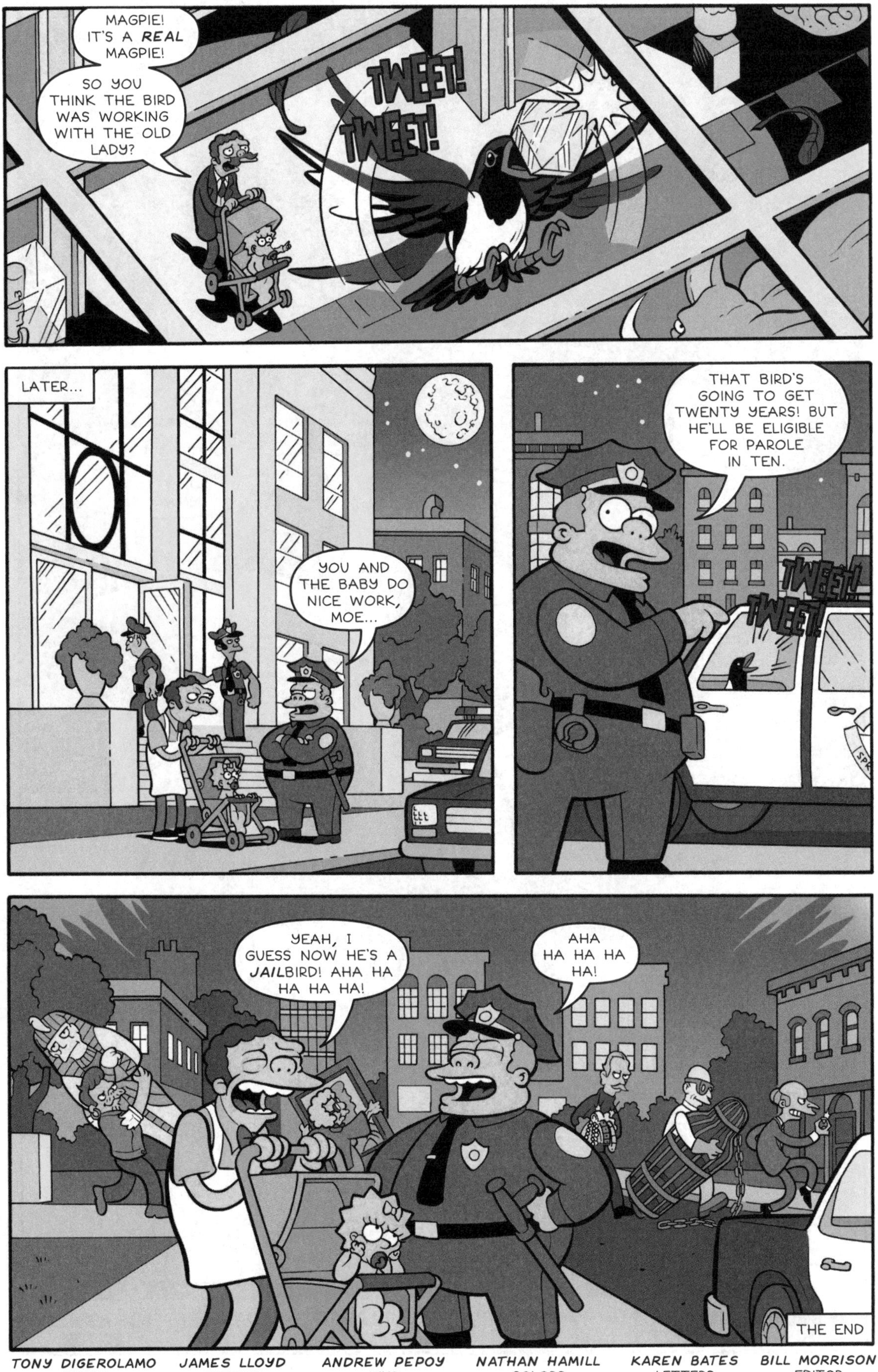

MAGPIE! IT'S A **REAL** MAGPIE!
SO YOU THINK THE BIRD WAS WORKING WITH THE OLD LADY?
TWEET! TWEET!
LATER...
YOU AND THE BABY DO NICE WORK, MOE...
THAT BIRD'S GOING TO GET TWENTY YEARS! BUT HE'LL BE ELIGIBLE FOR PAROLE IN TEN.
TWEET! TWEET!
YEAH, I GUESS NOW HE'S A **JAIL**BIRD! AHA HA HA HA HA!
AHA HA HA HA HA!
THE END

TONY DIGEROLAMO SCRIPT | ***JAMES LLOYD*** PENCILS | ***ANDREW PEPOY*** INKS | ***NATHAN HAMILL*** COLORS | ***KAREN BATES*** LETTERS | ***BILL MORRISON*** EDITOR

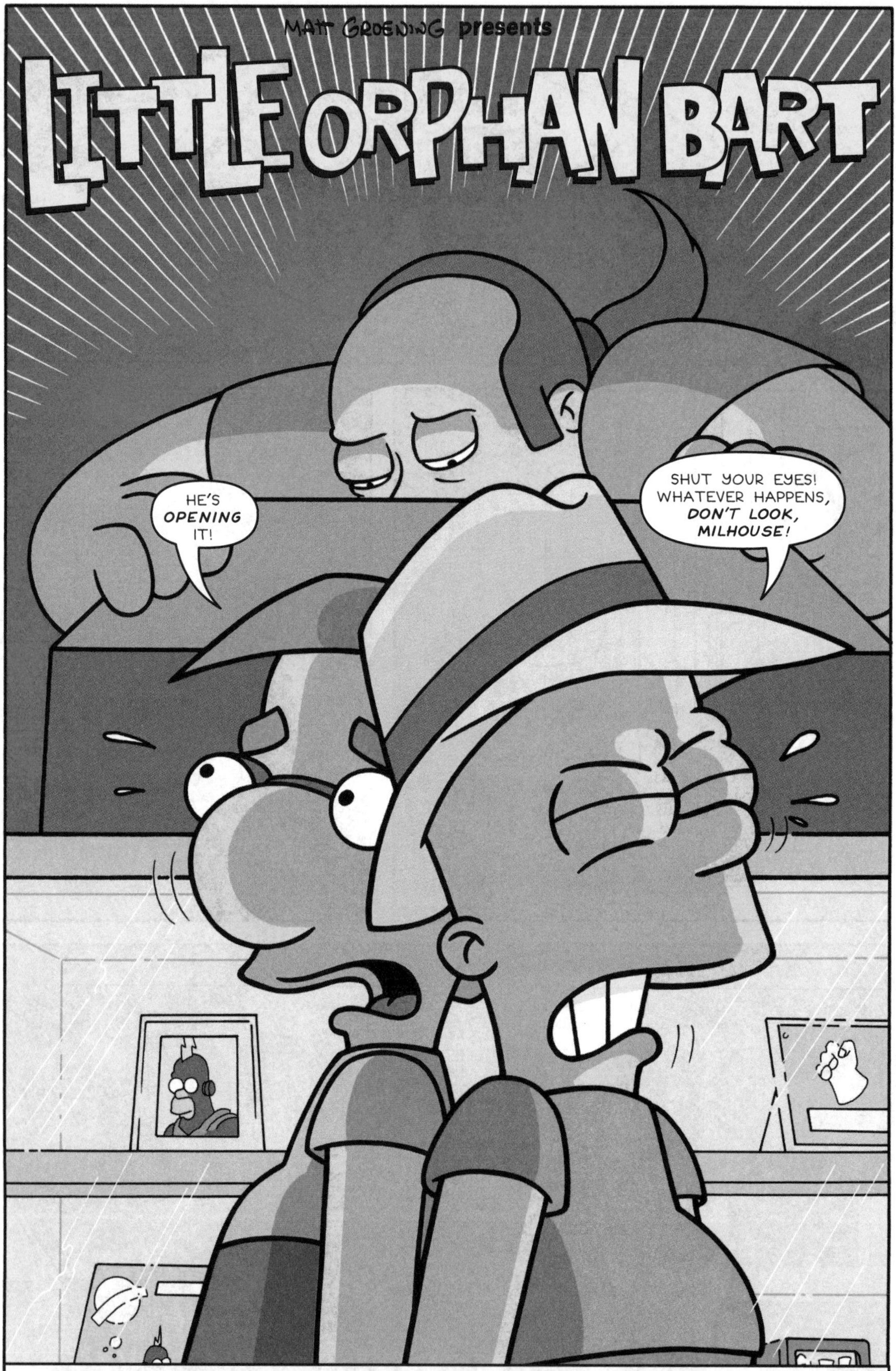
MATT GROENING presents
LITTLE ORPHAN BART
HE'S OPENING IT!
SHUT YOUR EYES! WHATEVER HAPPENS, DON'T LOOK, MILHOUSE!

IAN BOOTHBY	JOHN COSTANZA	PHYLLIS NOVIN	ART VILLANUEVA	KAREN BATES	BILL MORRISON
SCRIPT	PENCILS	INKS	COLORS	LETTERS	EDITOR

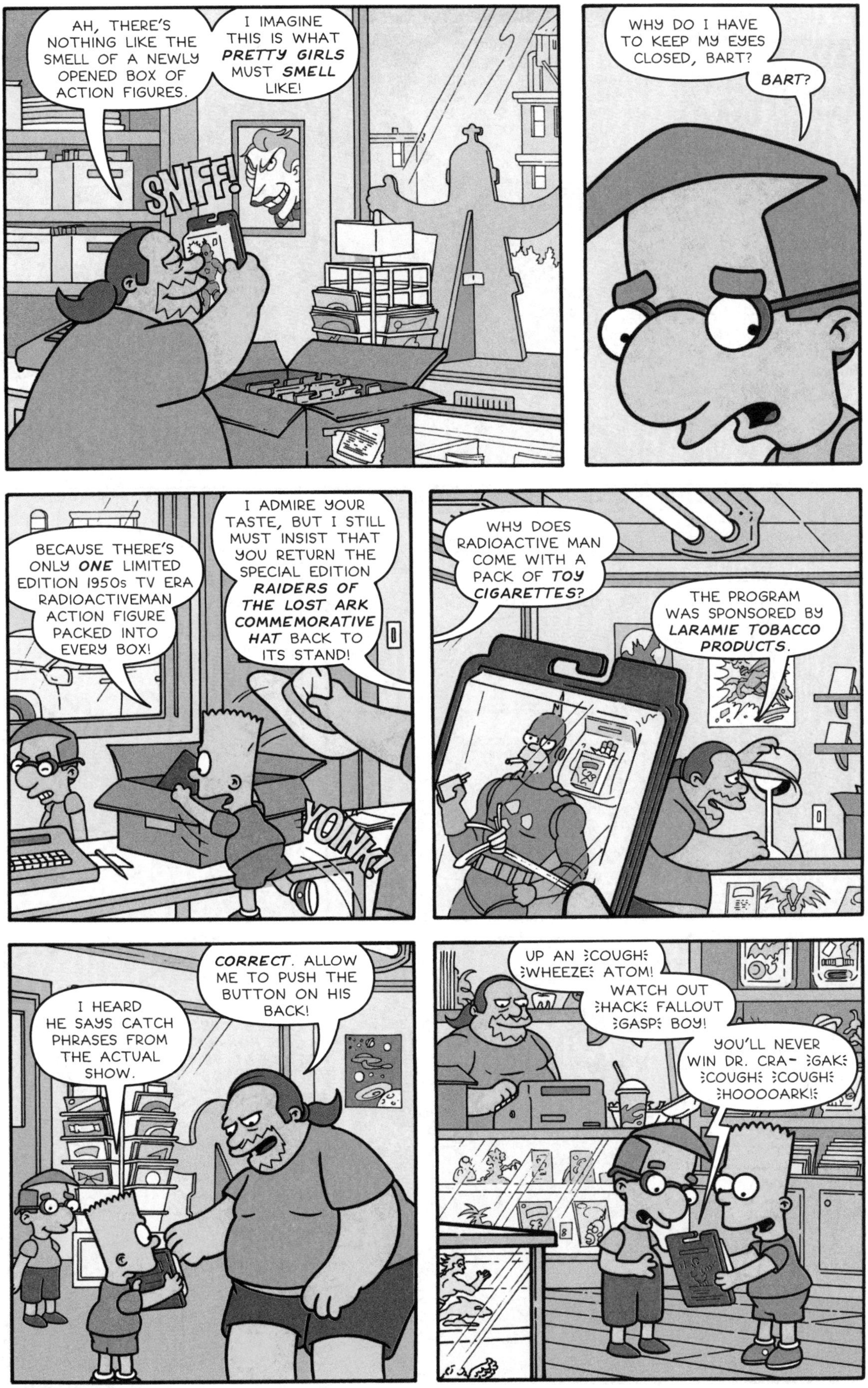
AH, THERE'S NOTHING LIKE THE SMELL OF A NEWLY OPENED BOX OF ACTION FIGURES.
I IMAGINE THIS IS WHAT PRETTY GIRLS MUST SMELL LIKE!
SNIFF!
WHY DO I HAVE TO KEEP MY EYES CLOSED, BART?
BART?
BECAUSE THERE'S ONLY ONE LIMITED EDITION 1950s TV ERA RADIOACTIVEMAN ACTION FIGURE PACKED INTO EVERY BOX!
I ADMIRE YOUR TASTE, BUT I STILL MUST INSIST THAT YOU RETURN THE SPECIAL EDITION RAIDERS OF THE LOST ARK COMMEMORATIVE HAT BACK TO ITS STAND!
YOINK!
WHY DOES RADIOACTIVE MAN COME WITH A PACK OF TOY CIGARETTES?
THE PROGRAM WAS SPONSORED BY LARAMIE TOBACCO PRODUCTS.
I HEARD HE SAYS CATCH PHRASES FROM THE ACTUAL SHOW.
CORRECT. ALLOW ME TO PUSH THE BUTTON ON HIS BACK!
UP AN ⁝COUGH⁝ ⁝WHEEZE⁝ ATOM!
WATCH OUT ⁝HACK⁝ FALLOUT ⁝GASP⁝ BOY!
YOU'LL NEVER WIN DR. CRA- ⁝GAK⁝ ⁝COUGH⁝ ⁝COUGH⁝ ⁝HOOOOARK!⁝

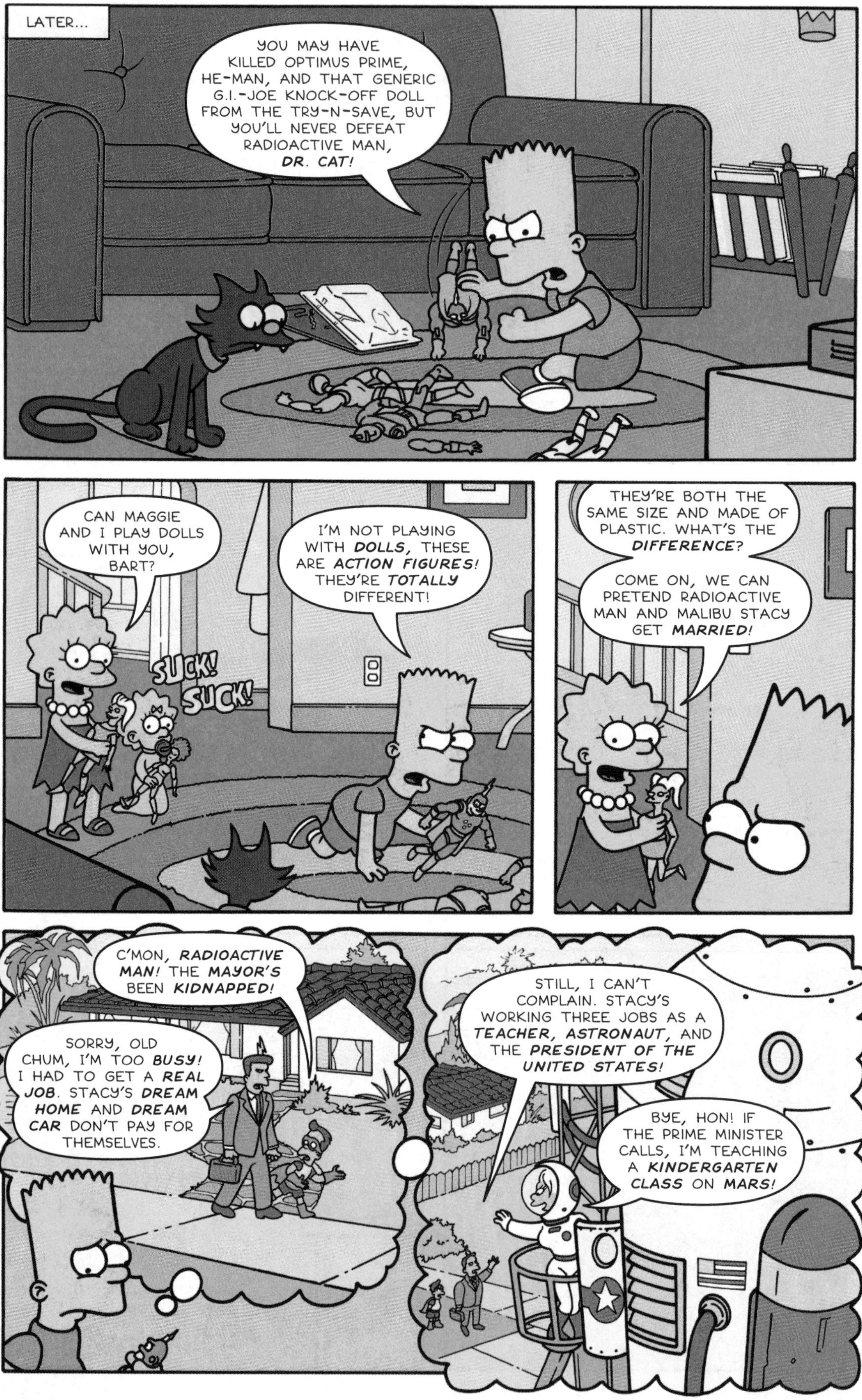

LATER...
YOU MAY HAVE KILLED OPTIMUS PRIME, HE-MAN, AND THAT GENERIC G.I.-JOE KNOCK-OFF DOLL FROM THE TRY-N-SAVE, BUT YOU'LL NEVER DEFEAT RADIOACTIVE MAN, **DR. CAT!**
CAN MAGGIE AND I PLAY DOLLS WITH YOU, BART?
SUCK! SUCK!
I'M NOT PLAYING WITH **DOLLS,** THESE ARE **ACTION FIGURES!** THEY'RE **TOTALLY** DIFFERENT!
THEY'RE BOTH THE SAME SIZE AND MADE OF PLASTIC. WHAT'S THE **DIFFERENCE?**
COME ON, WE CAN PRETEND RADIOACTIVE MAN AND MALIBU STACY GET **MARRIED!**
C'MON, **RADIOACTIVE MAN!** THE **MAYOR'S** BEEN **KIDNAPPED!**
SORRY, OLD CHUM, I'M TOO **BUSY!** I HAD TO GET A **REAL JOB.** STACY'S **DREAM HOME** AND **DREAM CAR** DON'T PAY FOR THEMSELVES.
STILL, I CAN'T COMPLAIN. STACY'S WORKING THREE JOBS AS A **TEACHER, ASTRONAUT,** AND THE **PRESIDENT OF THE UNITED STATES!**
BYE, HON! IF THE PRIME MINISTER CALLS, I'M TEACHING A **KINDERGARTEN CLASS** ON **MARS!**

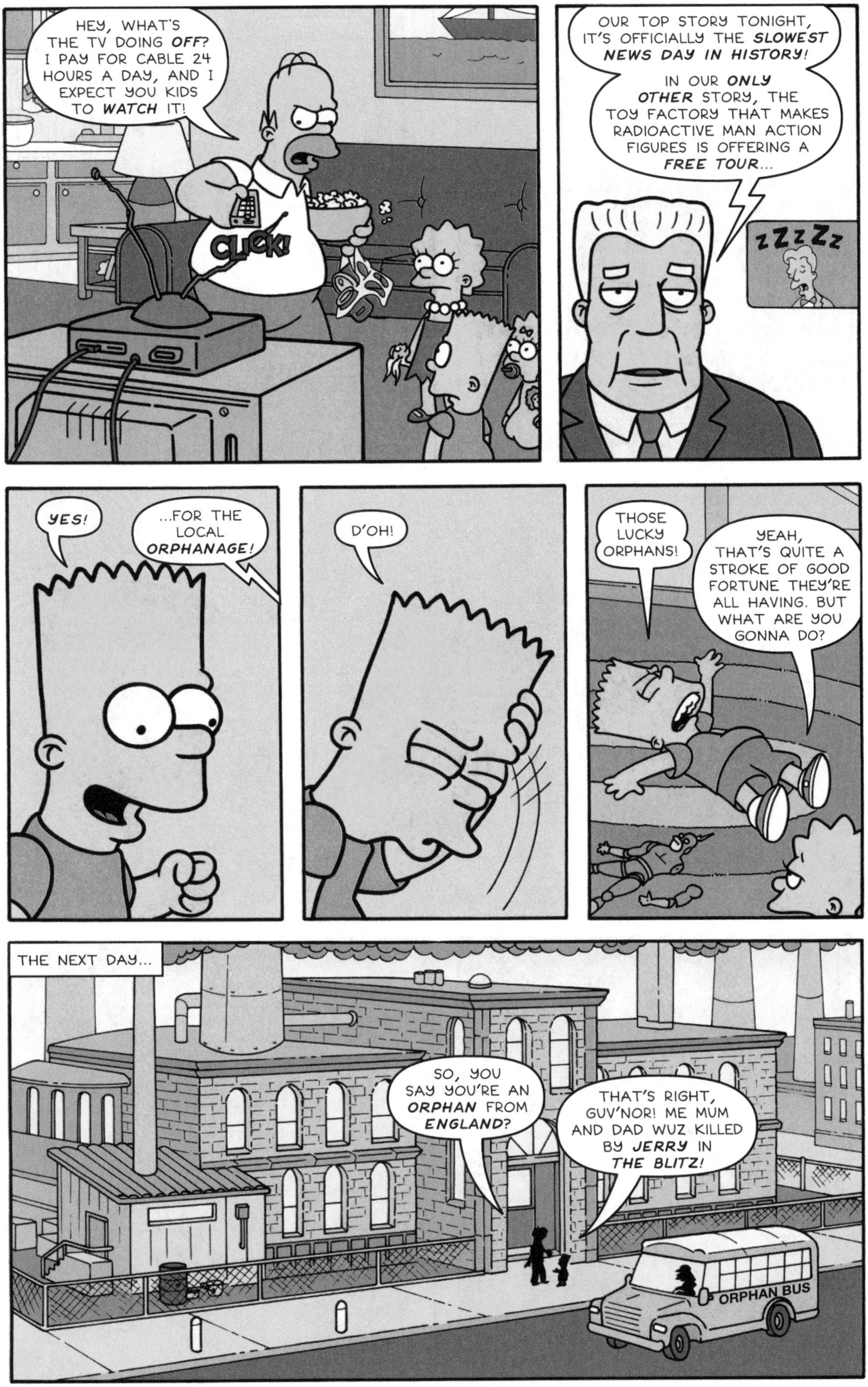
HEY, WHAT'S THE TV DOING OFF? I PAY FOR CABLE 24 HOURS A DAY, AND I EXPECT YOU KIDS TO WATCH IT!
CLICK!
OUR TOP STORY TONIGHT, IT'S OFFICIALLY THE SLOWEST NEWS DAY IN HISTORY!
IN OUR ONLY OTHER STORY, THE TOY FACTORY THAT MAKES RADIOACTIVE MAN ACTION FIGURES IS OFFERING A FREE TOUR...
ZZZZZ
YES!
...FOR THE LOCAL ORPHANAGE!
D'OH!
THOSE LUCKY ORPHANS!
YEAH, THAT'S QUITE A STROKE OF GOOD FORTUNE THEY'RE ALL HAVING. BUT WHAT ARE YOU GONNA DO?
THE NEXT DAY...
SO, YOU SAY YOU'RE AN ORPHAN FROM ENGLAND?
THAT'S RIGHT, GUV'NOR! ME MUM AND DAD WUZ KILLED BY JERRY IN THE BLITZ!
ORPHAN BUS

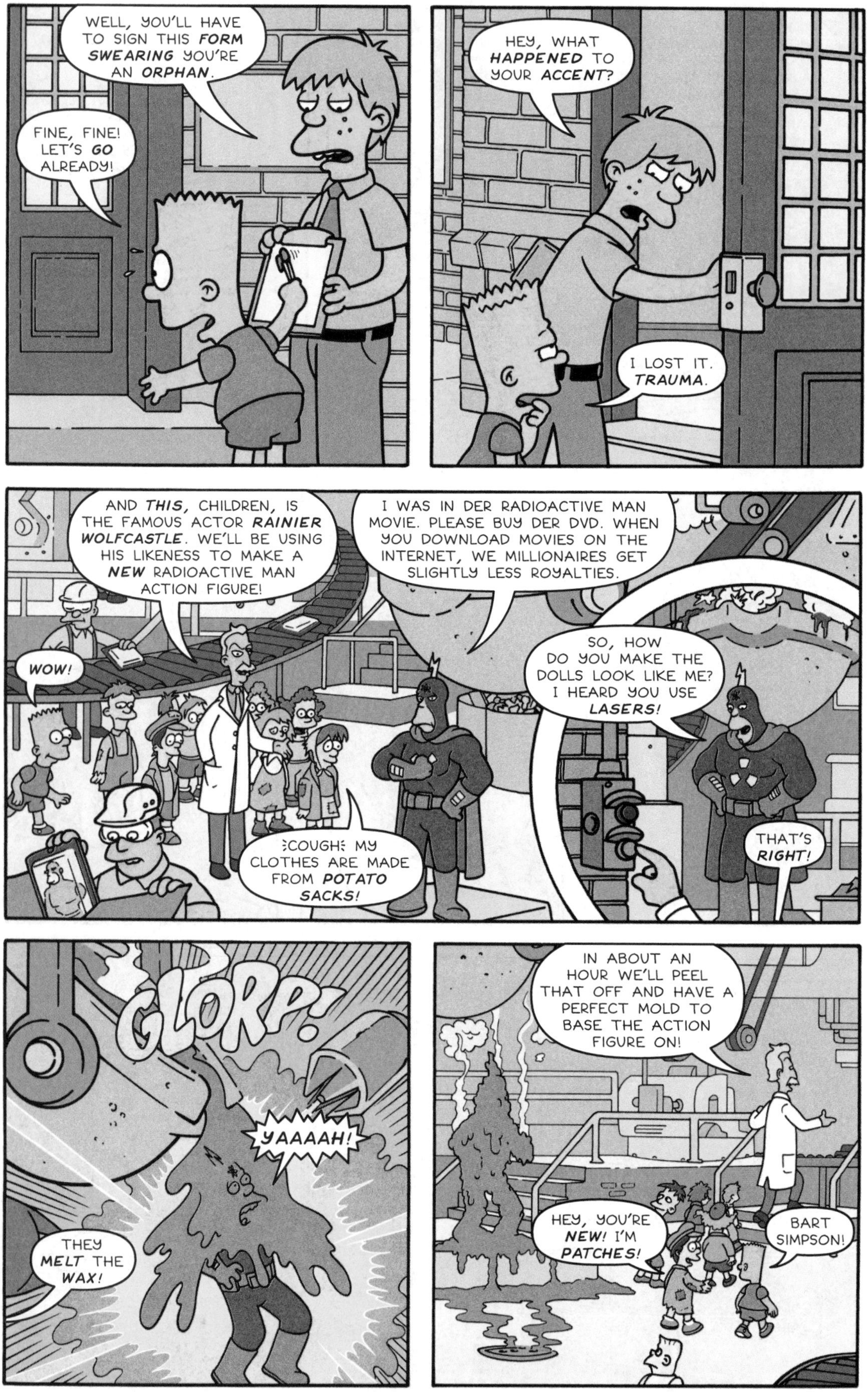
WELL, YOU'LL HAVE TO SIGN THIS FORM SWEARING YOU'RE AN ORPHAN.
FINE, FINE! LET'S GO ALREADY!
HEY, WHAT HAPPENED TO YOUR ACCENT?
I LOST IT. TRAUMA.
AND THIS, CHILDREN, IS THE FAMOUS ACTOR RAINIER WOLFCASTLE. WE'LL BE USING HIS LIKENESS TO MAKE A NEW RADIOACTIVE MAN ACTION FIGURE!
WOW!
I WAS IN DER RADIOACTIVE MAN MOVIE. PLEASE BUY DER DVD. WHEN YOU DOWNLOAD MOVIES ON THE INTERNET, WE MILLIONAIRES GET SLIGHTLY LESS ROYALTIES.
COUGH MY CLOTHES ARE MADE FROM POTATO SACKS!
SO, HOW DO YOU MAKE THE DOLLS LOOK LIKE ME? I HEARD YOU USE LASERS!
THAT'S RIGHT!
GLORP!
YAAAAH!
THEY MELT THE WAX!
IN ABOUT AN HOUR WE'LL PEEL THAT OFF AND HAVE A PERFECT MOLD TO BASE THE ACTION FIGURE ON!
HEY, YOU'RE NEW! I'M PATCHES!
BART SIMPSON!

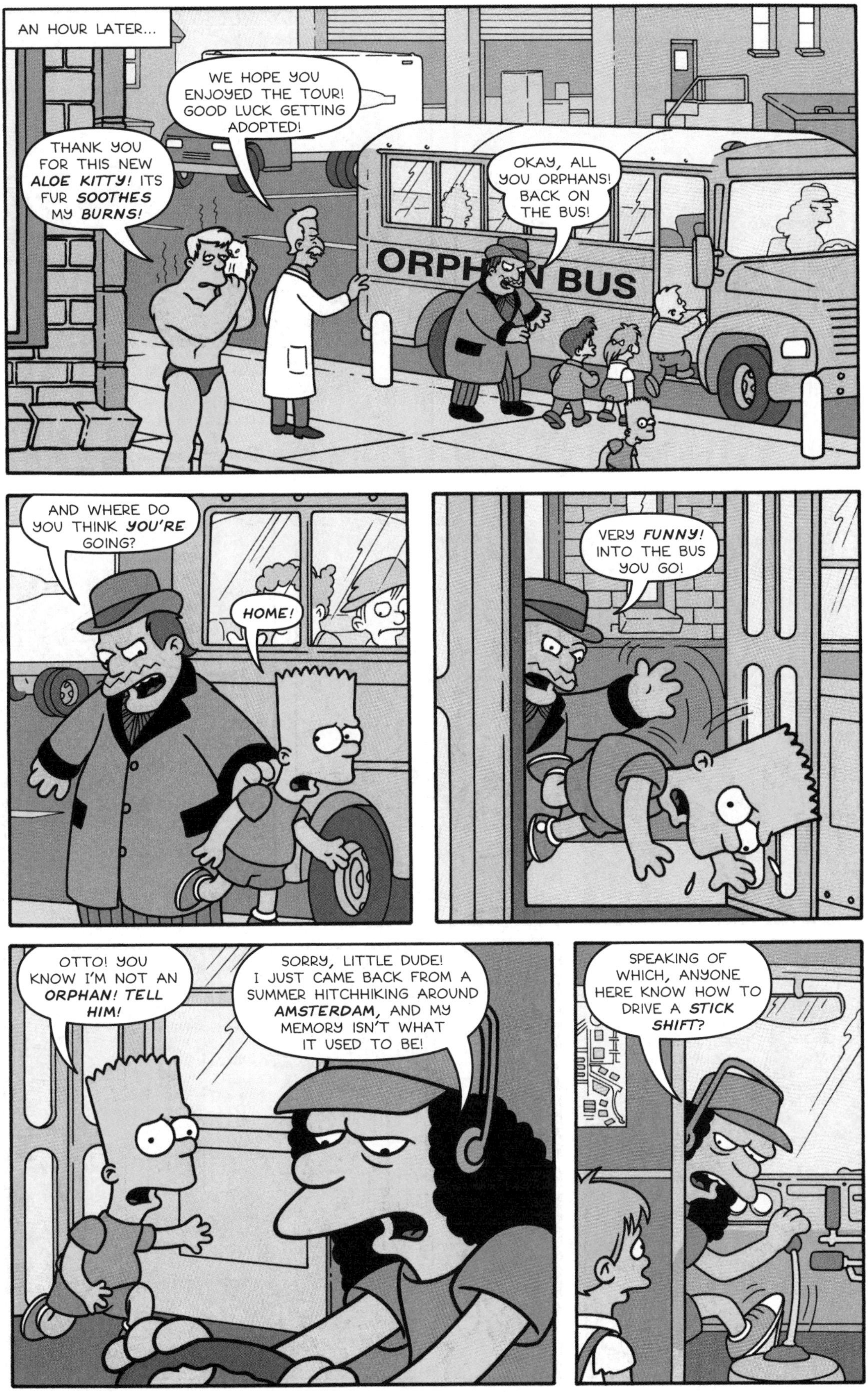
AN HOUR LATER...
THANK YOU FOR THIS NEW ALOE KITTY! ITS FUR SOOTHES MY BURNS!
WE HOPE YOU ENJOYED THE TOUR! GOOD LUCK GETTING ADOPTED!
OKAY, ALL YOU ORPHANS! BACK ON THE BUS!
ORPHAN BUS
AND WHERE DO YOU THINK YOU'RE GOING?
HOME!
VERY FUNNY! INTO THE BUS YOU GO!
OTTO! YOU KNOW I'M NOT AN ORPHAN! TELL HIM!
SORRY, LITTLE DUDE! I JUST CAME BACK FROM A SUMMER HITCHHIKING AROUND AMSTERDAM, AND MY MEMORY ISN'T WHAT IT USED TO BE!
SPEAKING OF WHICH, ANYONE HERE KNOW HOW TO DRIVE A STICK SHIFT?

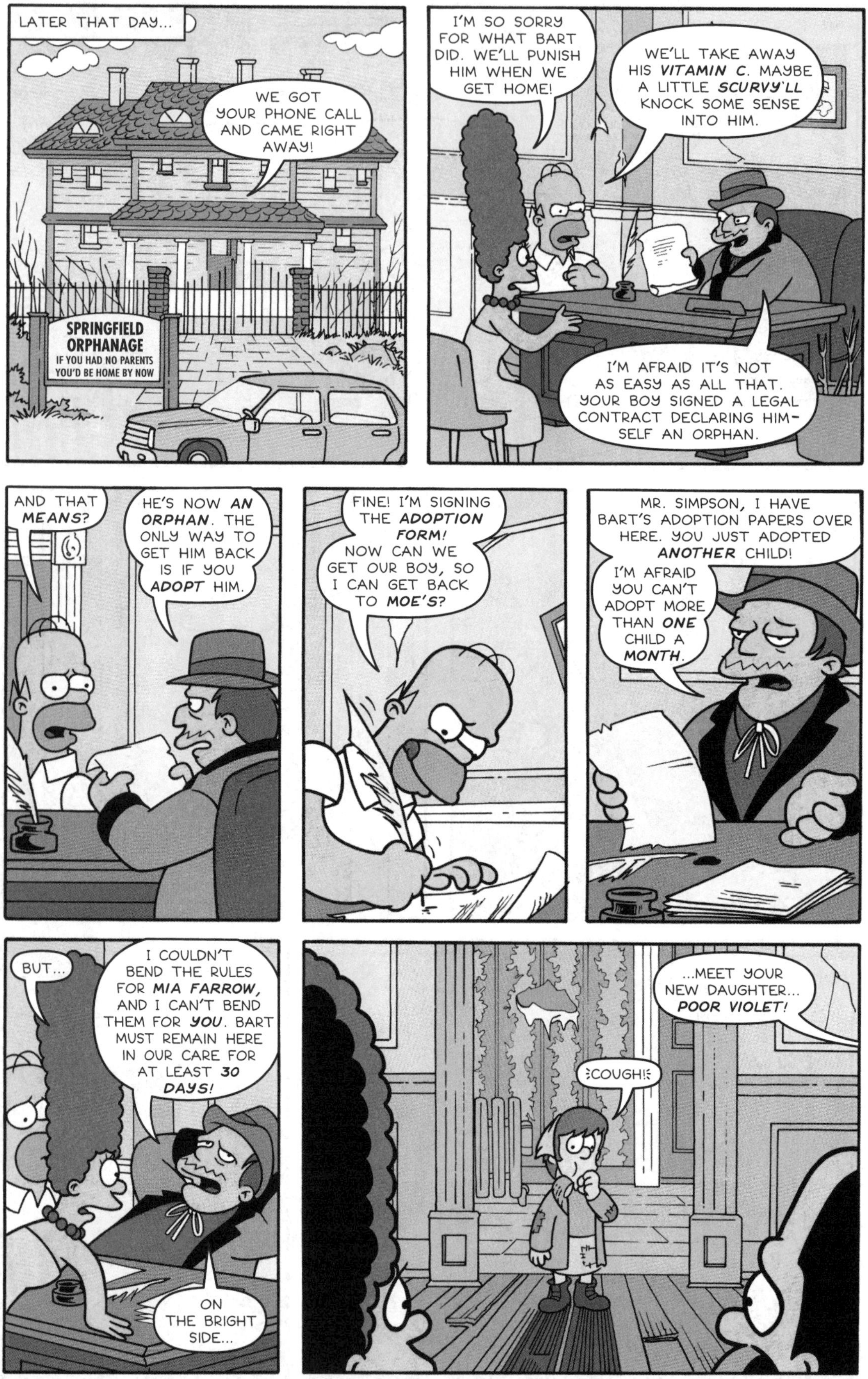
LATER THAT DAY...
WE GOT YOUR PHONE CALL AND CAME RIGHT AWAY!
SPRINGFIELD ORPHANAGE
IF YOU HAD NO PARENTS YOU'D BE HOME BY NOW
I'M SO SORRY FOR WHAT BART DID. WE'LL PUNISH HIM WHEN WE GET HOME!
WE'LL TAKE AWAY HIS VITAMIN C. MAYBE A LITTLE SCURVY'LL KNOCK SOME SENSE INTO HIM.
I'M AFRAID IT'S NOT AS EASY AS ALL THAT. YOUR BOY SIGNED A LEGAL CONTRACT DECLARING HIM-SELF AN ORPHAN.
AND THAT MEANS?
HE'S NOW AN ORPHAN. THE ONLY WAY TO GET HIM BACK IS IF YOU ADOPT HIM.
FINE! I'M SIGNING THE ADOPTION FORM! NOW CAN WE GET OUR BOY, SO I CAN GET BACK TO MOE'S?
MR. SIMPSON, I HAVE BART'S ADOPTION PAPERS OVER HERE. YOU JUST ADOPTED ANOTHER CHILD!
I'M AFRAID YOU CAN'T ADOPT MORE THAN ONE CHILD A MONTH.
BUT...
I COULDN'T BEND THE RULES FOR MIA FARROW, AND I CAN'T BEND THEM FOR YOU. BART MUST REMAIN HERE IN OUR CARE FOR AT LEAST 30 DAYS!
ON THE BRIGHT SIDE...
...MEET YOUR NEW DAUGHTER... POOR VIOLET!
COUGH!

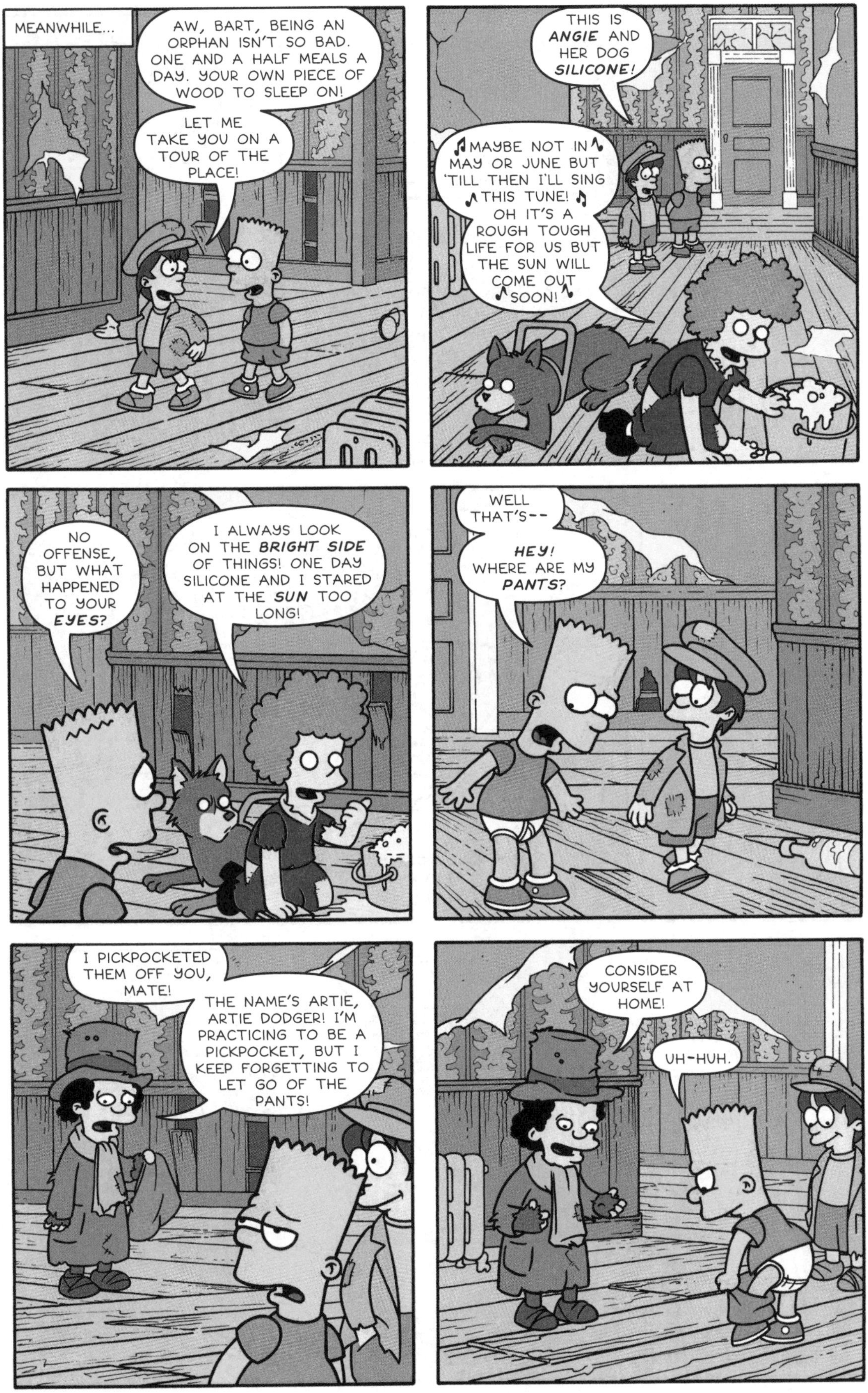
MEANWHILE...
AW, BART, BEING AN ORPHAN ISN'T SO BAD. ONE AND A HALF MEALS A DAY. YOUR OWN PIECE OF WOOD TO SLEEP ON!
LET ME TAKE YOU ON A TOUR OF THE PLACE!
THIS IS ANGIE AND HER DOG SILICONE!
♪MAYBE NOT IN MAY OR JUNE BUT 'TILL THEN I'LL SING THIS TUNE! ♪ OH IT'S A ROUGH TOUGH LIFE FOR US BUT THE SUN WILL COME OUT SOON!♪
NO OFFENSE, BUT WHAT HAPPENED TO YOUR EYES?
I ALWAYS LOOK ON THE BRIGHT SIDE OF THINGS! ONE DAY SILICONE AND I STARED AT THE SUN TOO LONG!
WELL THAT'S--
HEY! WHERE ARE MY PANTS?
I PICKPOCKETED THEM OFF YOU, MATE!
THE NAME'S ARTIE, ARTIE DODGER! I'M PRACTICING TO BE A PICKPOCKET, BUT I KEEP FORGETTING TO LET GO OF THE PANTS!
CONSIDER YOURSELF AT HOME!
UH-HUH.

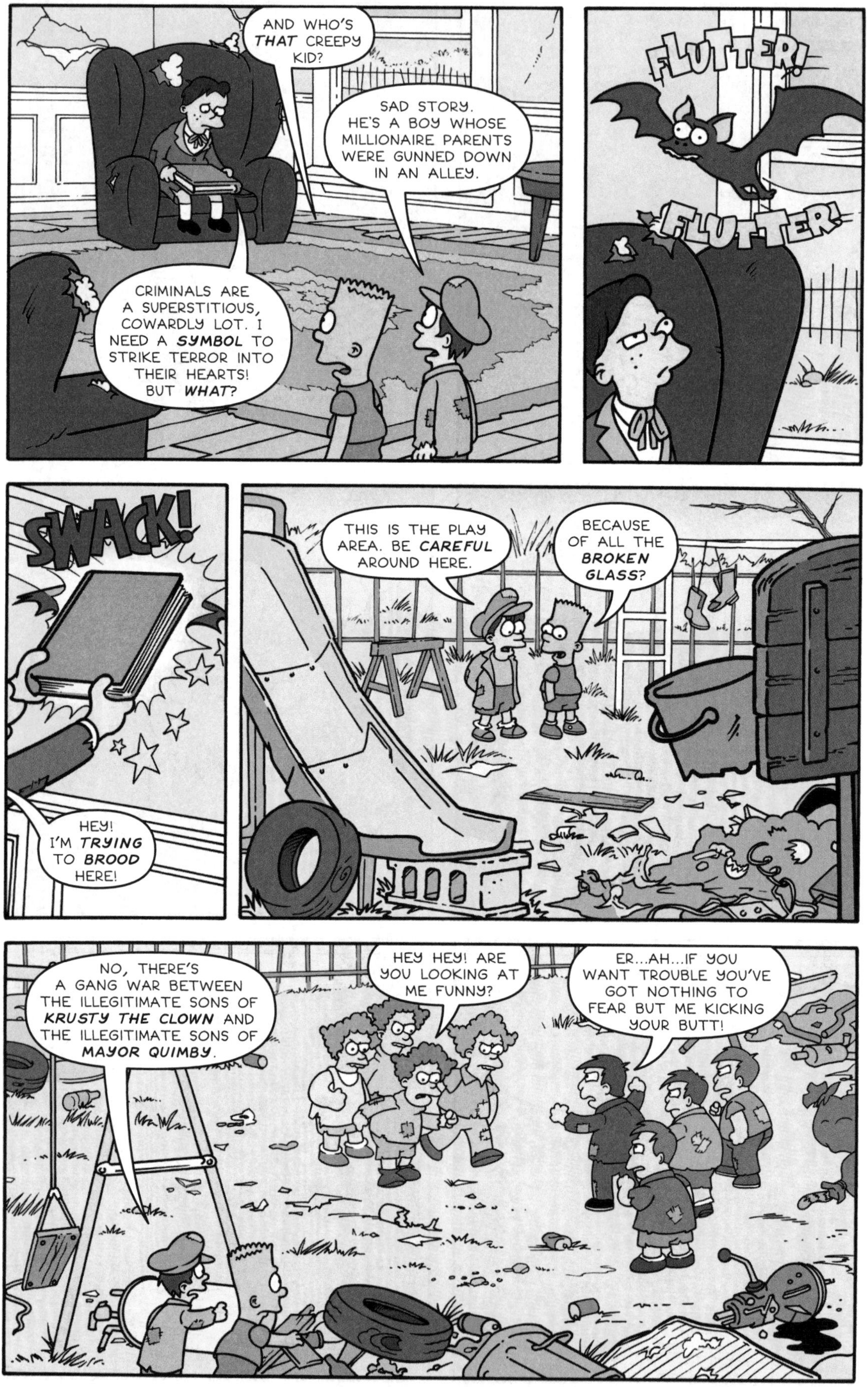
AND WHO'S THAT CREEPY KID?
SAD STORY. HE'S A BOY WHOSE MILLIONAIRE PARENTS WERE GUNNED DOWN IN AN ALLEY.
CRIMINALS ARE A SUPERSTITIOUS, COWARDLY LOT. I NEED A SYMBOL TO STRIKE TERROR INTO THEIR HEARTS! BUT WHAT?
FLUTTER!
FLUTTER!
SWACK!
HEY! I'M TRYING TO BROOD HERE!
THIS IS THE PLAY AREA. BE CAREFUL AROUND HERE.
BECAUSE OF ALL THE BROKEN GLASS?
NO, THERE'S A GANG WAR BETWEEN THE ILLEGITIMATE SONS OF KRUSTY THE CLOWN AND THE ILLEGITIMATE SONS OF MAYOR QUIMBY.
HEY HEY! ARE YOU LOOKING AT ME FUNNY?
ER...AH...IF YOU WANT TROUBLE YOU'VE GOT NOTHING TO FEAR BUT ME KICKING YOUR BUTT!

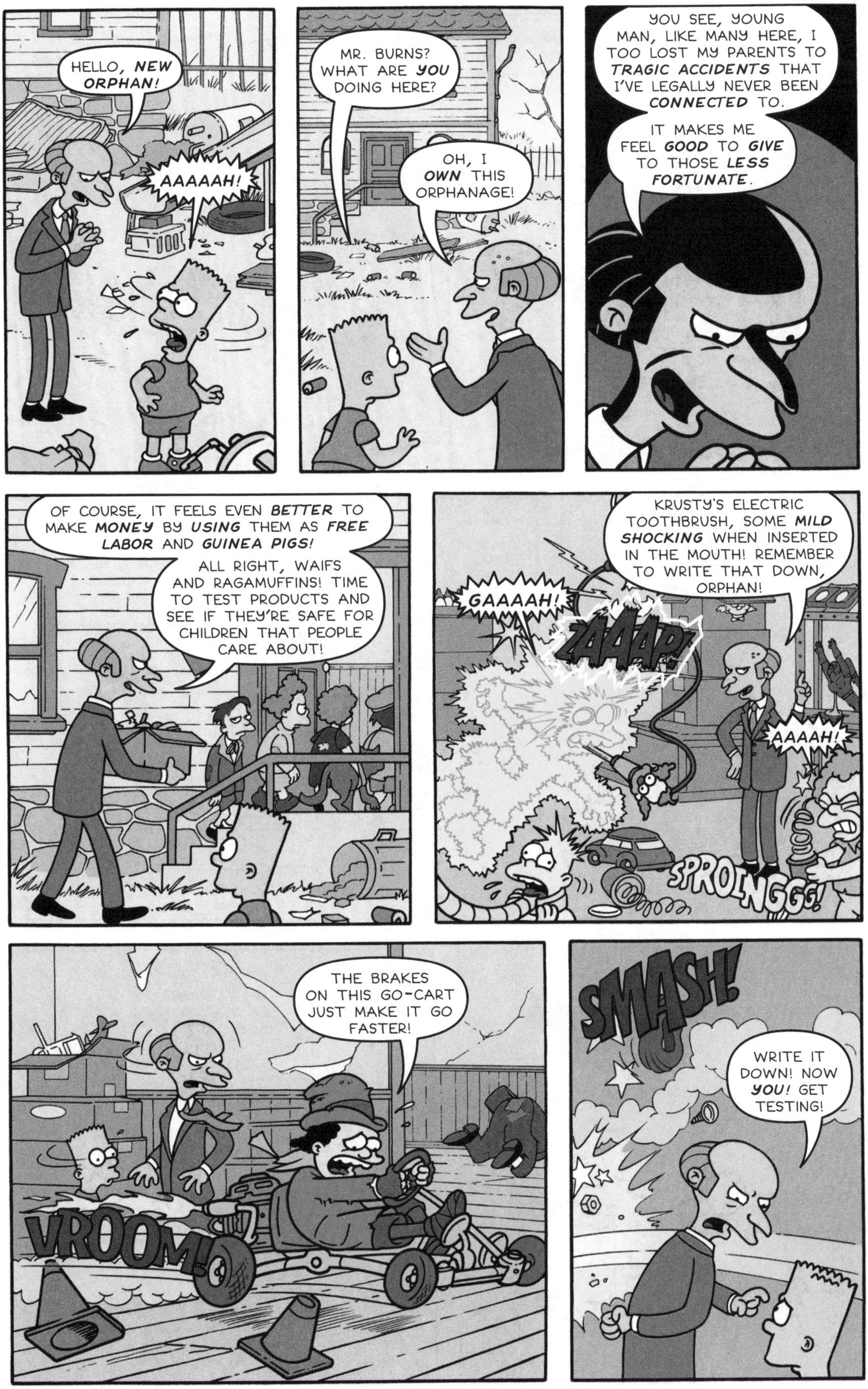
HELLO, NEW ORPHAN!
AAAAAH!
MR. BURNS? WHAT ARE YOU DOING HERE?
OH, I OWN THIS ORPHANAGE!
YOU SEE, YOUNG MAN, LIKE MANY HERE, I TOO LOST MY PARENTS TO TRAGIC ACCIDENTS THAT I'VE LEGALLY NEVER BEEN CONNECTED TO.
IT MAKES ME FEEL GOOD TO GIVE TO THOSE LESS FORTUNATE.
OF COURSE, IT FEELS EVEN BETTER TO MAKE MONEY BY USING THEM AS FREE LABOR AND GUINEA PIGS!
ALL RIGHT, WAIFS AND RAGAMUFFINS! TIME TO TEST PRODUCTS AND SEE IF THEY'RE SAFE FOR CHILDREN THAT PEOPLE CARE ABOUT!
KRUSTY'S ELECTRIC TOOTHBRUSH, SOME MILD SHOCKING WHEN INSERTED IN THE MOUTH! REMEMBER TO WRITE THAT DOWN, ORPHAN!
GAAAAH!
ZAAAP!
AAAAH!
SPROINGGG!
THE BRAKES ON THIS GO-CART JUST MAKE IT GO FASTER!
VROOM!
SMASH!
WRITE IT DOWN! NOW YOU! GET TESTING!

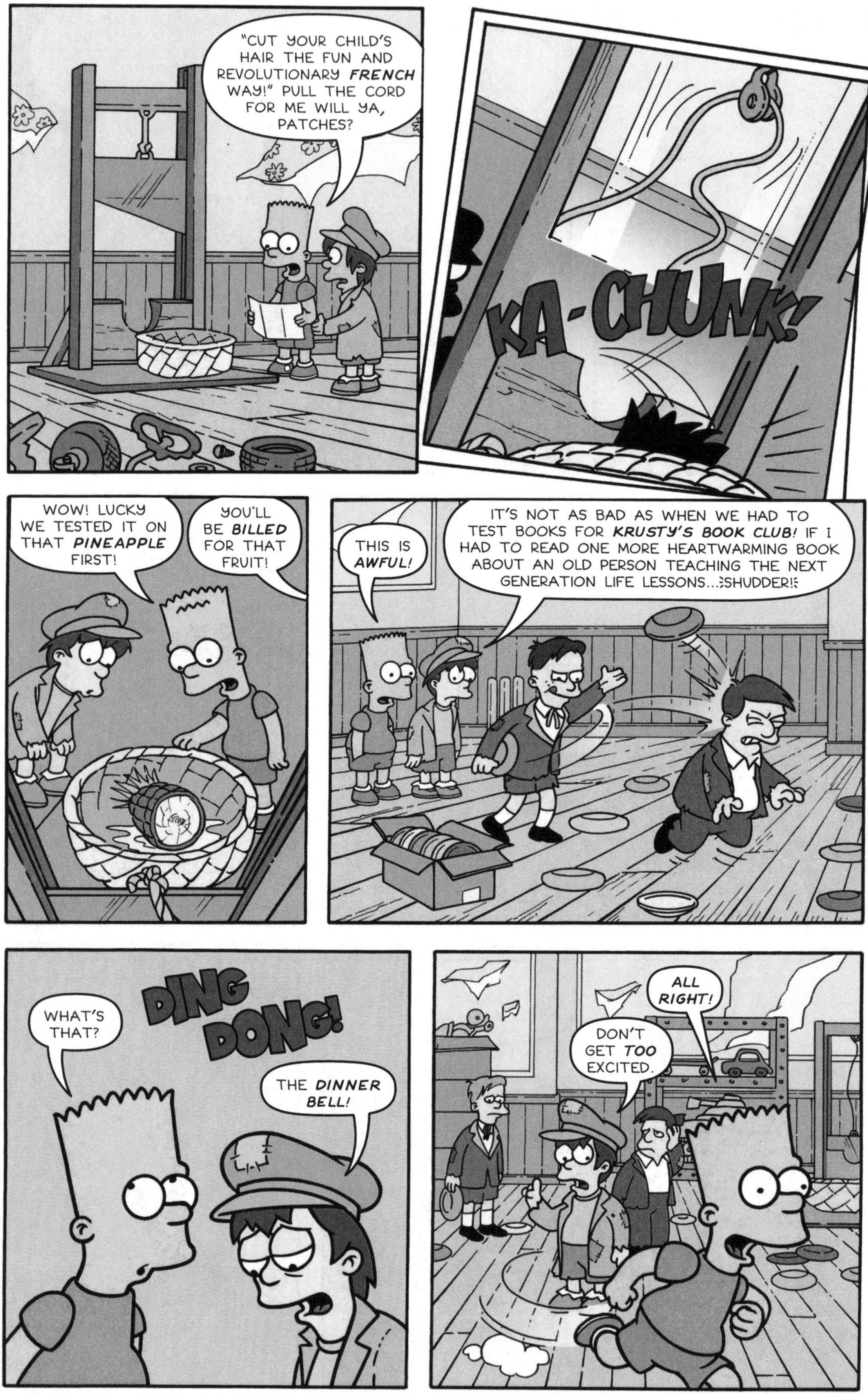
"CUT YOUR CHILD'S HAIR THE FUN AND REVOLUTIONARY FRENCH WAY!" PULL THE CORD FOR ME WILL YA, PATCHES?
KA-CHUNK!
WOW! LUCKY WE TESTED IT ON THAT PINEAPPLE FIRST!
YOU'LL BE BILLED FOR THAT FRUIT!
THIS IS AWFUL!
IT'S NOT AS BAD AS WHEN WE HAD TO TEST BOOKS FOR KRUSTY'S BOOK CLUB! IF I HAD TO READ ONE MORE HEARTWARMING BOOK ABOUT AN OLD PERSON TEACHING THE NEXT GENERATION LIFE LESSONS...SHUDDER!
WHAT'S THAT?
DING DONG!
THE DINNER BELL!
ALL RIGHT!
DON'T GET TOO EXCITED.

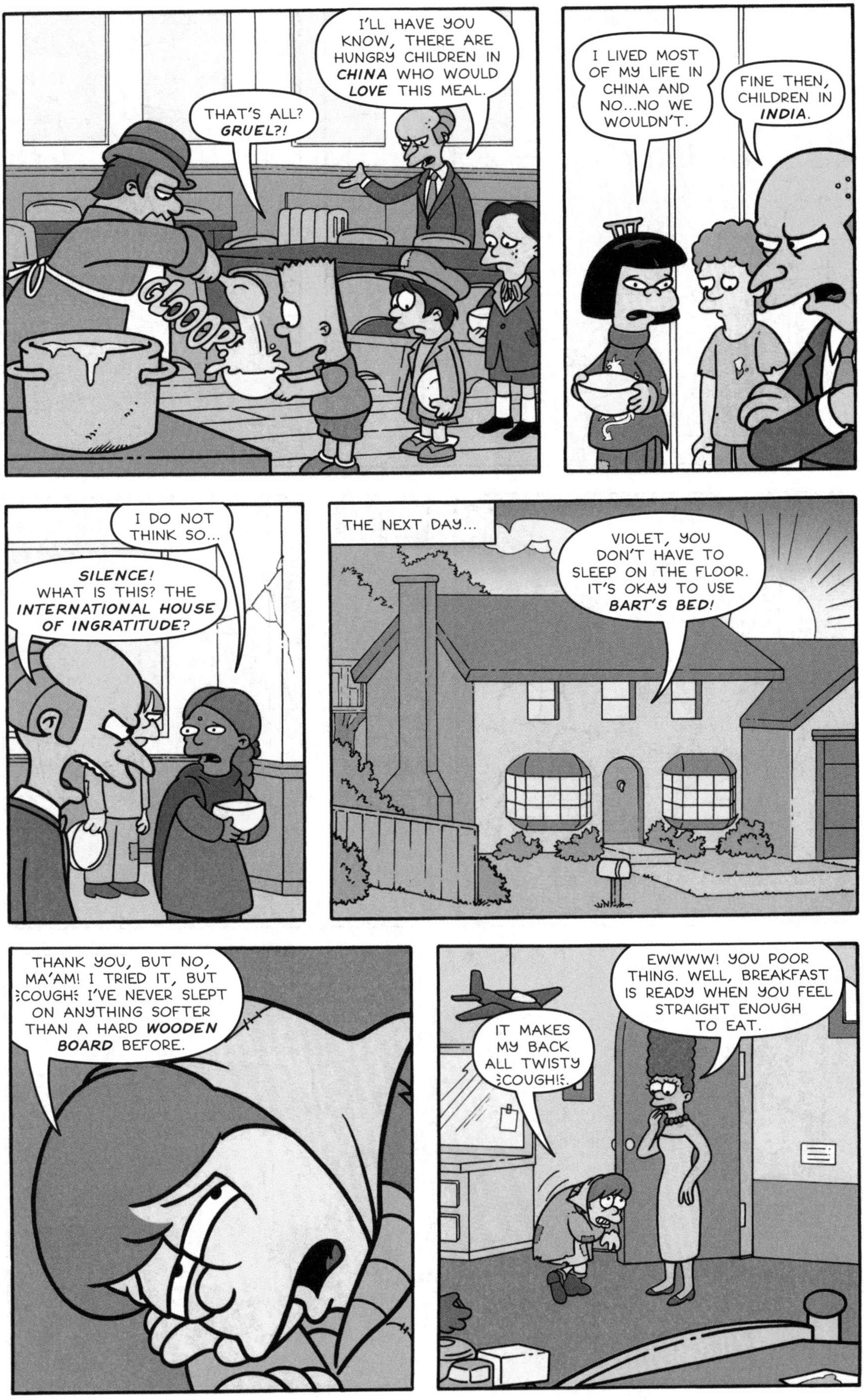

THAT'S ALL? GRUEL?!
I'LL HAVE YOU KNOW, THERE ARE HUNGRY CHILDREN IN CHINA WHO WOULD LOVE THIS MEAL.
GLOOOP!
I LIVED MOST OF MY LIFE IN CHINA AND NO...NO WE WOULDN'T.
FINE THEN, CHILDREN IN INDIA.
I DO NOT THINK SO...
SILENCE! WHAT IS THIS? THE INTERNATIONAL HOUSE OF INGRATITUDE?
THE NEXT DAY...
VIOLET, YOU DON'T HAVE TO SLEEP ON THE FLOOR. IT'S OKAY TO USE BART'S BED!
THANK YOU, BUT NO, MA'AM! I TRIED IT, BUT COUGH I'VE NEVER SLEPT ON ANYTHING SOFTER THAN A HARD WOODEN BOARD BEFORE.
IT MAKES MY BACK ALL TWISTY COUGH!.
EWWWW! YOU POOR THING. WELL, BREAKFAST IS READY WHEN YOU FEEL STRAIGHT ENOUGH TO EAT.

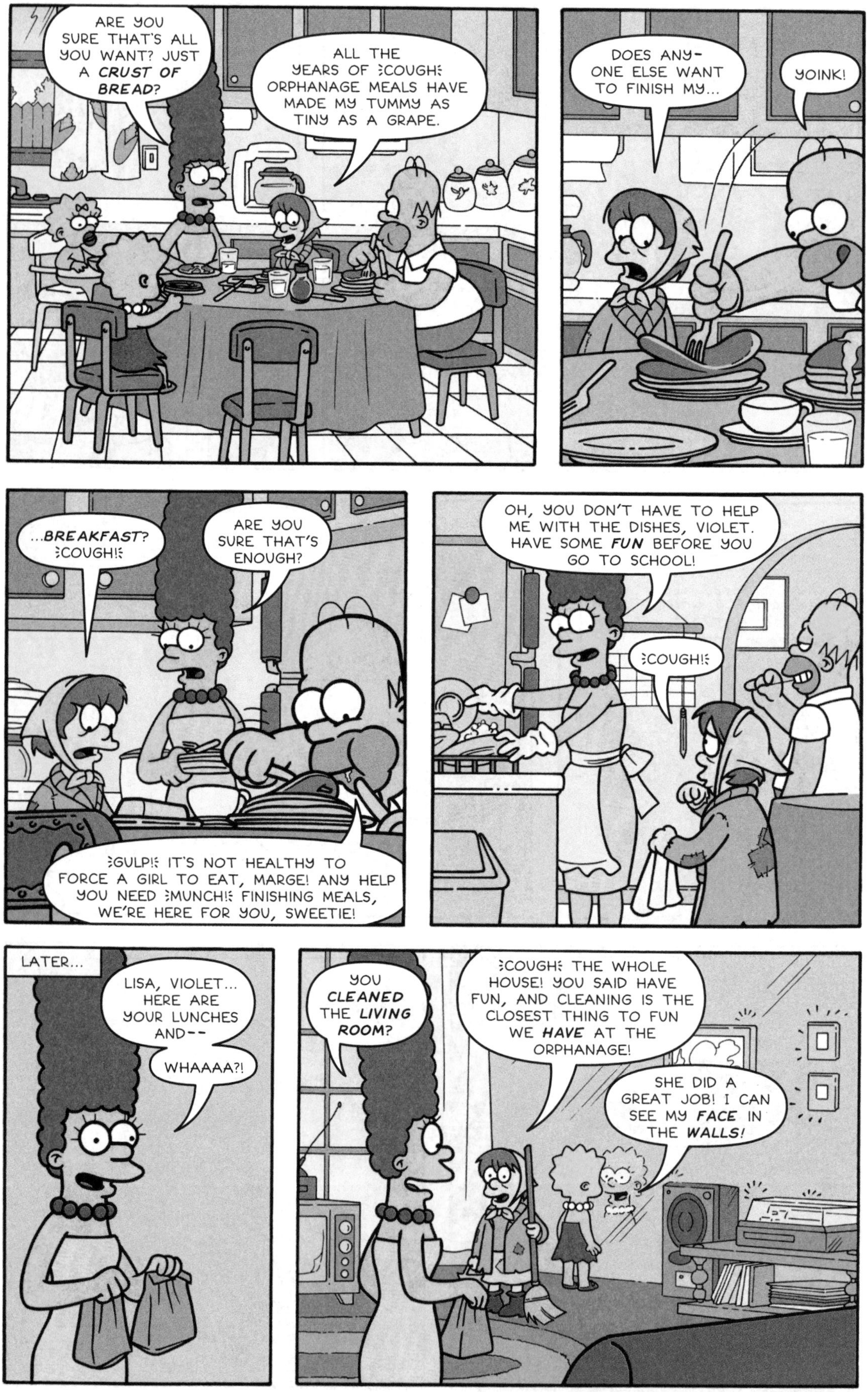
ARE YOU SURE THAT'S ALL YOU WANT? JUST A *CRUST OF BREAD*?
ALL THE YEARS OF ⁝COUGH⁝ ORPHANAGE MEALS HAVE MADE MY TUMMY AS TINY AS A GRAPE.
DOES ANY-ONE ELSE WANT TO FINISH MY...
YOINK!
...*BREAKFAST*? ⁝COUGH!⁝
ARE YOU SURE THAT'S ENOUGH?
⁝GULP!⁝ IT'S NOT HEALTHY TO FORCE A GIRL TO EAT, MARGE! ANY HELP YOU NEED ⁝MUNCH!⁝ FINISHING MEALS, WE'RE HERE FOR YOU, SWEETIE!
OH, YOU DON'T HAVE TO HELP ME WITH THE DISHES, VIOLET. HAVE SOME *FUN* BEFORE YOU GO TO SCHOOL!
⁝COUGH!⁝
LATER...
LISA, VIOLET... HERE ARE YOUR LUNCHES AND--
WHAAAA?!
YOU *CLEANED* THE *LIVING ROOM*?
⁝COUGH⁝ THE WHOLE HOUSE! YOU SAID HAVE FUN, AND CLEANING IS THE CLOSEST THING TO FUN WE *HAVE* AT THE ORPHANAGE!
SHE DID A GREAT JOB! I CAN SEE MY *FACE* IN THE *WALLS*!

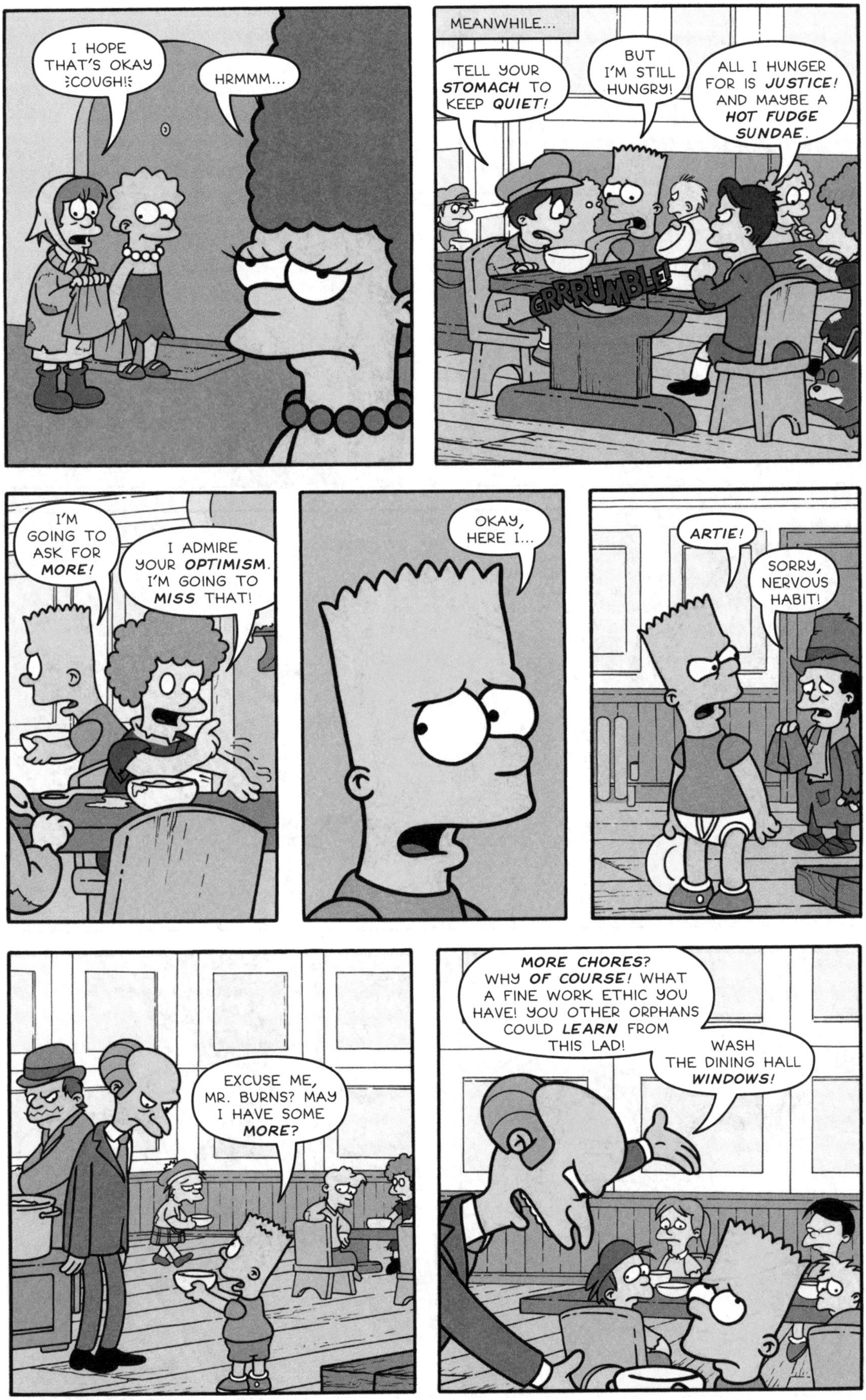
I HOPE THAT'S OKAY *COUGH!*
HRMMM...
MEANWHILE...
TELL YOUR STOMACH TO KEEP QUIET!
BUT I'M STILL HUNGRY!
ALL I HUNGER FOR IS JUSTICE! AND MAYBE A HOT FUDGE SUNDAE.
GRRRUMBLE!
I'M GOING TO ASK FOR MORE!
I ADMIRE YOUR OPTIMISM. I'M GOING TO MISS THAT!
OKAY, HERE I...
ARTIE!
SORRY, NERVOUS HABIT!
EXCUSE ME, MR. BURNS? MAY I HAVE SOME MORE?
MORE CHORES? WHY OF COURSE! WHAT A FINE WORK ETHIC YOU HAVE! YOU OTHER ORPHANS COULD LEARN FROM THIS LAD!
WASH THE DINING HALL WINDOWS!

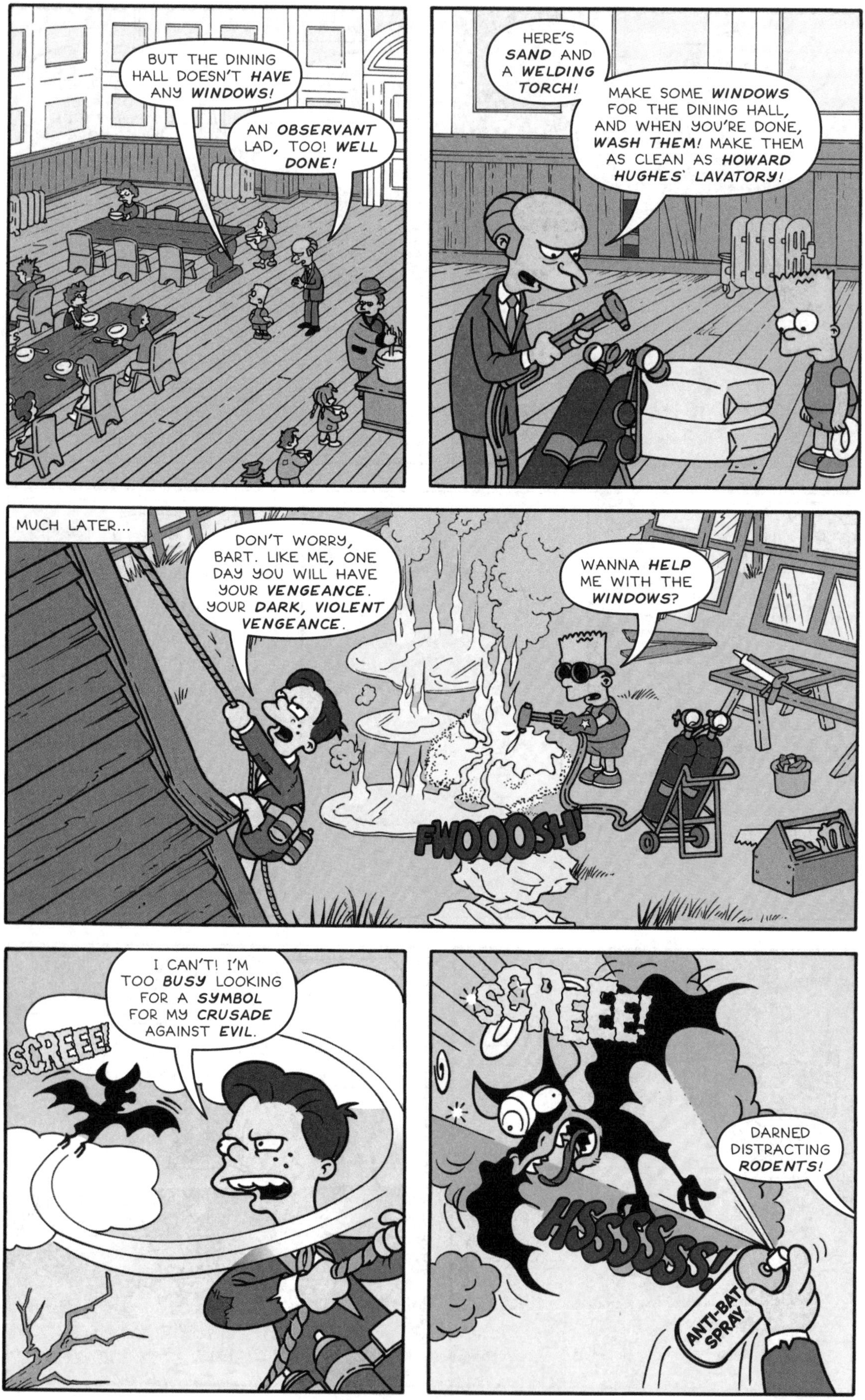
BUT THE DINING HALL DOESN'T HAVE ANY WINDOWS!
AN OBSERVANT LAD, TOO! WELL DONE!
HERE'S SAND AND A WELDING TORCH!
MAKE SOME WINDOWS FOR THE DINING HALL, AND WHEN YOU'RE DONE, WASH THEM! MAKE THEM AS CLEAN AS HOWARD HUGHES' LAVATORY!
MUCH LATER...
DON'T WORRY, BART. LIKE ME, ONE DAY YOU WILL HAVE YOUR VENGEANCE. YOUR DARK, VIOLENT VENGEANCE.
WANNA HELP ME WITH THE WINDOWS?
FWOOOSH!
I CAN'T! I'M TOO BUSY LOOKING FOR A SYMBOL FOR MY CRUSADE AGAINST EVIL.
SCREEE!
SCREEE!
HSSSSSS!
ANTI-BAT SPRAY
DARNED DISTRACTING RODENTS!

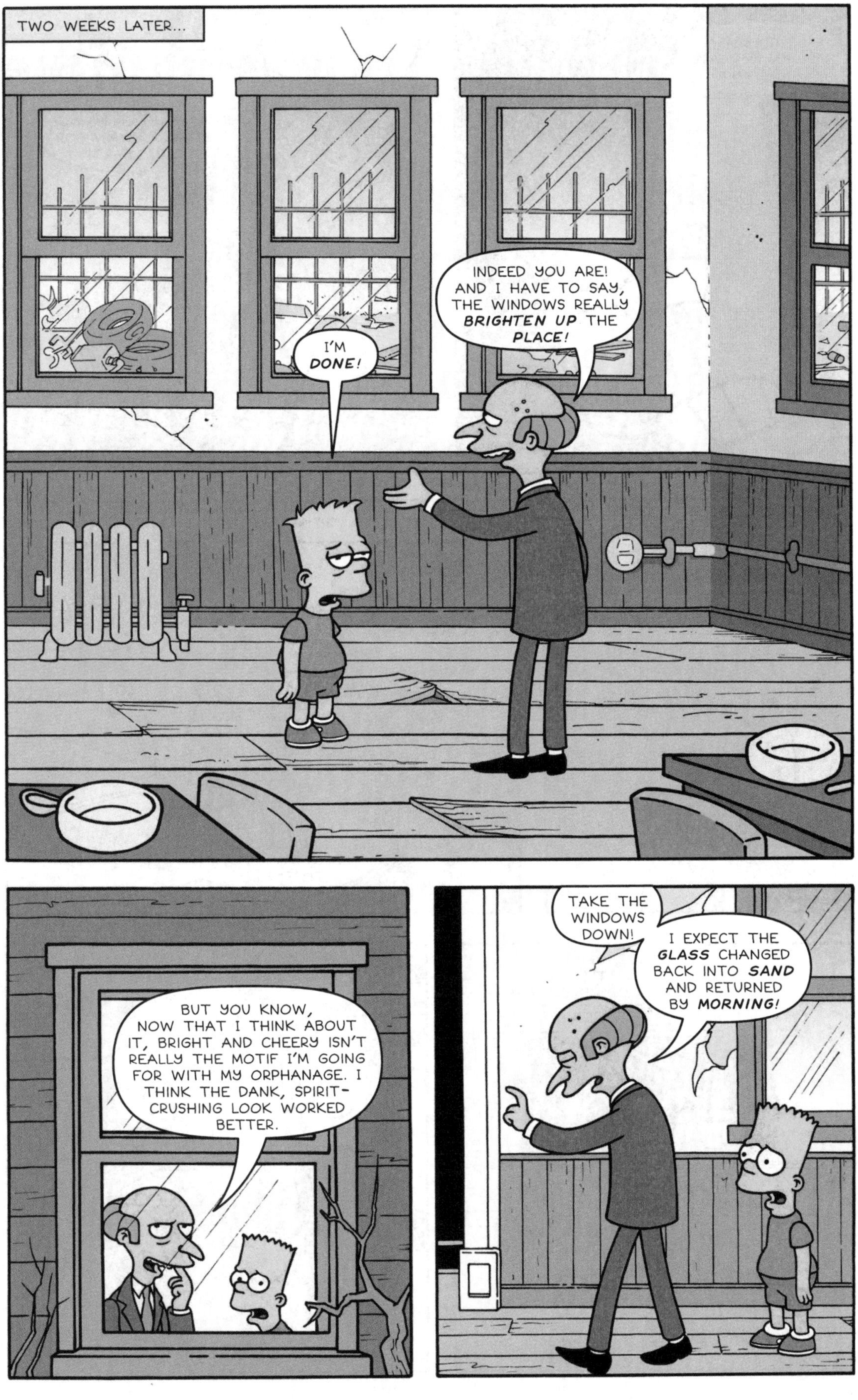
TWO WEEKS LATER...
I'M DONE!
INDEED YOU ARE! AND I HAVE TO SAY, THE WINDOWS REALLY BRIGHTEN UP THE PLACE!
BUT YOU KNOW, NOW THAT I THINK ABOUT IT, BRIGHT AND CHEERY ISN'T REALLY THE MOTIF I'M GOING FOR WITH MY ORPHANAGE. I THINK THE DANK, SPIRIT-CRUSHING LOOK WORKED BETTER.
TAKE THE WINDOWS DOWN!
I EXPECT THE GLASS CHANGED BACK INTO SAND AND RETURNED BY MORNING!

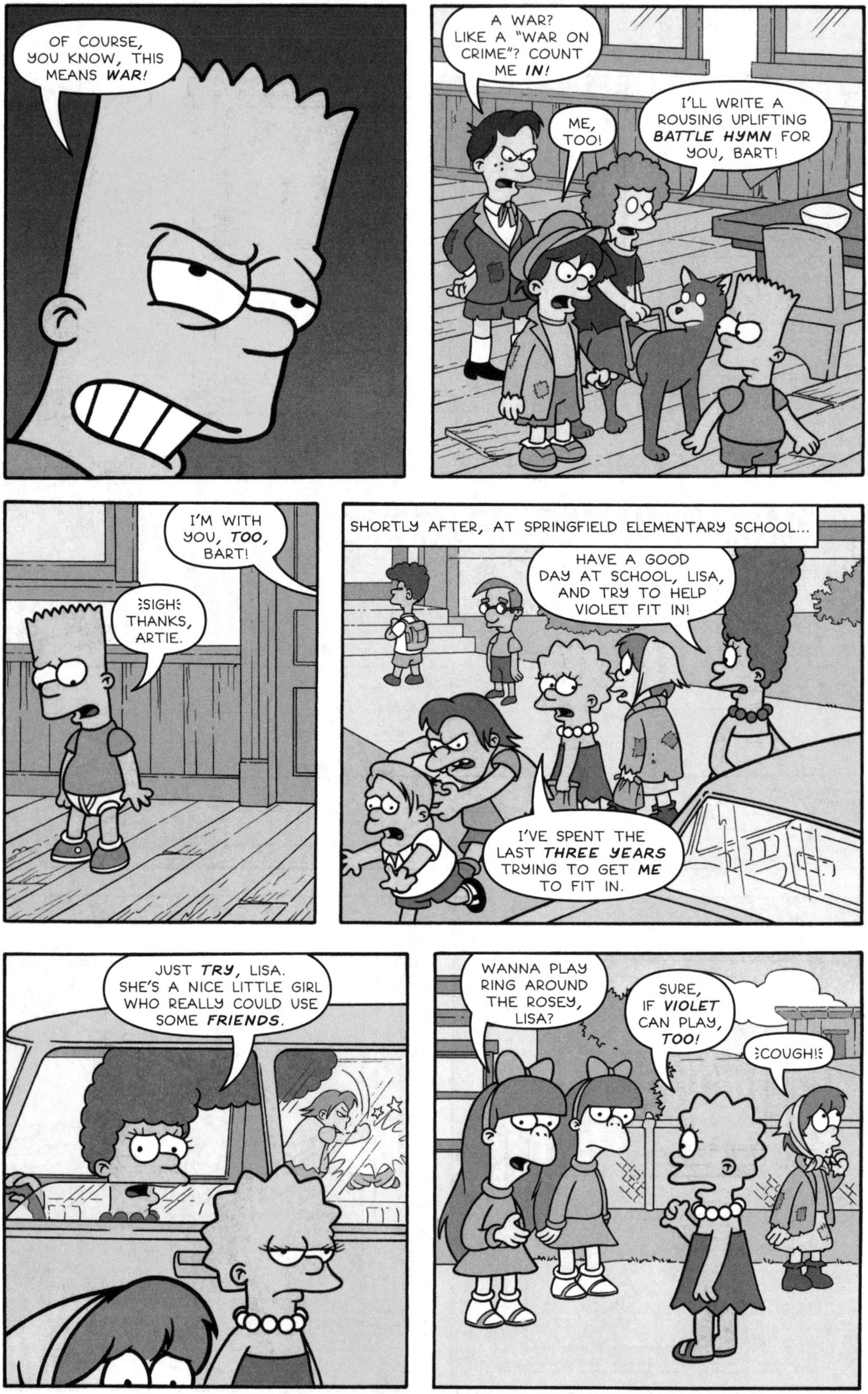
OF COURSE, YOU KNOW, THIS MEANS WAR!
A WAR? LIKE A "WAR ON CRIME"? COUNT ME IN!
ME, TOO!
I'LL WRITE A ROUSING UPLIFTING BATTLE HYMN FOR YOU, BART!
I'M WITH YOU, TOO, BART!
SIGH THANKS, ARTIE.
SHORTLY AFTER, AT SPRINGFIELD ELEMENTARY SCHOOL...
HAVE A GOOD DAY AT SCHOOL, LISA, AND TRY TO HELP VIOLET FIT IN!
I'VE SPENT THE LAST THREE YEARS TRYING TO GET ME TO FIT IN.
JUST TRY, LISA. SHE'S A NICE LITTLE GIRL WHO REALLY COULD USE SOME FRIENDS.
WANNA PLAY RING AROUND THE ROSEY, LISA?
SURE, IF VIOLET CAN PLAY, TOO!
COUGH!

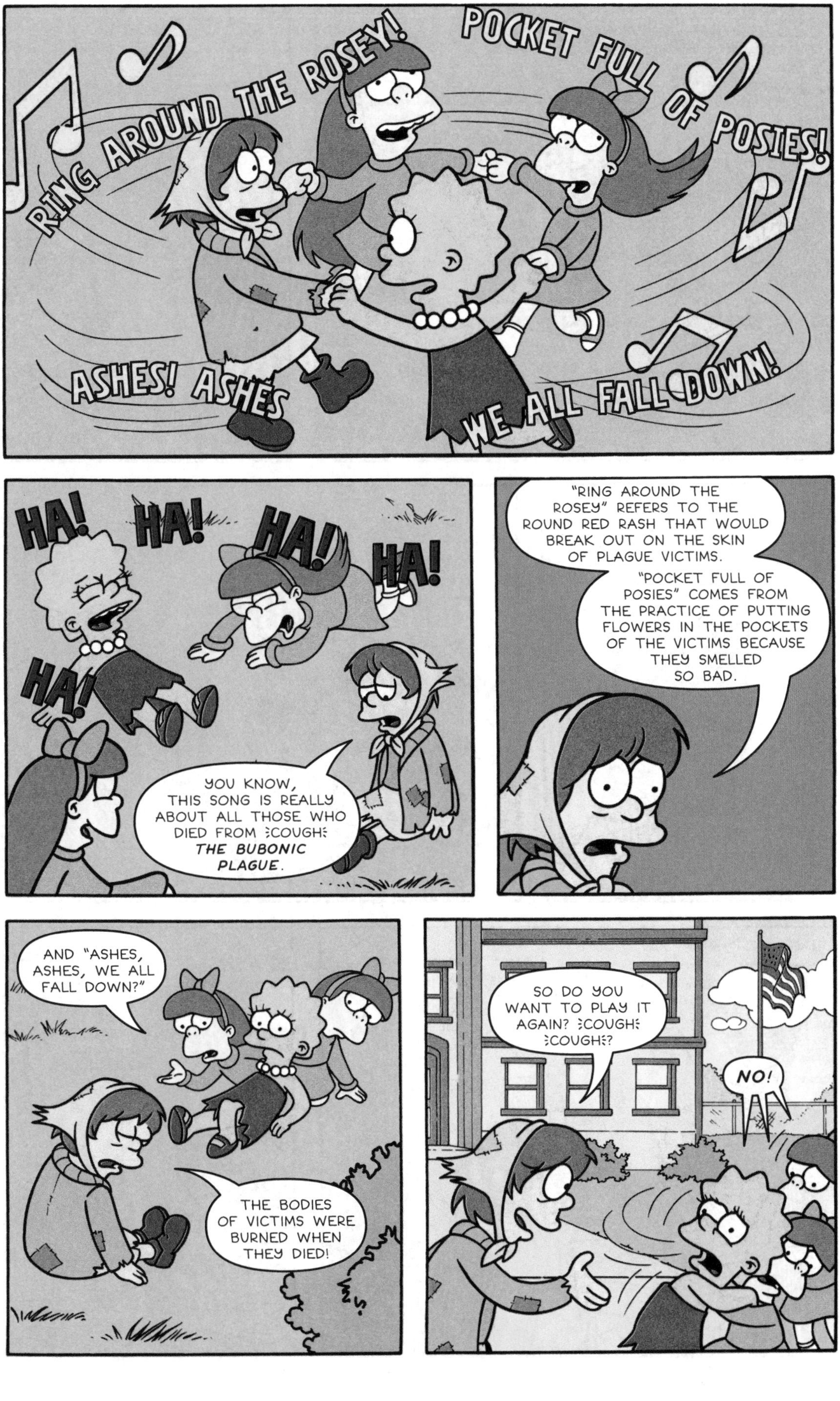
RING AROUND THE ROSEY!
POCKET FULL OF POSIES!
ASHES! ASHES
WE ALL FALL DOWN!
HA! HA! HA! HA!
HA!
YOU KNOW, THIS SONG IS REALLY ABOUT ALL THOSE WHO DIED FROM ⁝COUGH⁝ *THE BUBONIC PLAGUE*.
"RING AROUND THE ROSEY" REFERS TO THE ROUND RED RASH THAT WOULD BREAK OUT ON THE SKIN OF PLAGUE VICTIMS.
"POCKET FULL OF POSIES" COMES FROM THE PRACTICE OF PUTTING FLOWERS IN THE POCKETS OF THE VICTIMS BECAUSE THEY SMELLED SO BAD.
AND "ASHES, ASHES, WE ALL FALL DOWN?"
THE BODIES OF VICTIMS WERE BURNED WHEN THEY DIED!
SO DO YOU WANT TO PLAY IT AGAIN? ⁝COUGH⁝ ⁝COUGH⁝?
NO!

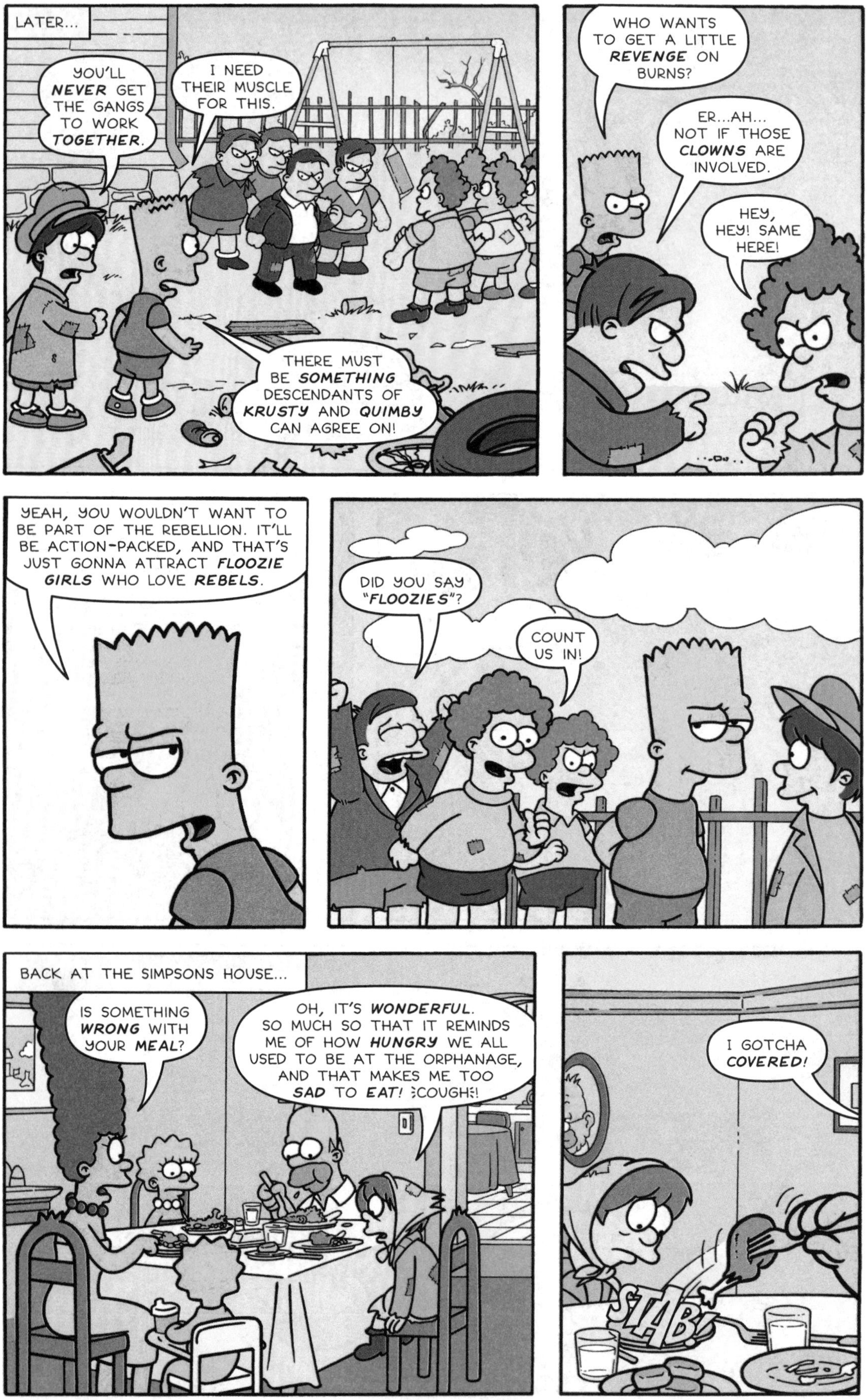
LATER...
YOU'LL NEVER GET THE GANGS TO WORK TOGETHER.
I NEED THEIR MUSCLE FOR THIS.
THERE MUST BE SOMETHING DESCENDANTS OF KRUSTY AND QUIMBY CAN AGREE ON!
WHO WANTS TO GET A LITTLE REVENGE ON BURNS?
ER...AH... NOT IF THOSE CLOWNS ARE INVOLVED.
HEY, HEY! SAME HERE!
YEAH, YOU WOULDN'T WANT TO BE PART OF THE REBELLION. IT'LL BE ACTION-PACKED, AND THAT'S JUST GONNA ATTRACT FLOOZIE GIRLS WHO LOVE REBELS.
DID YOU SAY "FLOOZIES"?
COUNT US IN!
BACK AT THE SIMPSONS HOUSE...
IS SOMETHING WRONG WITH YOUR MEAL?
OH, IT'S WONDERFUL. SO MUCH SO THAT IT REMINDS ME OF HOW HUNGRY WE ALL USED TO BE AT THE ORPHANAGE, AND THAT MAKES ME TOO SAD TO EAT! COUGH!
I GOTCHA COVERED!
STAB!

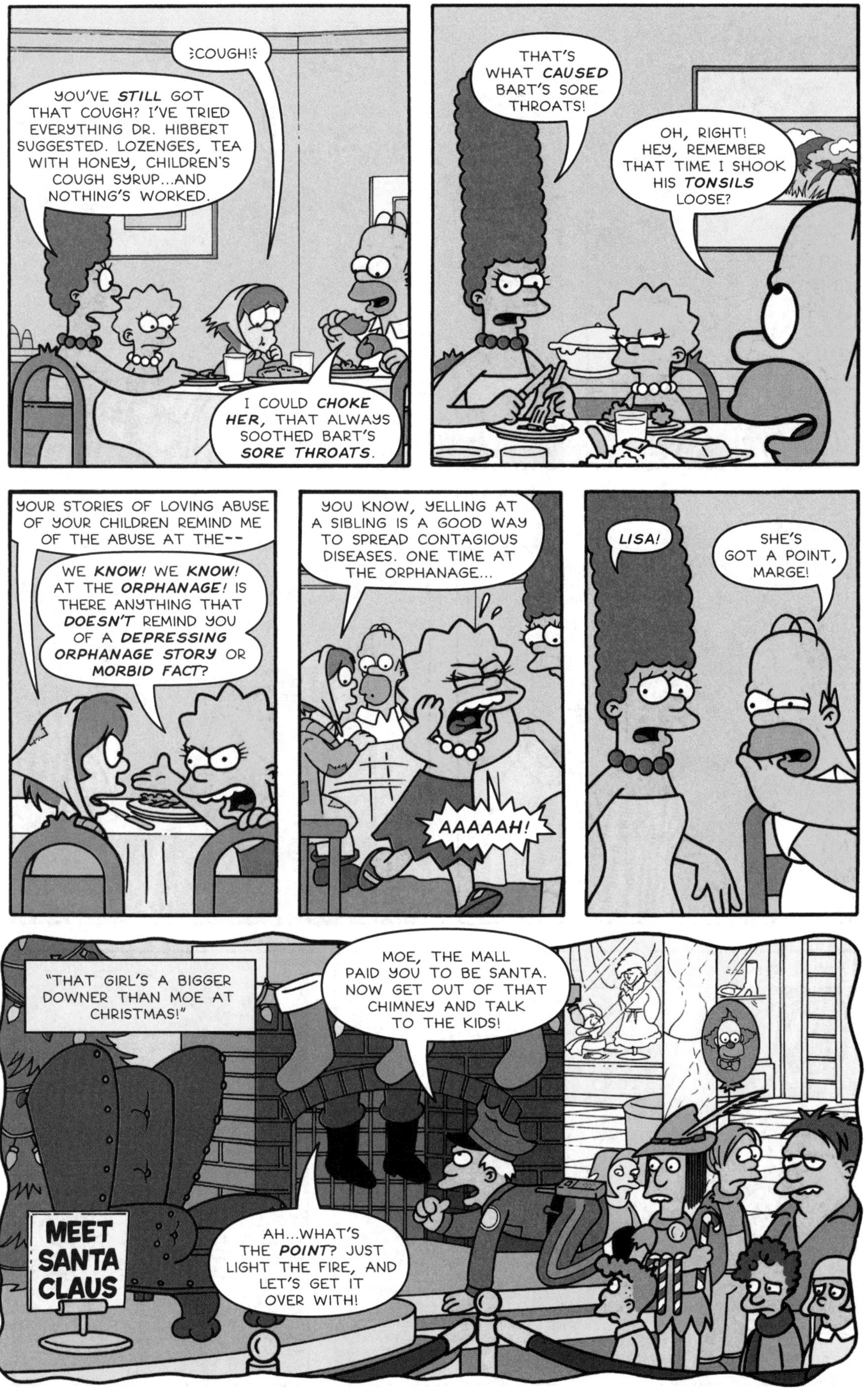

YOU'VE STILL GOT THAT COUGH? I'VE TRIED EVERYTHING DR. HIBBERT SUGGESTED. LOZENGES, TEA WITH HONEY, CHILDREN'S COUGH SYRUP...AND NOTHING'S WORKED.
COUGH!
I COULD CHOKE HER, THAT ALWAYS SOOTHED BART'S SORE THROATS.
THAT'S WHAT CAUSED BART'S SORE THROATS!
OH, RIGHT! HEY, REMEMBER THAT TIME I SHOOK HIS TONSILS LOOSE?
YOUR STORIES OF LOVING ABUSE OF YOUR CHILDREN REMIND ME OF THE ABUSE AT THE--
WE KNOW! WE KNOW! AT THE ORPHANAGE! IS THERE ANYTHING THAT DOESN'T REMIND YOU OF A DEPRESSING ORPHANAGE STORY OR MORBID FACT?
YOU KNOW, YELLING AT A SIBLING IS A GOOD WAY TO SPREAD CONTAGIOUS DISEASES. ONE TIME AT THE ORPHANAGE...
AAAAAH!
LISA!
SHE'S GOT A POINT, MARGE!
"THAT GIRL'S A BIGGER DOWNER THAN MOE AT CHRISTMAS!"
MOE, THE MALL PAID YOU TO BE SANTA. NOW GET OUT OF THAT CHIMNEY AND TALK TO THE KIDS!
MEET SANTA CLAUS
AH...WHAT'S THE POINT? JUST LIGHT THE FIRE, AND LET'S GET IT OVER WITH!

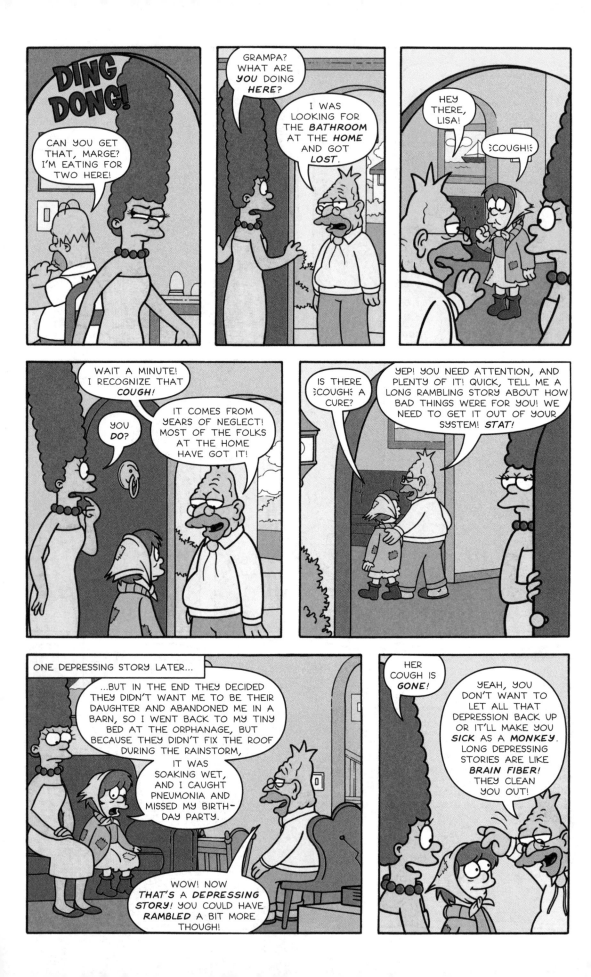

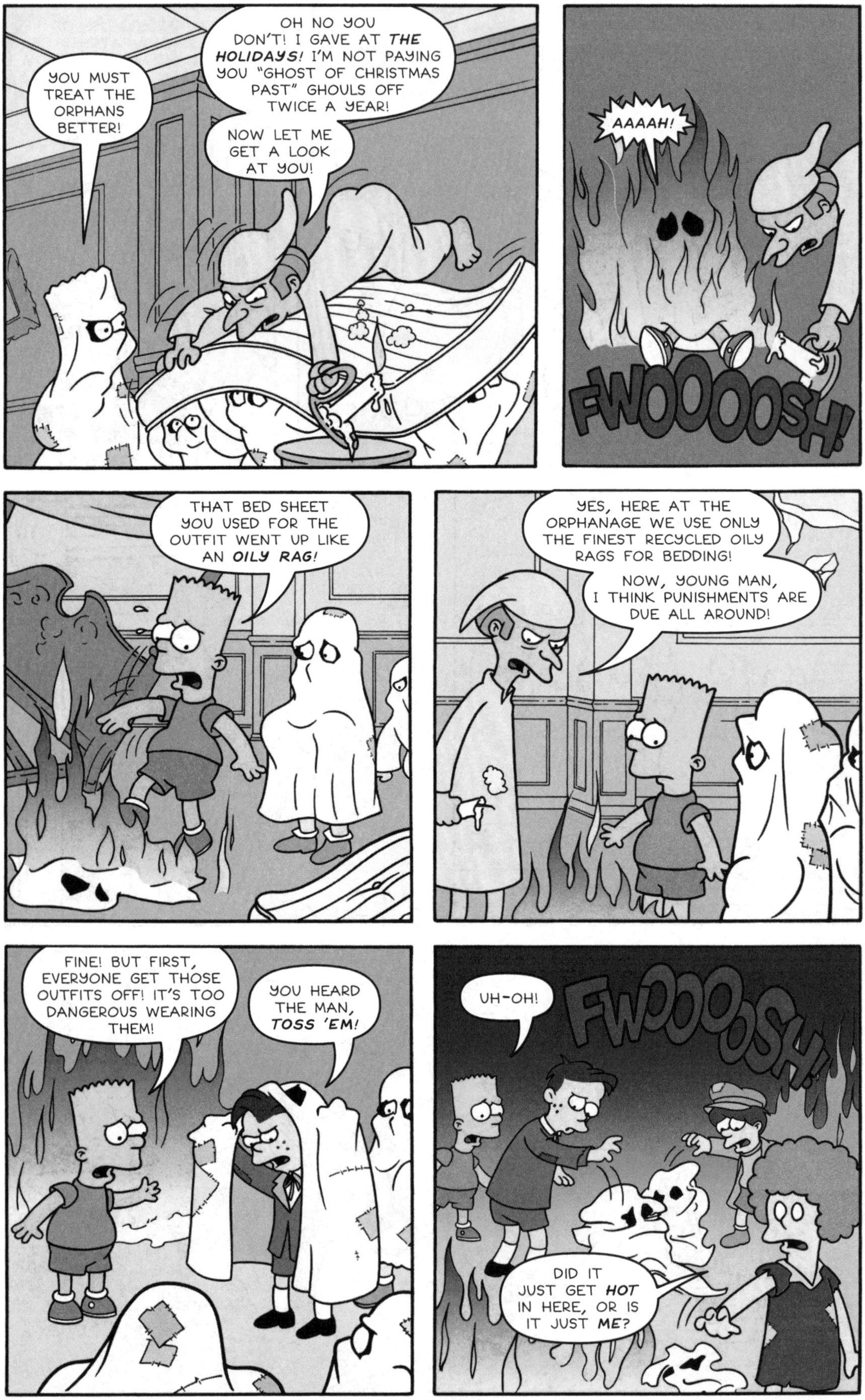
YOU MUST TREAT THE ORPHANS BETTER!
OH NO YOU DON'T! I GAVE AT *THE HOLIDAYS!* I'M NOT PAYING YOU "GHOST OF CHRISTMAS PAST" GHOULS OFF TWICE A YEAR!
NOW LET ME GET A LOOK AT YOU!
AAAAH!
FWOOOOOSH!
THAT BED SHEET YOU USED FOR THE OUTFIT WENT UP LIKE AN *OILY RAG!*
YES, HERE AT THE ORPHANAGE WE USE ONLY THE FINEST RECYCLED OILY RAGS FOR BEDDING!
NOW, YOUNG MAN, I THINK PUNISHMENTS ARE DUE ALL AROUND!
FINE! BUT FIRST, EVERYONE GET THOSE OUTFITS OFF! IT'S TOO DANGEROUS WEARING THEM!
YOU HEARD THE MAN, *TOSS 'EM!*
UH-OH!
FWOOOOOSH!
DID IT JUST GET *HOT* IN HERE, OR IS IT JUST *ME?*

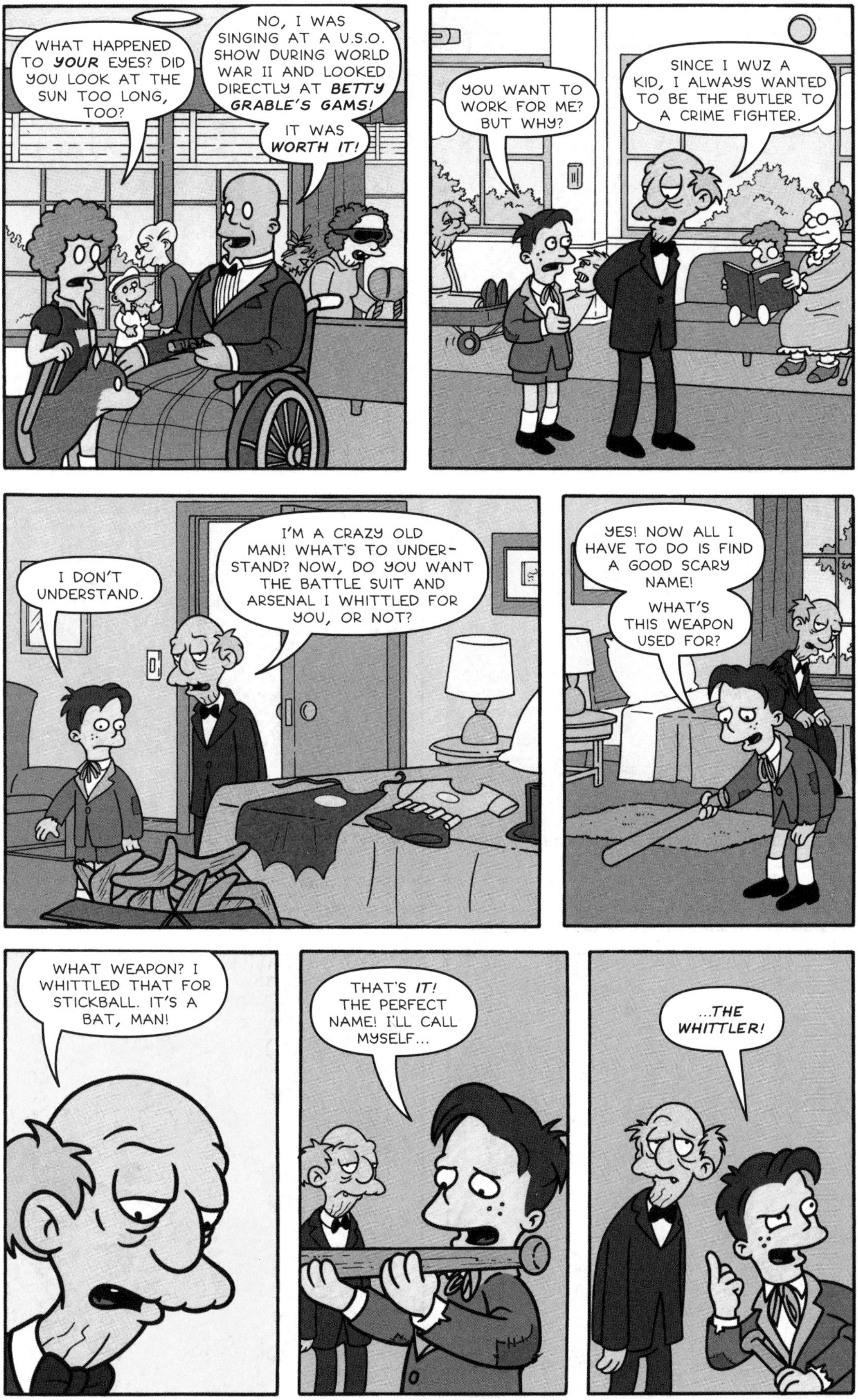
WHAT HAPPENED TO *YOUR* EYES? DID YOU LOOK AT THE SUN TOO LONG, TOO?
NO, I WAS SINGING AT A U.S.O. SHOW DURING WORLD WAR II AND LOOKED DIRECTLY AT *BETTY GRABLE'S GAMS!*
IT WAS *WORTH IT!*
YOU WANT TO WORK FOR ME? BUT WHY?
SINCE I WUZ A KID, I ALWAYS WANTED TO BE THE BUTLER TO A CRIME FIGHTER.
I DON'T UNDERSTAND.
I'M A CRAZY OLD MAN! WHAT'S TO UNDERSTAND? NOW, DO YOU WANT THE BATTLE SUIT AND ARSENAL I WHITTLED FOR YOU, OR NOT?
YES! NOW ALL I HAVE TO DO IS FIND A GOOD SCARY NAME!
WHAT'S THIS WEAPON USED FOR?
WHAT WEAPON? I WHITTLED THAT FOR STICKBALL. IT'S A BAT, MAN!
THAT'S *IT!* THE PERFECT NAME! I'LL CALL MYSELF...
...THE WHITTLER!

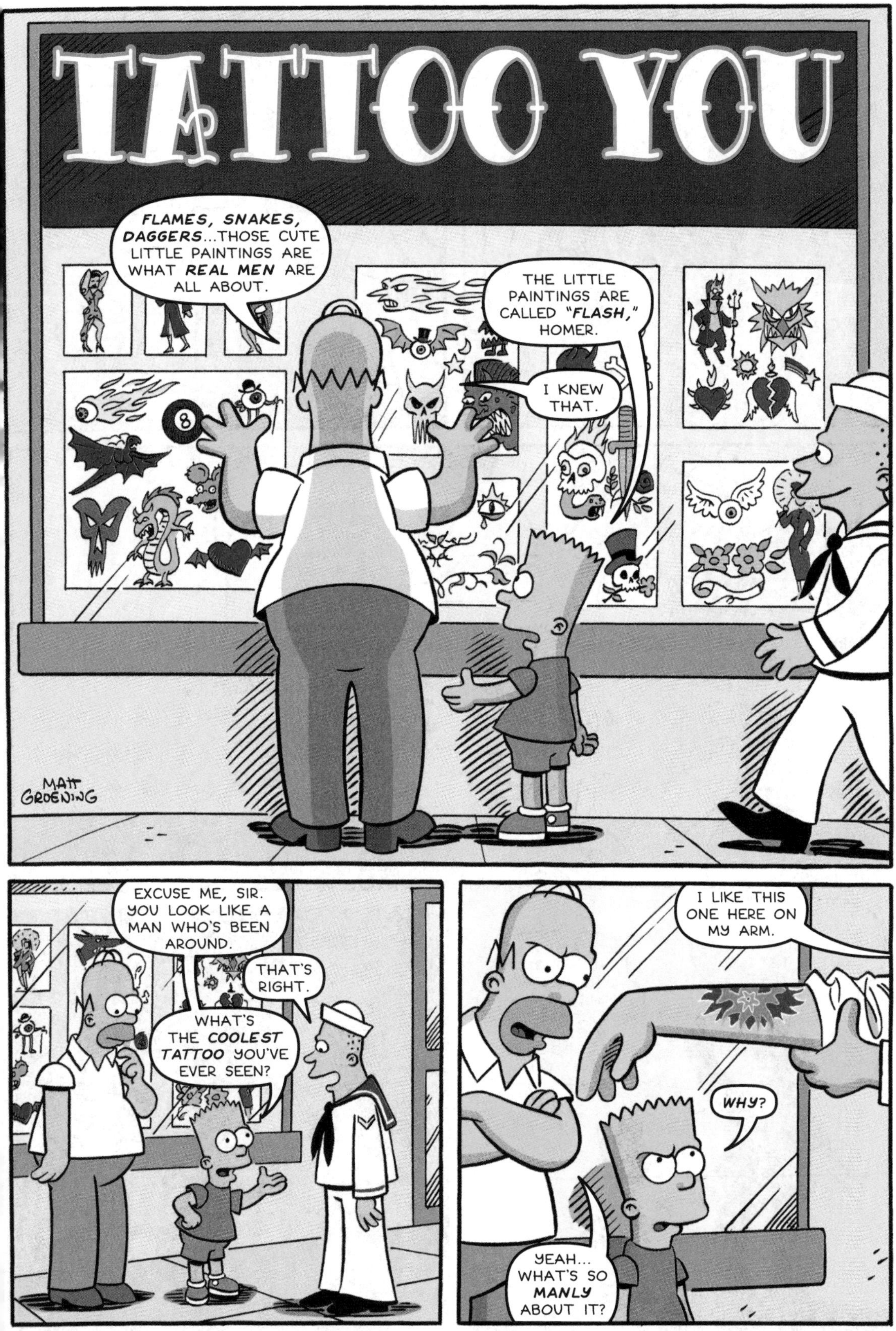
TATTOO YOU
FLAMES, SNAKES, DAGGERS...THOSE CUTE LITTLE PAINTINGS ARE WHAT REAL MEN ARE ALL ABOUT.
THE LITTLE PAINTINGS ARE CALLED "FLASH," HOMER.
I KNEW THAT.
MATT GROENING
EXCUSE ME, SIR. YOU LOOK LIKE A MAN WHO'S BEEN AROUND.
THAT'S RIGHT.
WHAT'S THE COOLEST TATTOO YOU'VE EVER SEEN?
I LIKE THIS ONE HERE ON MY ARM.
WHY?
YEAH... WHAT'S SO MANLY ABOUT IT?

CAROL LAY
SCRIPT & ART

NATHAN HAMILL
COLORS

KAREN BATES
LETTERS

BILL MORRISON
EDITOR

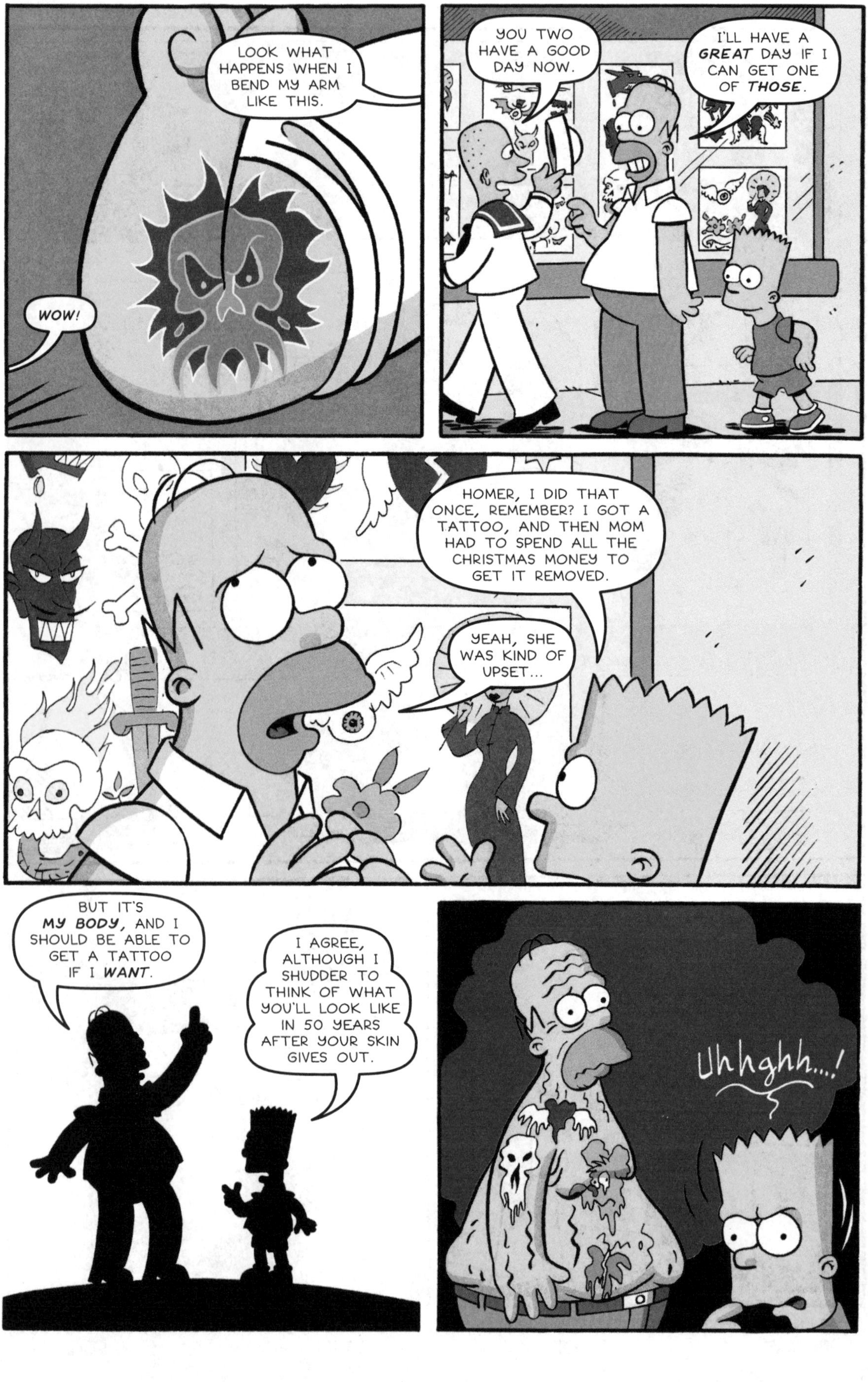
LOOK WHAT HAPPENS WHEN I BEND MY ARM LIKE THIS.
WOW!
YOU TWO HAVE A GOOD DAY NOW.
I'LL HAVE A GREAT DAY IF I CAN GET ONE OF THOSE.
HOMER, I DID THAT ONCE, REMEMBER? I GOT A TATTOO, AND THEN MOM HAD TO SPEND ALL THE CHRISTMAS MONEY TO GET IT REMOVED.
YEAH, SHE WAS KIND OF UPSET...
BUT IT'S MY BODY, AND I SHOULD BE ABLE TO GET A TATTOO IF I WANT.
I AGREE, ALTHOUGH I SHUDDER TO THINK OF WHAT YOU'LL LOOK LIKE IN 50 YEARS AFTER YOUR SKIN GIVES OUT.
Uhhghh...!

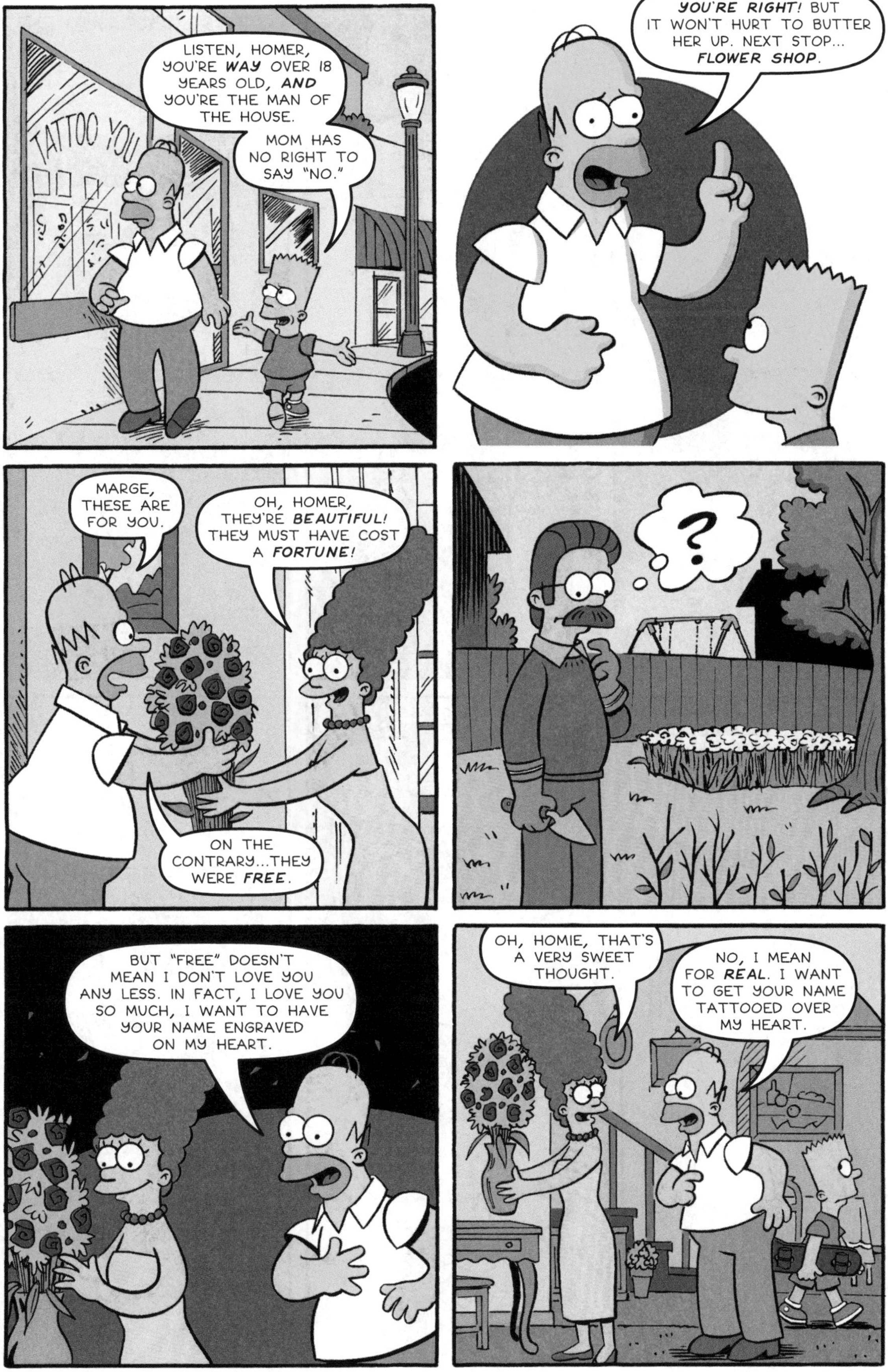
TATTOO YOU
LISTEN, HOMER, YOU'RE **WAY** OVER 18 YEARS OLD, **AND** YOU'RE THE MAN OF THE HOUSE.
MOM HAS NO RIGHT TO SAY "NO."
YOU'RE RIGHT! BUT IT WON'T HURT TO BUTTER HER UP. NEXT STOP... ***FLOWER SHOP***.
MARGE, THESE ARE FOR YOU.
OH, HOMER, THEY'RE ***BEAUTIFUL!*** THEY MUST HAVE COST A ***FORTUNE!***
ON THE CONTRARY...THEY WERE ***FREE***.
?
BUT "FREE" DOESN'T MEAN I DON'T LOVE YOU ANY LESS. IN FACT, I LOVE YOU SO MUCH, I WANT TO HAVE YOUR NAME ENGRAVED ON MY HEART.
OH, HOMIE, THAT'S A VERY SWEET THOUGHT.
NO, I MEAN FOR ***REAL***. I WANT TO GET YOUR NAME TATTOOED OVER MY HEART.

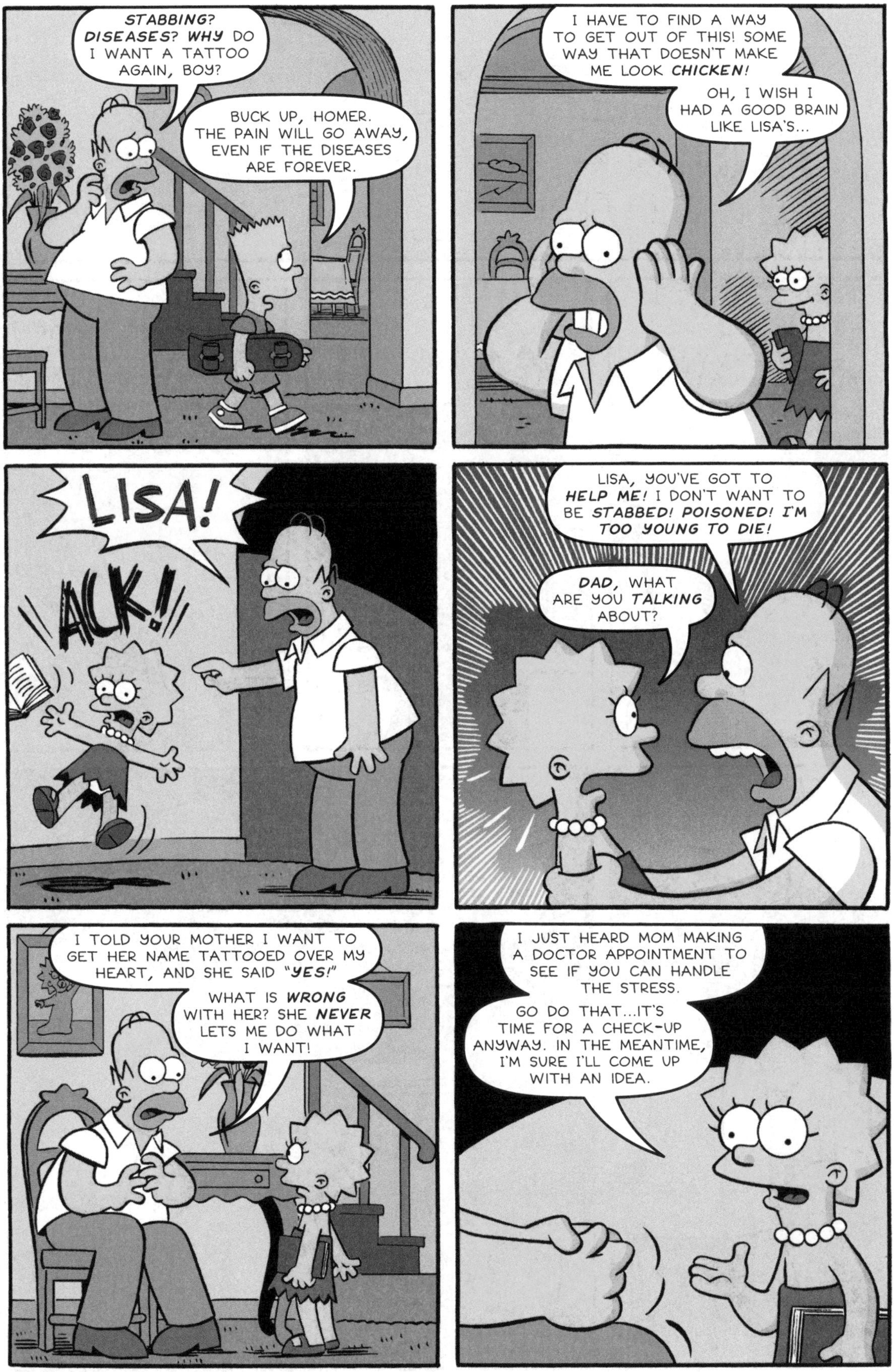
STABBING? DISEASES? WHY DO I WANT A TATTOO AGAIN, BOY?
BUCK UP, HOMER. THE PAIN WILL GO AWAY, EVEN IF THE DISEASES ARE FOREVER.
I HAVE TO FIND A WAY TO GET OUT OF THIS! SOME WAY THAT DOESN'T MAKE ME LOOK CHICKEN!
OH, I WISH I HAD A GOOD BRAIN LIKE LISA'S...
LISA!
ACK!!
LISA, YOU'VE GOT TO HELP ME! I DON'T WANT TO BE STABBED! POISONED! I'M TOO YOUNG TO DIE!
DAD, WHAT ARE YOU TALKING ABOUT?
I TOLD YOUR MOTHER I WANT TO GET HER NAME TATTOOED OVER MY HEART, AND SHE SAID "YES!"
WHAT IS WRONG WITH HER? SHE NEVER LETS ME DO WHAT I WANT!
I JUST HEARD MOM MAKING A DOCTOR APPOINTMENT TO SEE IF YOU CAN HANDLE THE STRESS.
GO DO THAT...IT'S TIME FOR A CHECK-UP ANYWAY. IN THE MEANTIME, I'M SURE I'LL COME UP WITH AN IDEA.

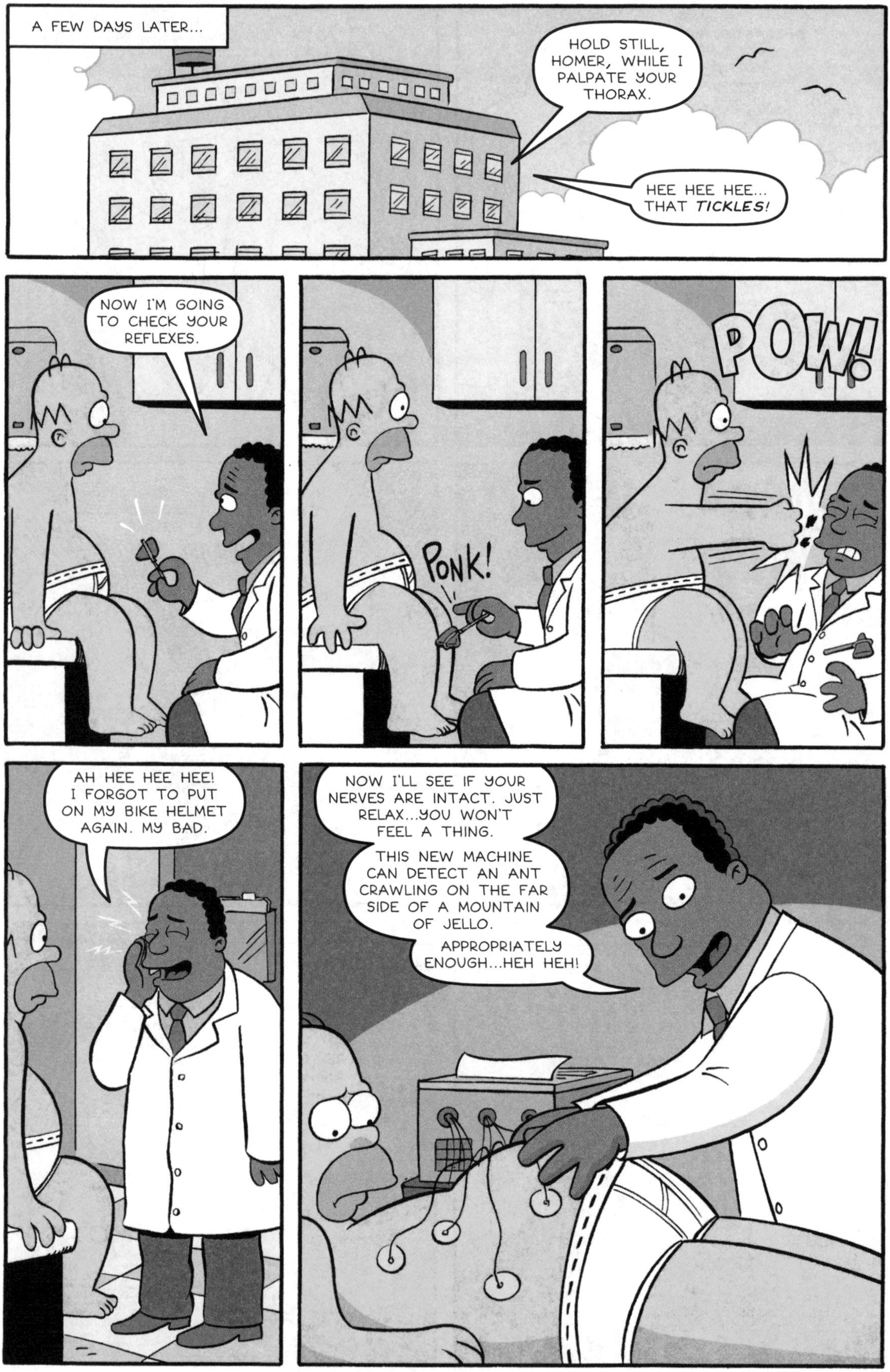
A FEW DAYS LATER...
HOLD STILL, HOMER, WHILE I PALPATE YOUR THORAX.
HEE HEE HEE... THAT TICKLES!
NOW I'M GOING TO CHECK YOUR REFLEXES.
PONK!
POW!
AH HEE HEE HEE! I FORGOT TO PUT ON MY BIKE HELMET AGAIN. MY BAD.
NOW I'LL SEE IF YOUR NERVES ARE INTACT. JUST RELAX...YOU WON'T FEEL A THING.
THIS NEW MACHINE CAN DETECT AN ANT CRAWLING ON THE FAR SIDE OF A MOUNTAIN OF JELLO.
APPROPRIATELY ENOUGH...HEH HEH!

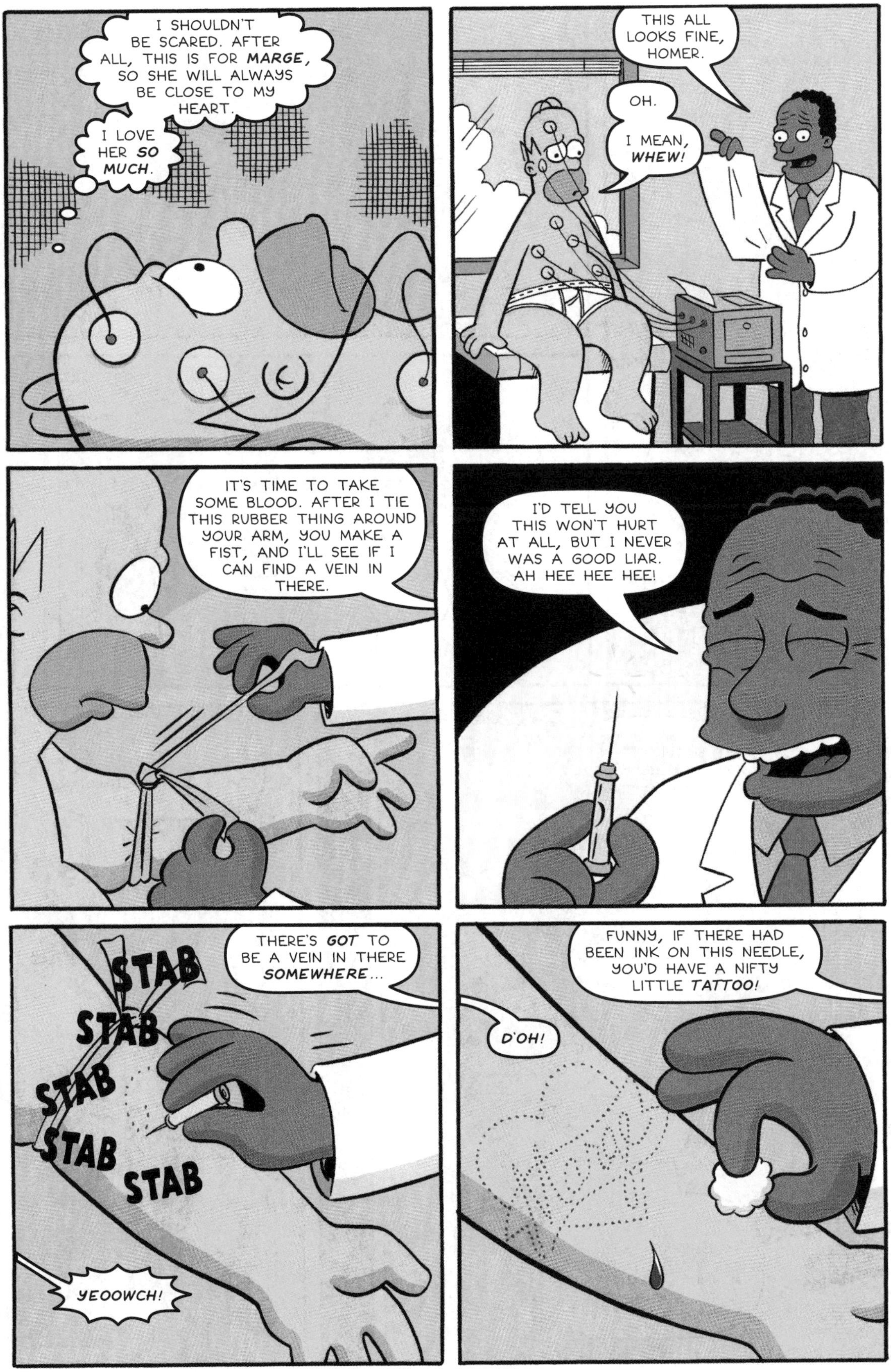
I SHOULDN'T BE SCARED. AFTER ALL, THIS IS FOR MARGE, SO SHE WILL ALWAYS BE CLOSE TO MY HEART.
I LOVE HER SO MUCH.
THIS ALL LOOKS FINE, HOMER.
OH.
I MEAN, WHEW!
IT'S TIME TO TAKE SOME BLOOD. AFTER I TIE THIS RUBBER THING AROUND YOUR ARM, YOU MAKE A FIST, AND I'LL SEE IF I CAN FIND A VEIN IN THERE.
I'D TELL YOU THIS WON'T HURT AT ALL, BUT I NEVER WAS A GOOD LIAR. AH HEE HEE HEE!
THERE'S GOT TO BE A VEIN IN THERE SOMEWHERE...
STAB
STAB
STAB
STAB
STAB
YEOOWCH!
FUNNY, IF THERE HAD BEEN INK ON THIS NEEDLE, YOU'D HAVE A NIFTY LITTLE TATTOO!
D'OH!

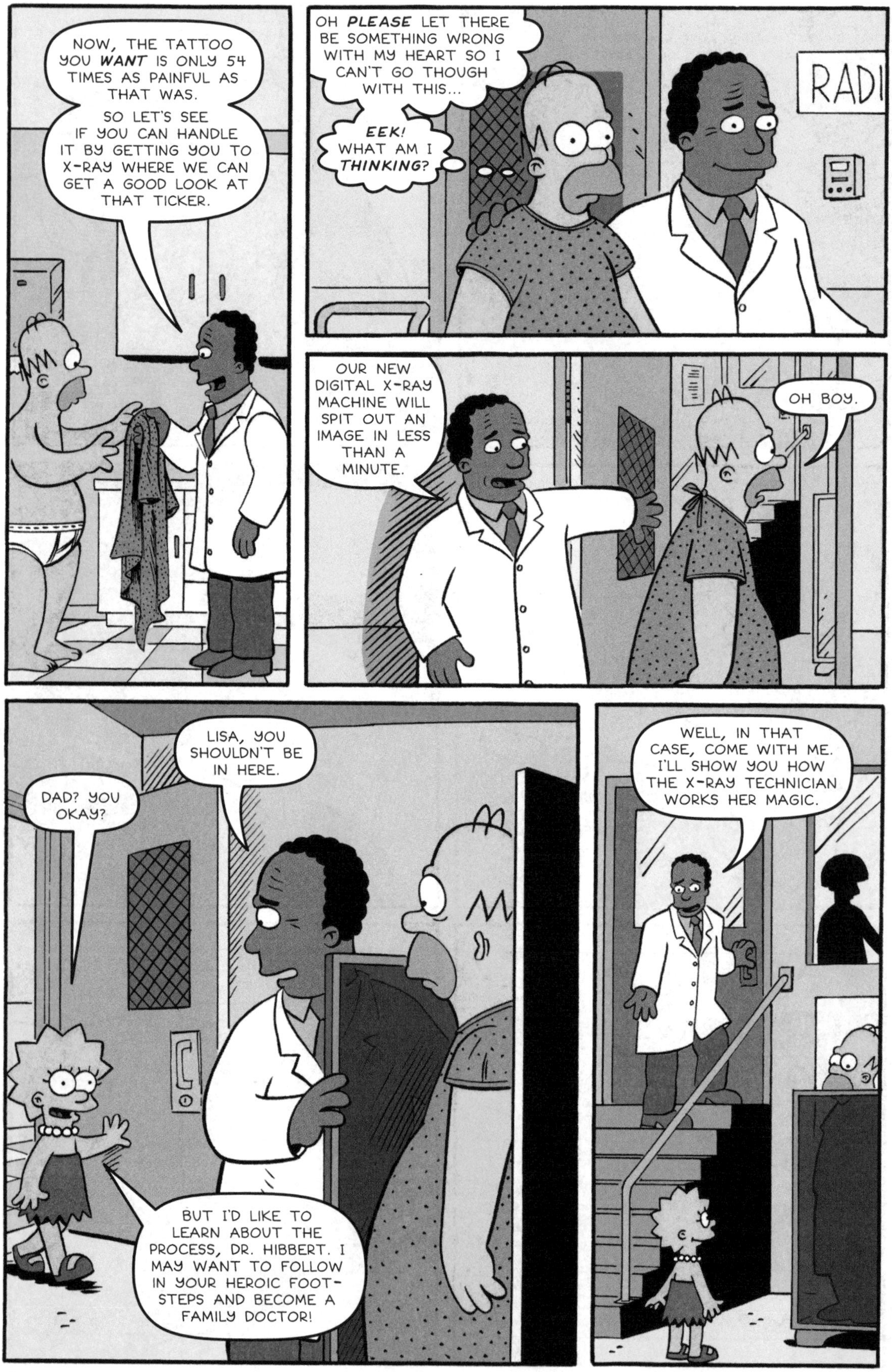
NOW, THE TATTOO YOU *WANT* IS ONLY 54 TIMES AS PAINFUL AS THAT WAS.
SO LET'S SEE IF YOU CAN HANDLE IT BY GETTING YOU TO X-RAY WHERE WE CAN GET A GOOD LOOK AT THAT TICKER.
OH *PLEASE* LET THERE BE SOMETHING WRONG WITH MY HEART SO I CAN'T GO THOUGH WITH THIS...
EEK! WHAT AM I *THINKING?*
RADI
OUR NEW DIGITAL X-RAY MACHINE WILL SPIT OUT AN IMAGE IN LESS THAN A MINUTE.
OH BOY.
DAD? YOU OKAY?
LISA, YOU SHOULDN'T BE IN HERE.
BUT I'D LIKE TO LEARN ABOUT THE PROCESS, DR. HIBBERT. I MAY WANT TO FOLLOW IN YOUR HEROIC FOOT-STEPS AND BECOME A FAMILY DOCTOR!
WELL, IN THAT CASE, COME WITH ME. I'LL SHOW YOU HOW THE X-RAY TECHNICIAN WORKS HER MAGIC.

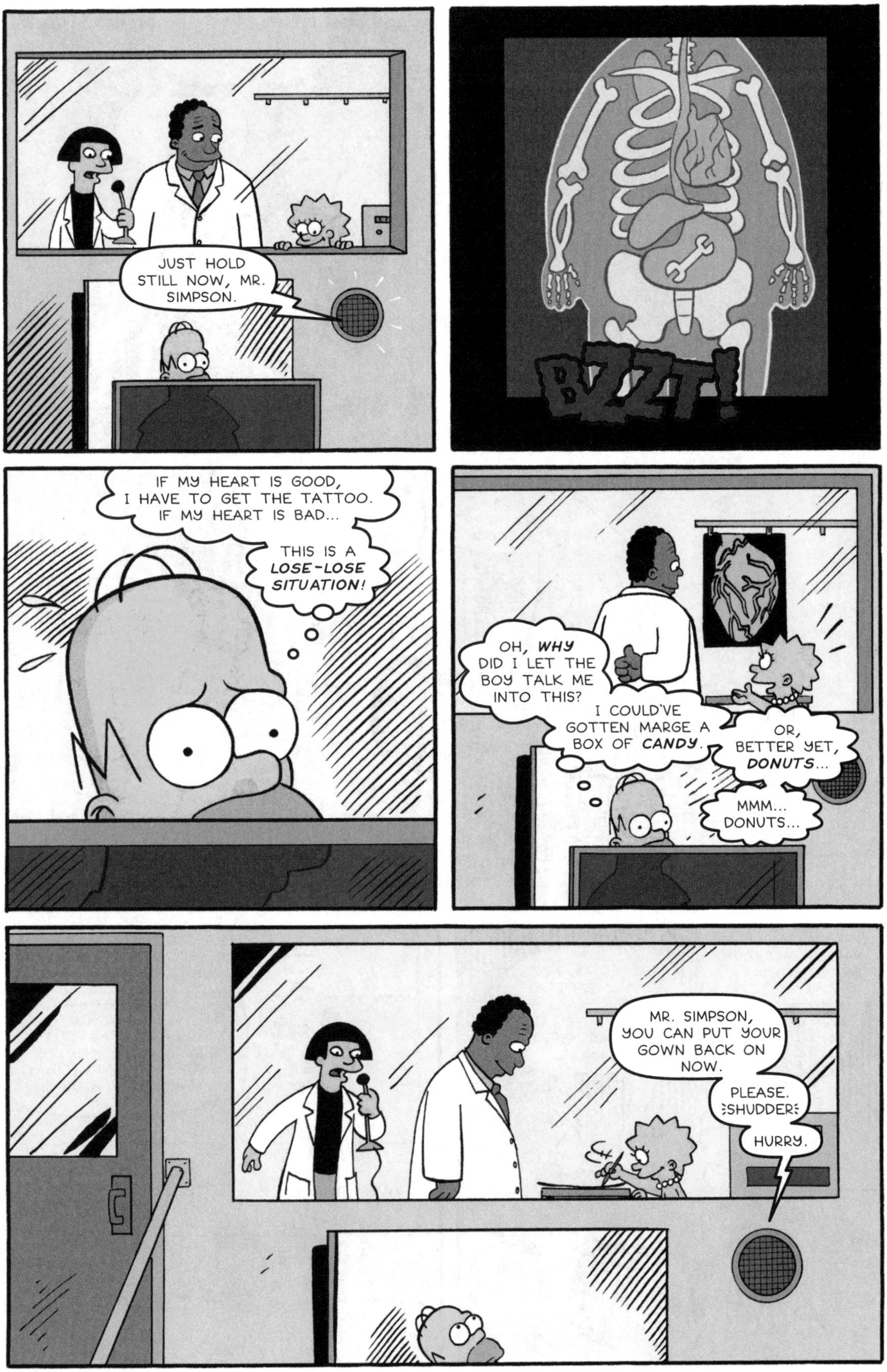
JUST HOLD STILL NOW, MR. SIMPSON.
BZZT!
IF MY HEART IS GOOD, I HAVE TO GET THE TATTOO. IF MY HEART IS BAD...
THIS IS A LOSE-LOSE SITUATION!
OH, WHY DID I LET THE BOY TALK ME INTO THIS?
I COULD'VE GOTTEN MARGE A BOX OF CANDY.
OR, BETTER YET, DONUTS...
MMM... DONUTS...
MR. SIMPSON, YOU CAN PUT YOUR GOWN BACK ON NOW.
PLEASE. ⸗SHUDDER⸗
HURRY.

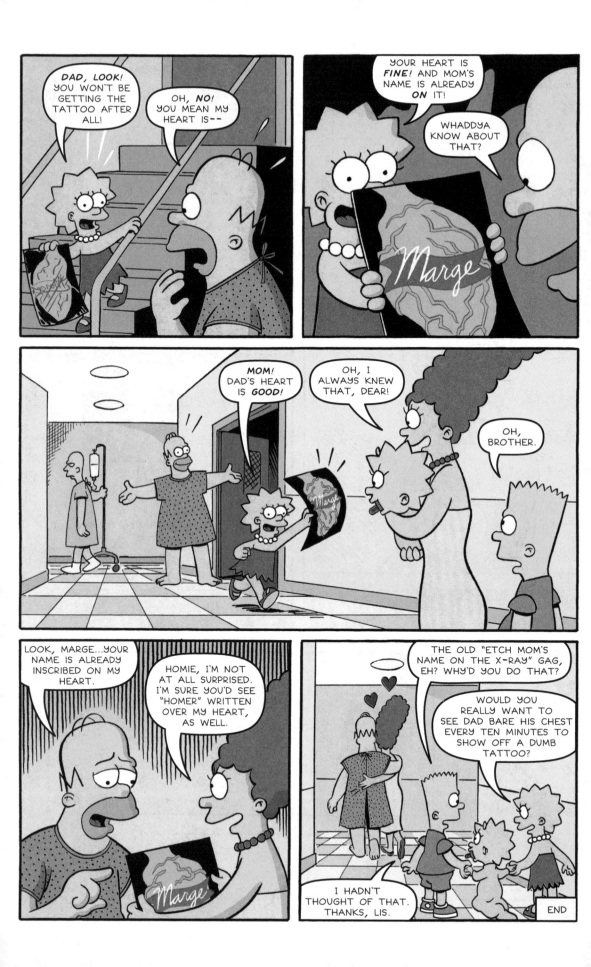

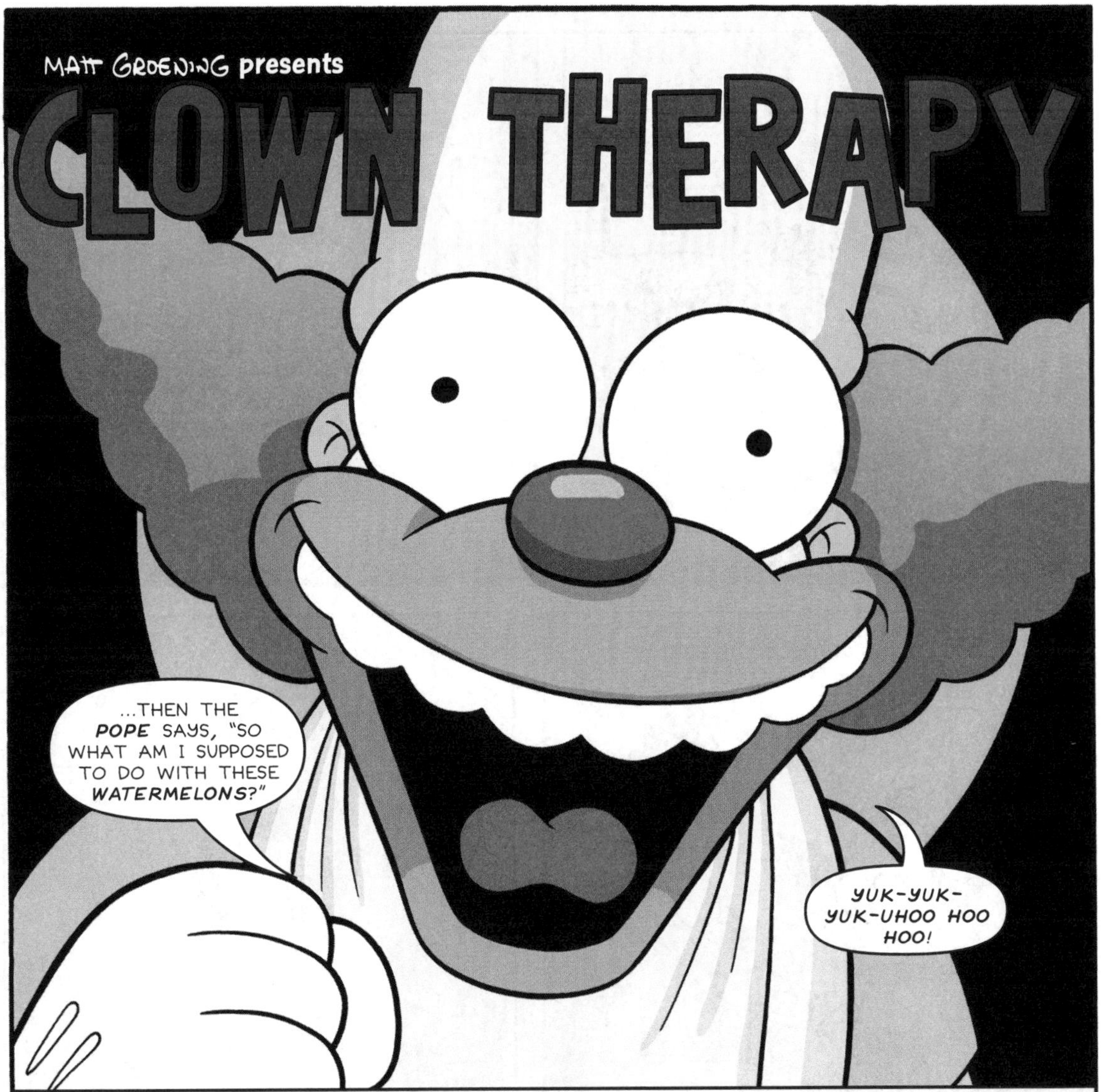
MATT GROENING presents
CLOWN THERAPY
...THEN THE POPE SAYS, "SO WHAT AM I SUPPOSED TO DO WITH THESE WATERMELONS?"
YUK-YUK-YUK-UHOO HOO HOO!

CHUCK DIXON	PHIL ORTIZ	MIKE DECARLO	ART VILLANUEVA	KAREN BATES	BILL MORRISON
SCRIPT	PENCILS	INKS	COLORS	LETTERS	EDITOR

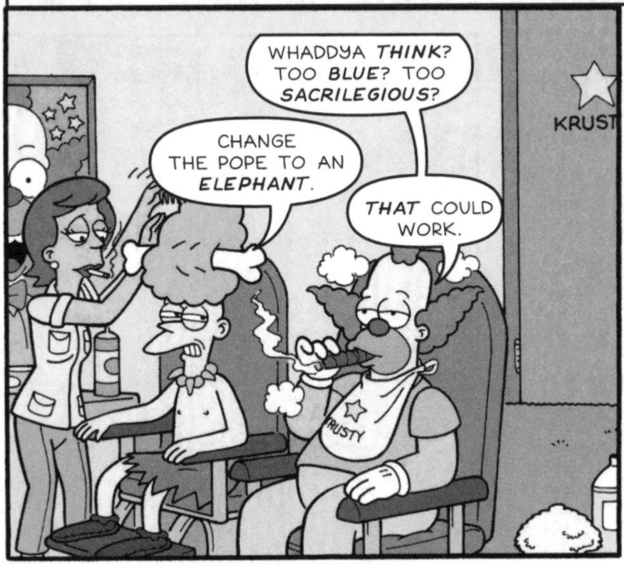
WHADDYA THINK? TOO BLUE? TOO SACRILEGIOUS?
CHANGE THE POPE TO AN ELEPHANT.
THAT COULD WORK.
KRUST
RUSTY

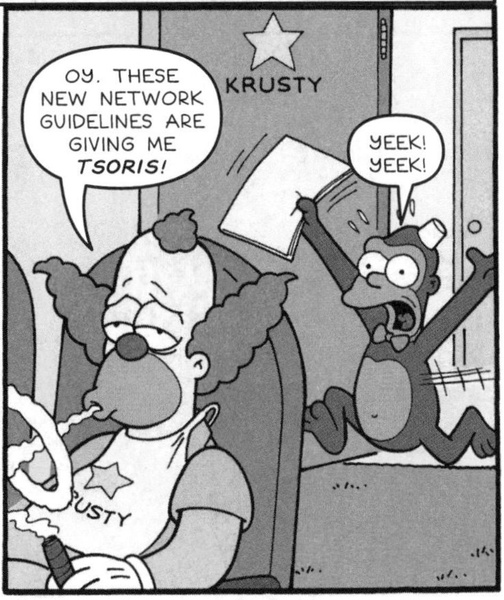
KRUSTY
OY. THESE NEW NETWORK GUIDELINES ARE GIVING ME TSORIS!
YEEK! YEEK!
RUSTY

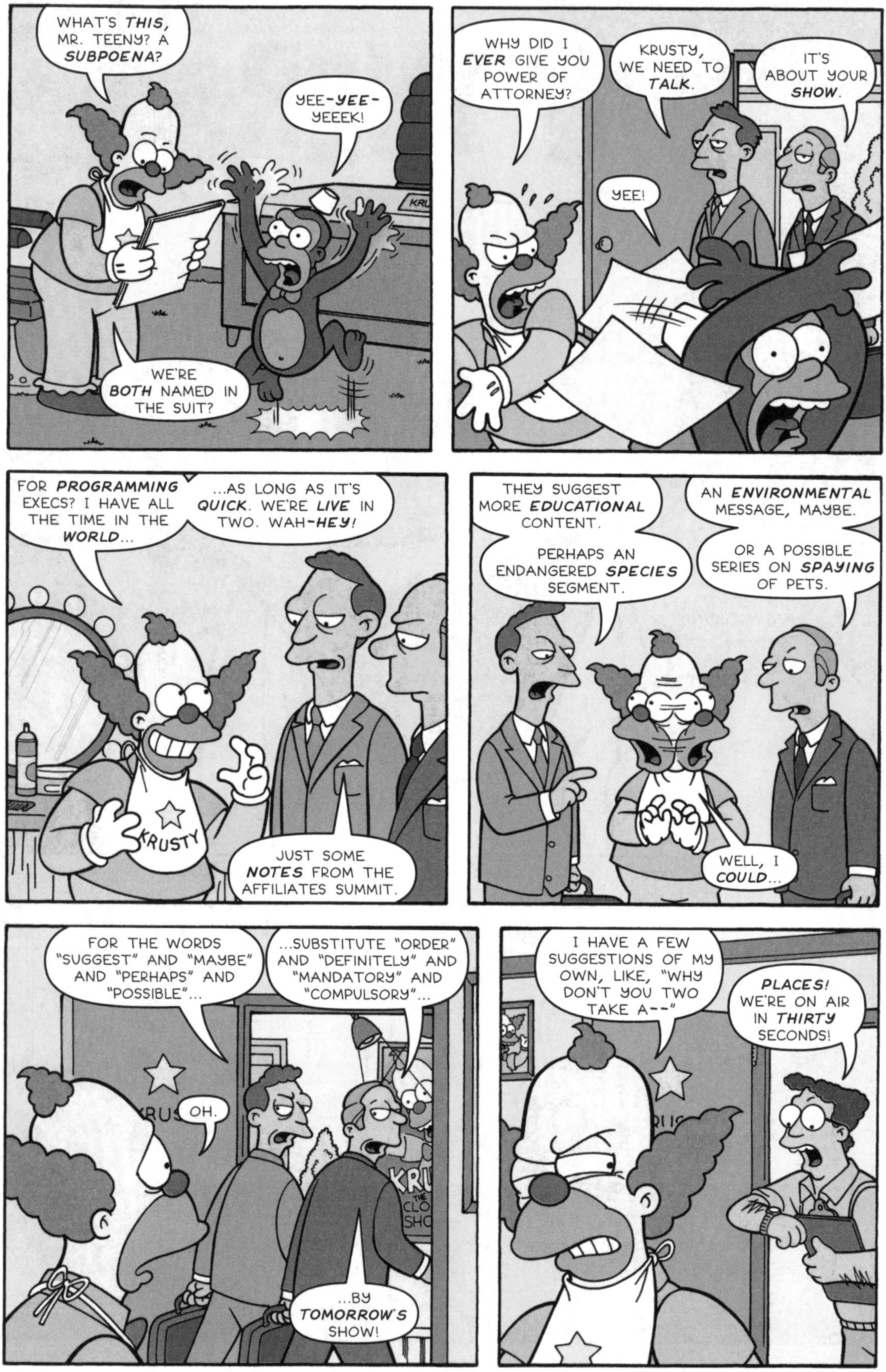
WHAT'S THIS, MR. TEENY? A SUBPOENA?
YEE-YEE-YEEEK!
WE'RE BOTH NAMED IN THE SUIT?
WHY DID I EVER GIVE YOU POWER OF ATTORNEY?
YEE!
KRUSTY, WE NEED TO TALK.
IT'S ABOUT YOUR SHOW.
FOR PROGRAMMING EXECS? I HAVE ALL THE TIME IN THE WORLD...
...AS LONG AS IT'S QUICK. WE'RE LIVE IN TWO. WAH-HEY!
KRUSTY
JUST SOME NOTES FROM THE AFFILIATES SUMMIT.
THEY SUGGEST MORE EDUCATIONAL CONTENT.
AN ENVIRONMENTAL MESSAGE, MAYBE.
PERHAPS AN ENDANGERED SPECIES SEGMENT.
OR A POSSIBLE SERIES ON SPAYING OF PETS.
WELL, I COULD...
FOR THE WORDS "SUGGEST" AND "MAYBE" AND "PERHAPS" AND "POSSIBLE"...
...SUBSTITUTE "ORDER" AND "DEFINITELY" AND "MANDATORY" AND "COMPULSORY"...
OH.
...BY TOMORROW'S SHOW!
I HAVE A FEW SUGGESTIONS OF MY OWN, LIKE, "WHY DON'T YOU TWO TAKE A--"
PLACES! WE'RE ON AIR IN THIRTY SECONDS!

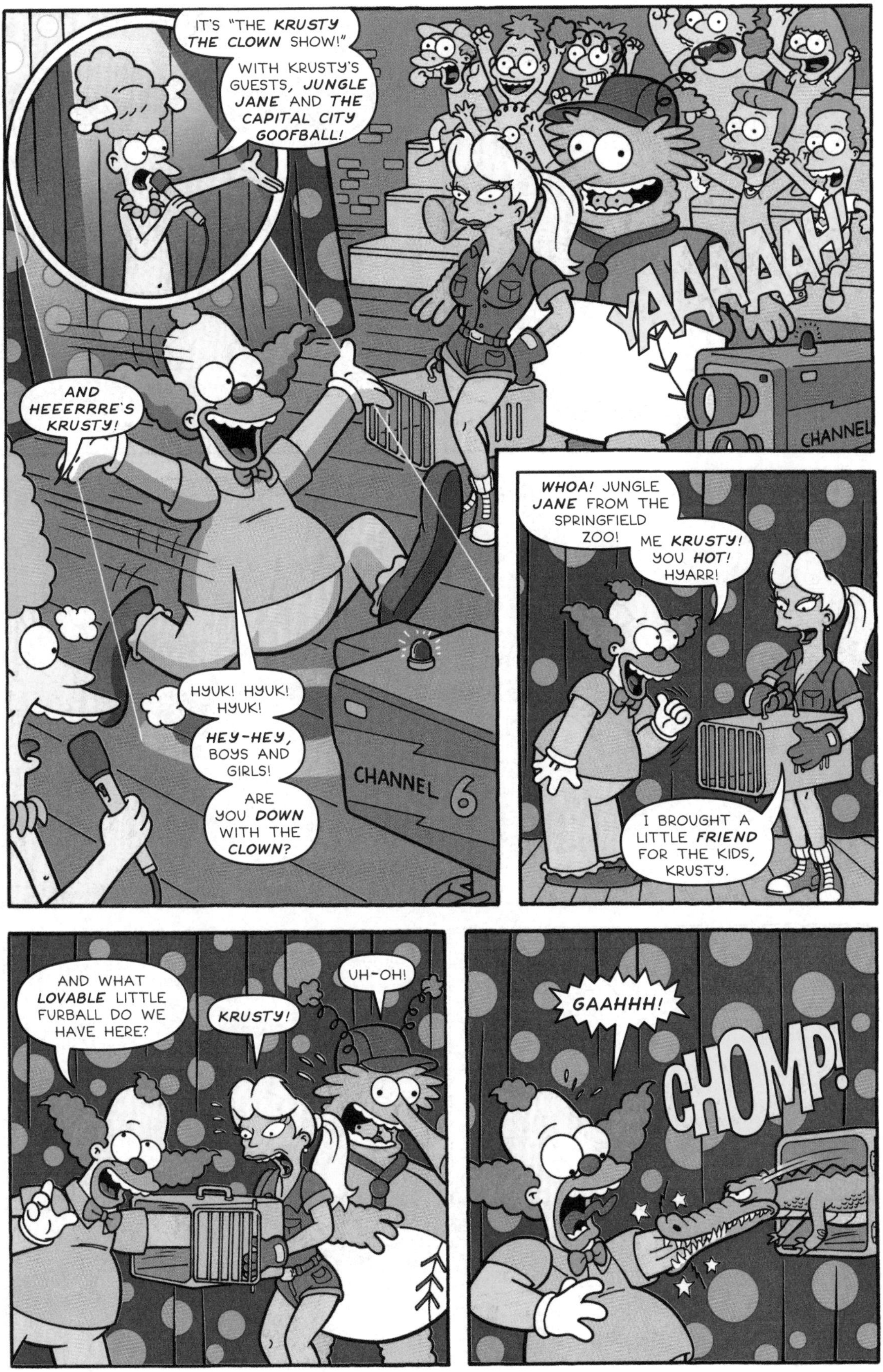

IT'S "THE KRUSTY THE CLOWN SHOW!"
WITH KRUSTY'S GUESTS, JUNGLE JANE AND THE CAPITAL CITY GOOFBALL!
YAAAAAH!
AND HEEERRRE'S KRUSTY!
HYUK! HYUK! HYUK!
HEY-HEY, BOYS AND GIRLS!
ARE YOU DOWN WITH THE CLOWN?
CHANNEL 6
WHOA! JUNGLE JANE FROM THE SPRINGFIELD ZOO!
ME KRUSTY! YOU HOT! HYARR!
I BROUGHT A LITTLE FRIEND FOR THE KIDS, KRUSTY.
AND WHAT LOVABLE LITTLE FURBALL DO WE HAVE HERE?
KRUSTY!
UH-OH!
GAAHHH!
CHOMP!

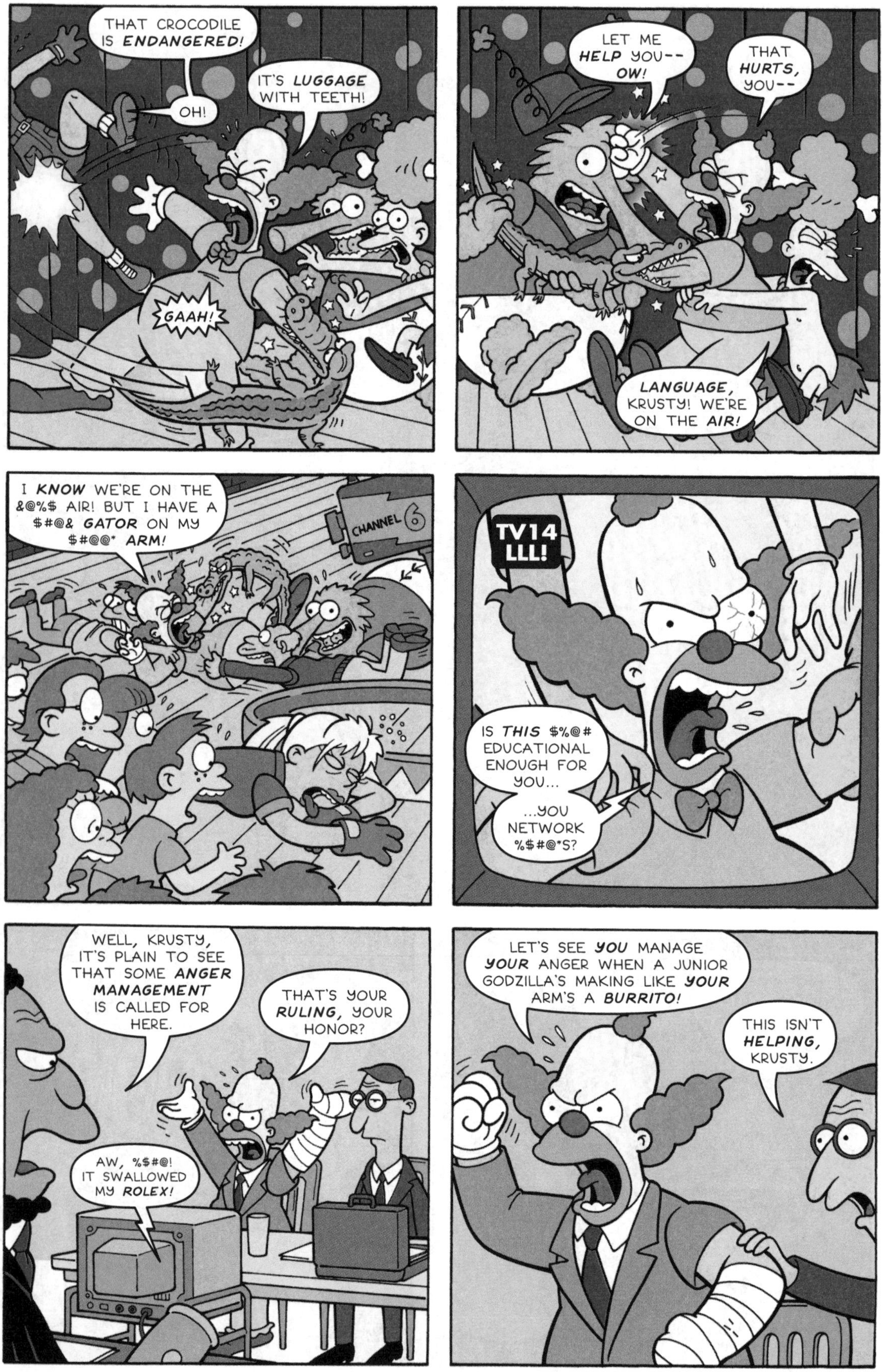
THAT CROCODILE IS ENDANGERED!
OH!
IT'S LUGGAGE WITH TEETH!
GAAH!
LET ME HELP YOU-- OW!
THAT HURTS, YOU--
LANGUAGE, KRUSTY! WE'RE ON THE AIR!
I KNOW WE'RE ON THE &@%$ AIR! BUT I HAVE A $#@& GATOR ON MY $#@@* ARM!
CHANNEL 6
TV14 LLL!
IS THIS $%@# EDUCATIONAL ENOUGH FOR YOU...
...YOU NETWORK %$#@*S?
WELL, KRUSTY, IT'S PLAIN TO SEE THAT SOME ANGER MANAGEMENT IS CALLED FOR HERE.
THAT'S YOUR RULING, YOUR HONOR?
AW, %$#@! IT SWALLOWED MY ROLEX!
LET'S SEE YOU MANAGE YOUR ANGER WHEN A JUNIOR GODZILLA'S MAKING LIKE YOUR ARM'S A BURRITO!
THIS ISN'T HELPING, KRUSTY.

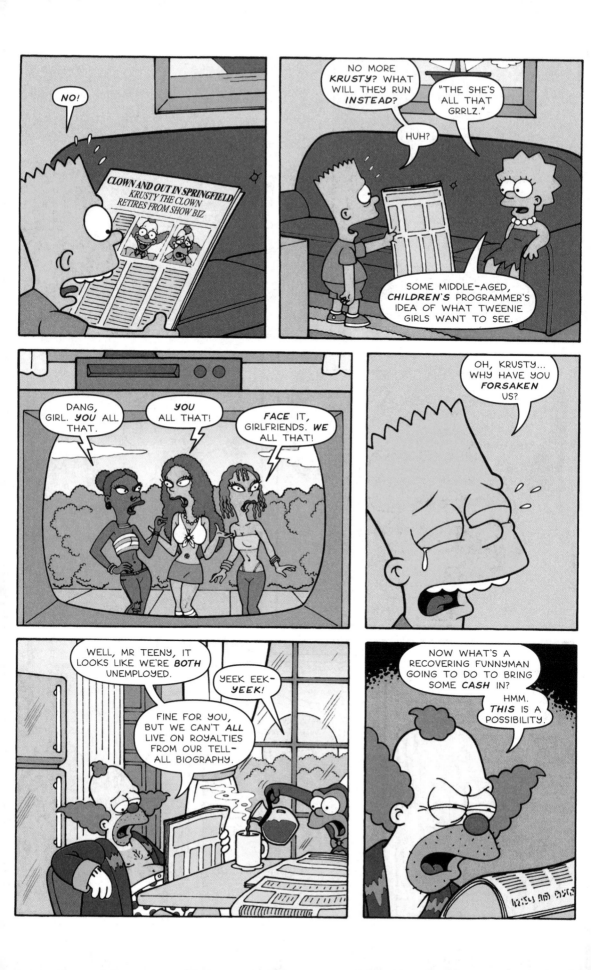

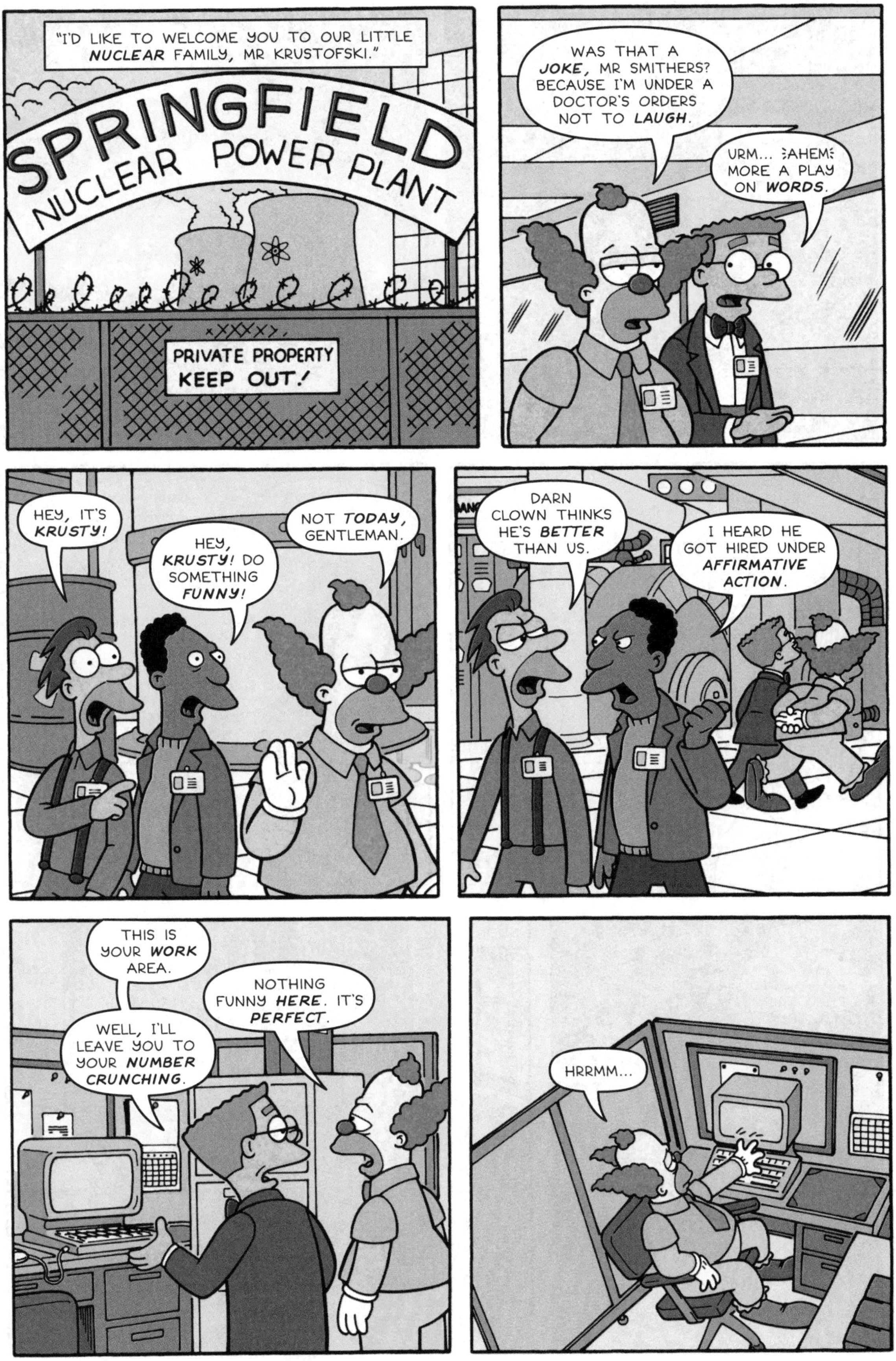
"I'D LIKE TO WELCOME YOU TO OUR LITTLE NUCLEAR FAMILY, MR KRUSTOFSKI."
SPRINGFIELD NUCLEAR POWER PLANT
PRIVATE PROPERTY KEEP OUT!
WAS THAT A JOKE, MR SMITHERS? BECAUSE I'M UNDER A DOCTOR'S ORDERS NOT TO LAUGH.
URM... AHEM MORE A PLAY ON WORDS.
HEY, IT'S KRUSTY!
HEY, KRUSTY! DO SOMETHING FUNNY!
NOT TODAY, GENTLEMAN.
DARN CLOWN THINKS HE'S BETTER THAN US.
I HEARD HE GOT HIRED UNDER AFFIRMATIVE ACTION.
THIS IS YOUR WORK AREA.
WELL, I'LL LEAVE YOU TO YOUR NUMBER CRUNCHING.
NOTHING FUNNY HERE. IT'S PERFECT.
HRRMM...

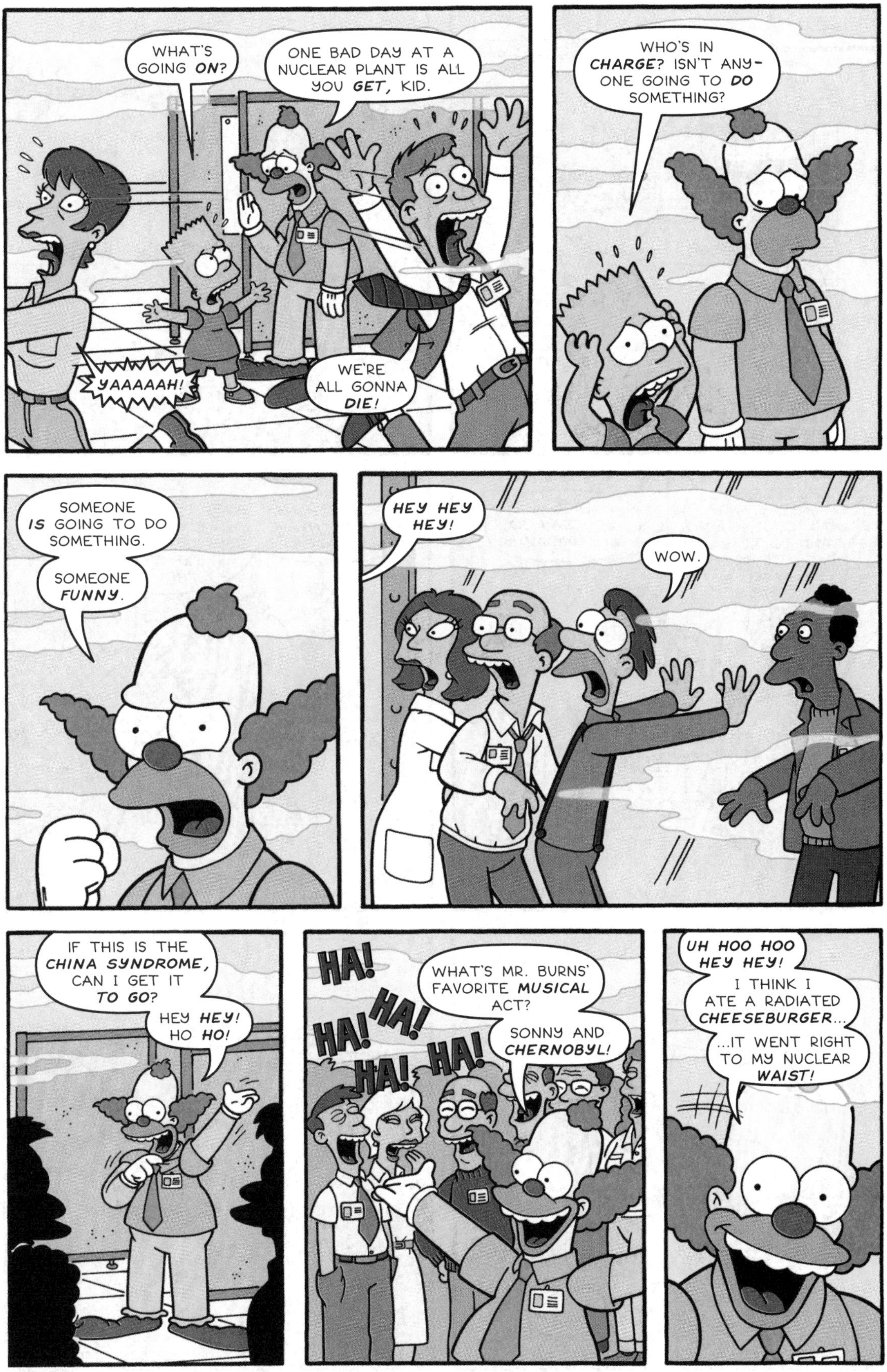
WHAT'S GOING ON?
ONE BAD DAY AT A NUCLEAR PLANT IS ALL YOU GET, KID.
YAAAAAH!
WE'RE ALL GONNA DIE!
WHO'S IN CHARGE? ISN'T ANY-ONE GOING TO DO SOMETHING?
SOMEONE IS GOING TO DO SOMETHING.
SOMEONE FUNNY.
HEY HEY HEY!
WOW.
IF THIS IS THE CHINA SYNDROME, CAN I GET IT TO GO?
HEY HEY! HO HO!
HA! HA! HA! HA! HA!
WHAT'S MR. BURNS' FAVORITE MUSICAL ACT?
SONNY AND CHERNOBYL!
UH HOO HOO HEY HEY!
I THINK I ATE A RADIATED CHEESEBURGER...
...IT WENT RIGHT TO MY NUCLEAR WAIST!

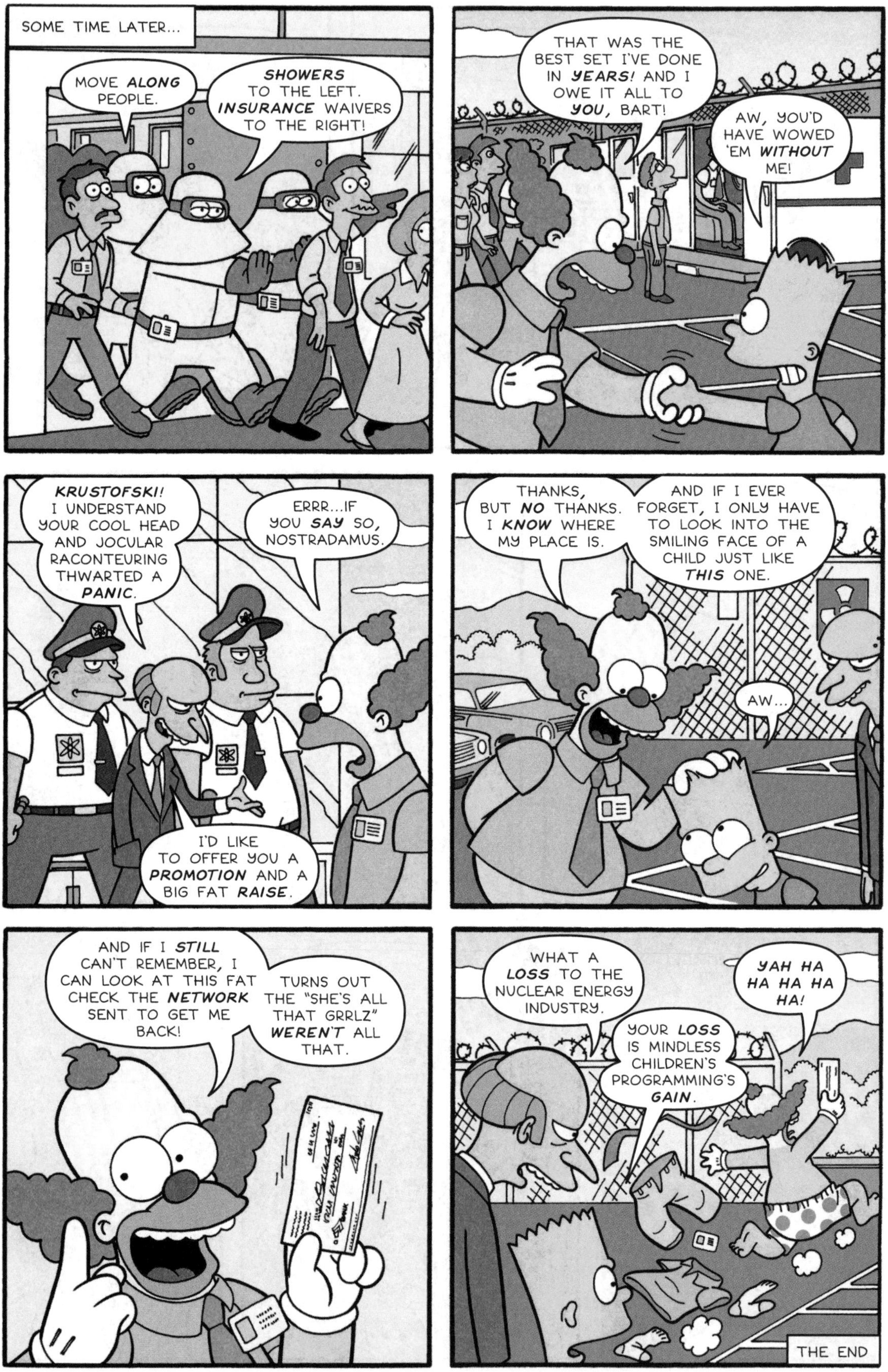
SOME TIME LATER...
MOVE ALONG PEOPLE.
SHOWERS TO THE LEFT. INSURANCE WAIVERS TO THE RIGHT!
THAT WAS THE BEST SET I'VE DONE IN YEARS! AND I OWE IT ALL TO YOU, BART!
AW, YOU'D HAVE WOWED 'EM WITHOUT ME!
KRUSTOFSKI! I UNDERSTAND YOUR COOL HEAD AND JOCULAR RACONTEURING THWARTED A PANIC.
ERRR...IF YOU SAY SO, NOSTRADAMUS.
I'D LIKE TO OFFER YOU A PROMOTION AND A BIG FAT RAISE.
THANKS, BUT NO THANKS. I KNOW WHERE MY PLACE IS.
AND IF I EVER FORGET, I ONLY HAVE TO LOOK INTO THE SMILING FACE OF A CHILD JUST LIKE THIS ONE.
AW...
AND IF I STILL CAN'T REMEMBER, I CAN LOOK AT THIS FAT CHECK THE NETWORK SENT TO GET ME BACK!
TURNS OUT THE "SHE'S ALL THAT GRRLZ" WEREN'T ALL THAT.
WHAT A LOSS TO THE NUCLEAR ENERGY INDUSTRY.
YOUR LOSS IS MINDLESS CHILDREN'S PROGRAMMING'S GAIN.
YAH HA HA HA HA HA!
THE END

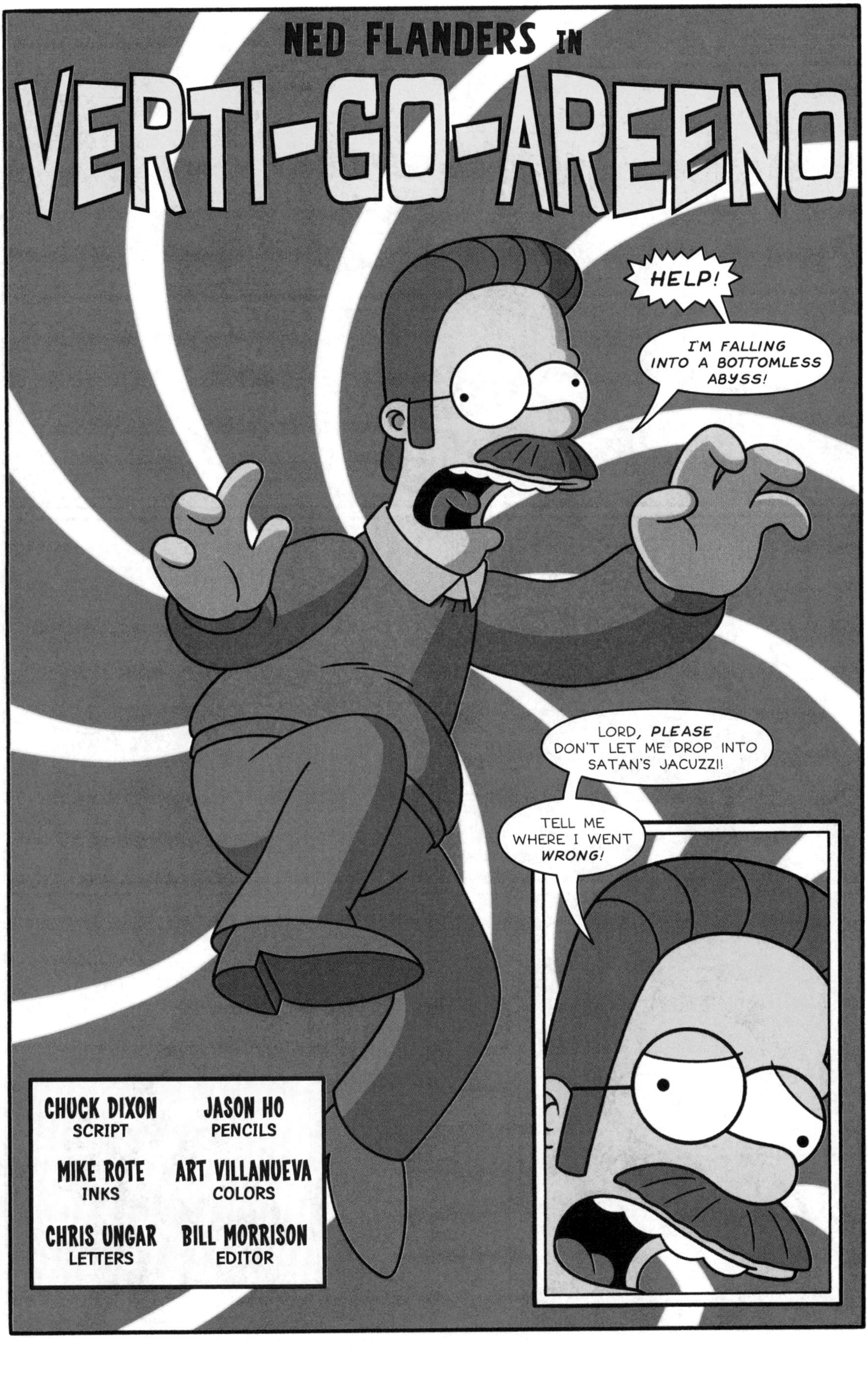
NED FLANDERS IN
VERTI-GO-AREENO
HELP!
I'M FALLING INTO A BOTTOMLESS ABYSS!
LORD, PLEASE DON'T LET ME DROP INTO SATAN'S JACUZZI!
TELL ME WHERE I WENT WRONG!
CHUCK DIXON SCRIPT
JASON HO PENCILS
MIKE ROTE INKS
ART VILLANUEVA COLORS
CHRIS UNGAR LETTERS
BILL MORRISON EDITOR

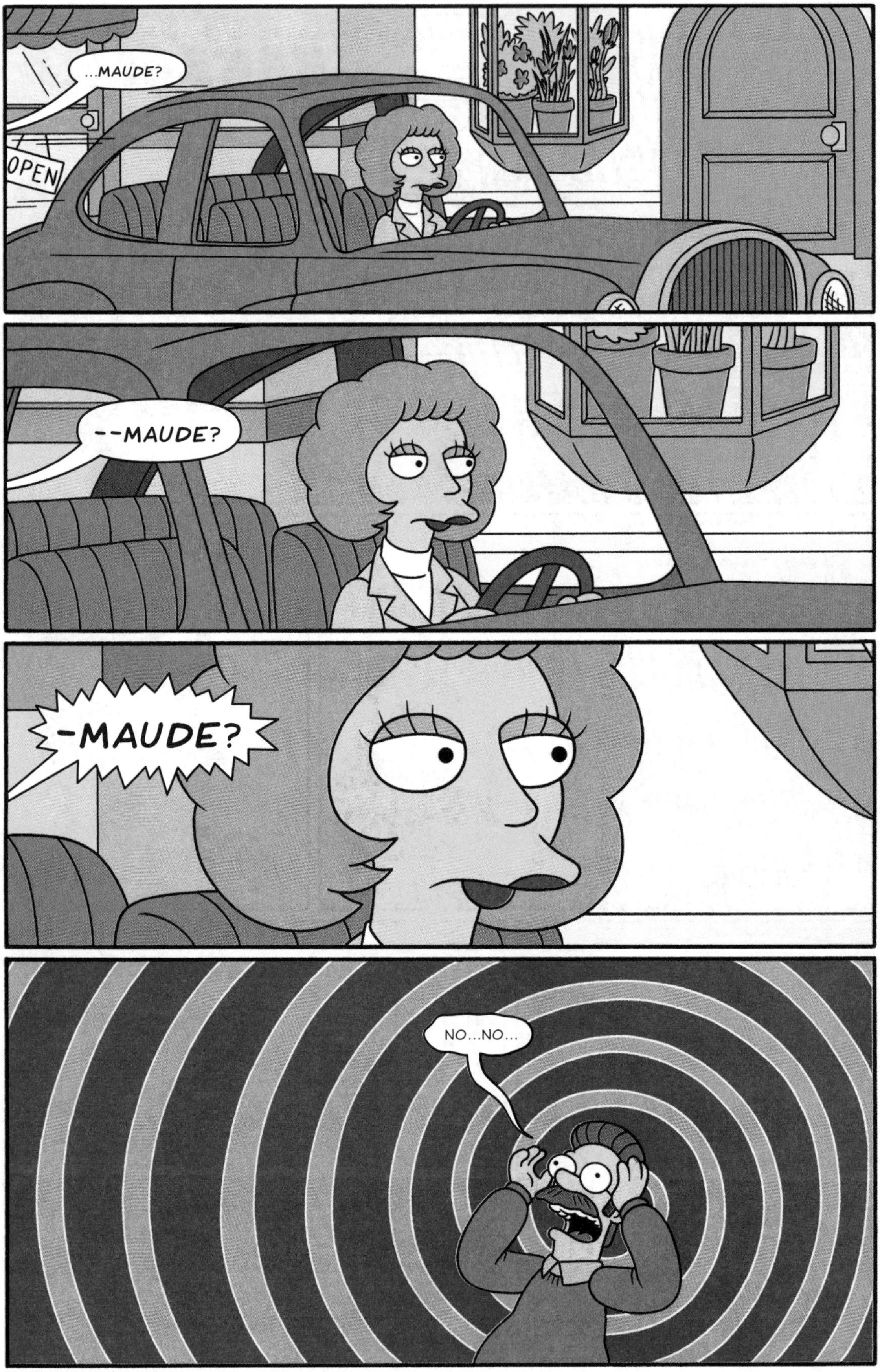
...MAUDE?
OPEN
--MAUDE?
-MAUDE?
NO...NO...

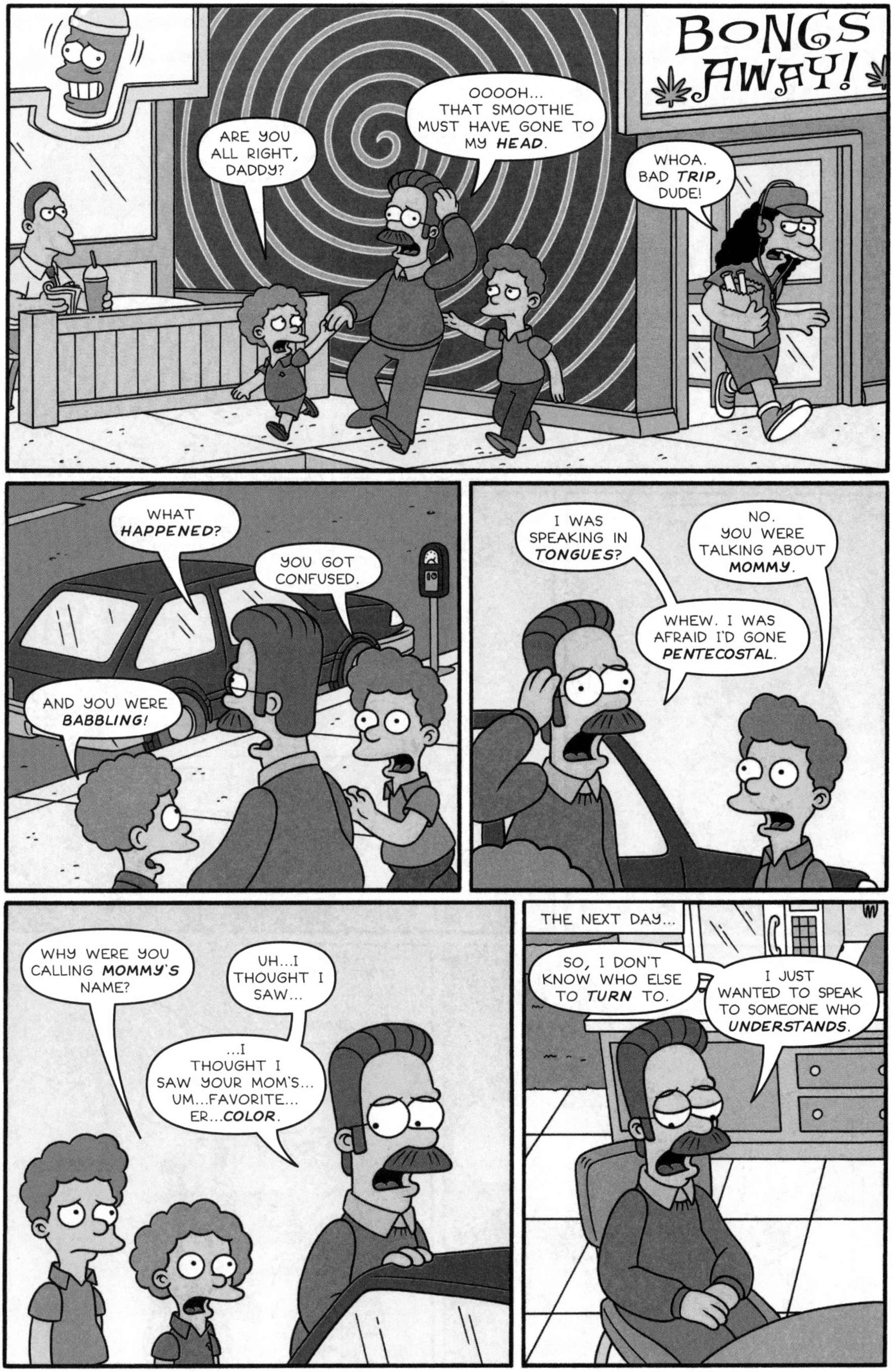
BONGS AWAY!
ARE YOU ALL RIGHT, DADDY?
OOOOH... THAT SMOOTHIE MUST HAVE GONE TO MY HEAD.
WHOA. BAD TRIP, DUDE!
WHAT HAPPENED?
YOU GOT CONFUSED.
AND YOU WERE BABBLING!
I WAS SPEAKING IN TONGUES?
NO. YOU WERE TALKING ABOUT MOMMY.
WHEW. I WAS AFRAID I'D GONE PENTECOSTAL.
WHY WERE YOU CALLING MOMMY'S NAME?
UH...I THOUGHT I SAW...
...I THOUGHT I SAW YOUR MOM'S... UM...FAVORITE... ER...COLOR.
THE NEXT DAY...
SO, I DON'T KNOW WHO ELSE TO TURN TO.
I JUST WANTED TO SPEAK TO SOMEONE WHO UNDERSTANDS.

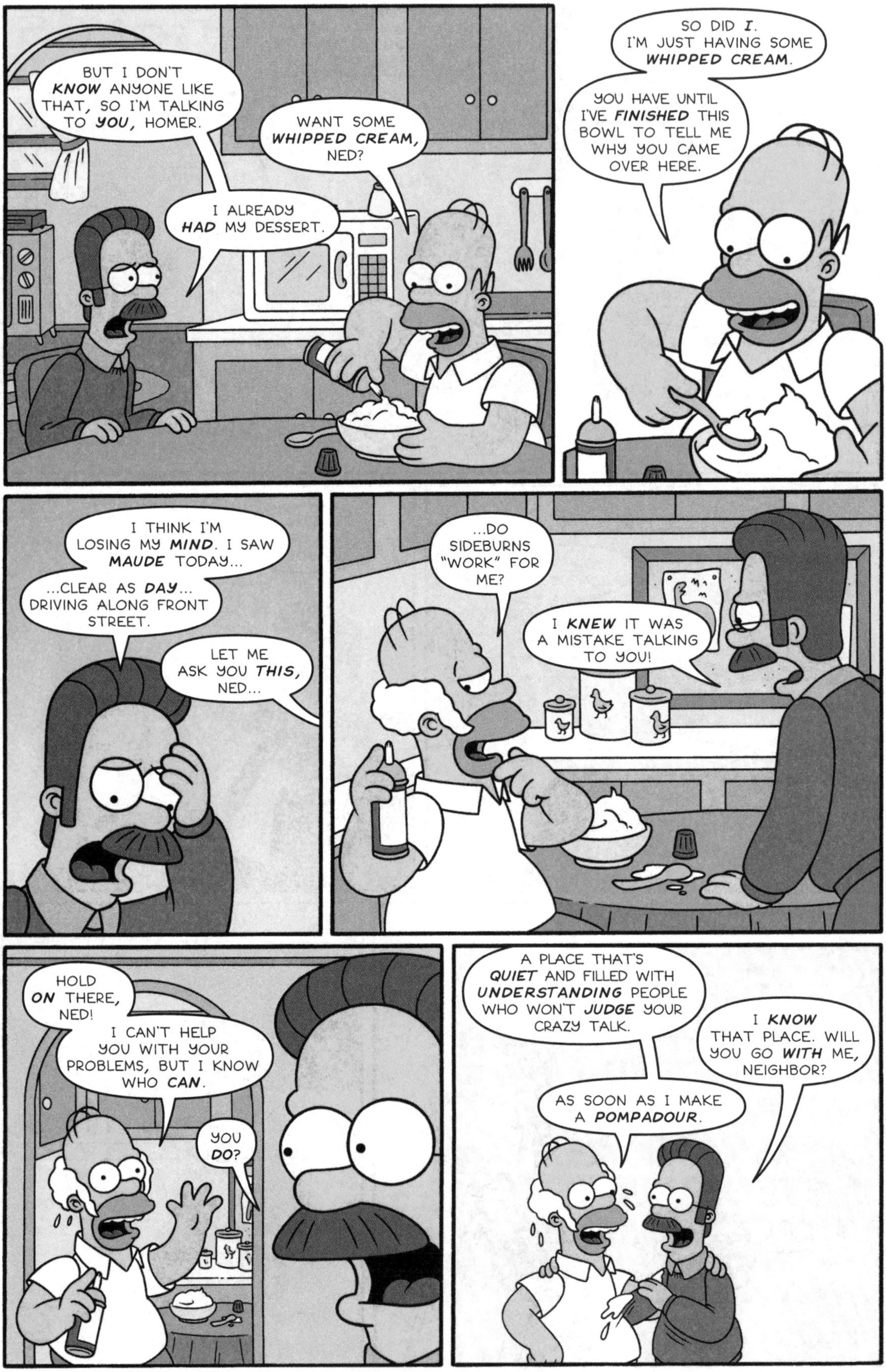
BUT I DON'T KNOW ANYONE LIKE THAT, SO I'M TALKING TO YOU, HOMER.
WANT SOME WHIPPED CREAM, NED?
I ALREADY HAD MY DESSERT.
SO DID I. I'M JUST HAVING SOME WHIPPED CREAM.
YOU HAVE UNTIL I'VE FINISHED THIS BOWL TO TELL ME WHY YOU CAME OVER HERE.
I THINK I'M LOSING MY MIND. I SAW MAUDE TODAY...
...CLEAR AS DAY... DRIVING ALONG FRONT STREET.
LET ME ASK YOU THIS, NED...
...DO SIDEBURNS "WORK" FOR ME?
I KNEW IT WAS A MISTAKE TALKING TO YOU!
HOLD ON THERE, NED!
I CAN'T HELP YOU WITH YOUR PROBLEMS, BUT I KNOW WHO CAN.
YOU DO?
A PLACE THAT'S QUIET AND FILLED WITH UNDERSTANDING PEOPLE WHO WON'T JUDGE YOUR CRAZY TALK.
I KNOW THAT PLACE. WILL YOU GO WITH ME, NEIGHBOR?
AS SOON AS I MAKE A POMPADOUR.

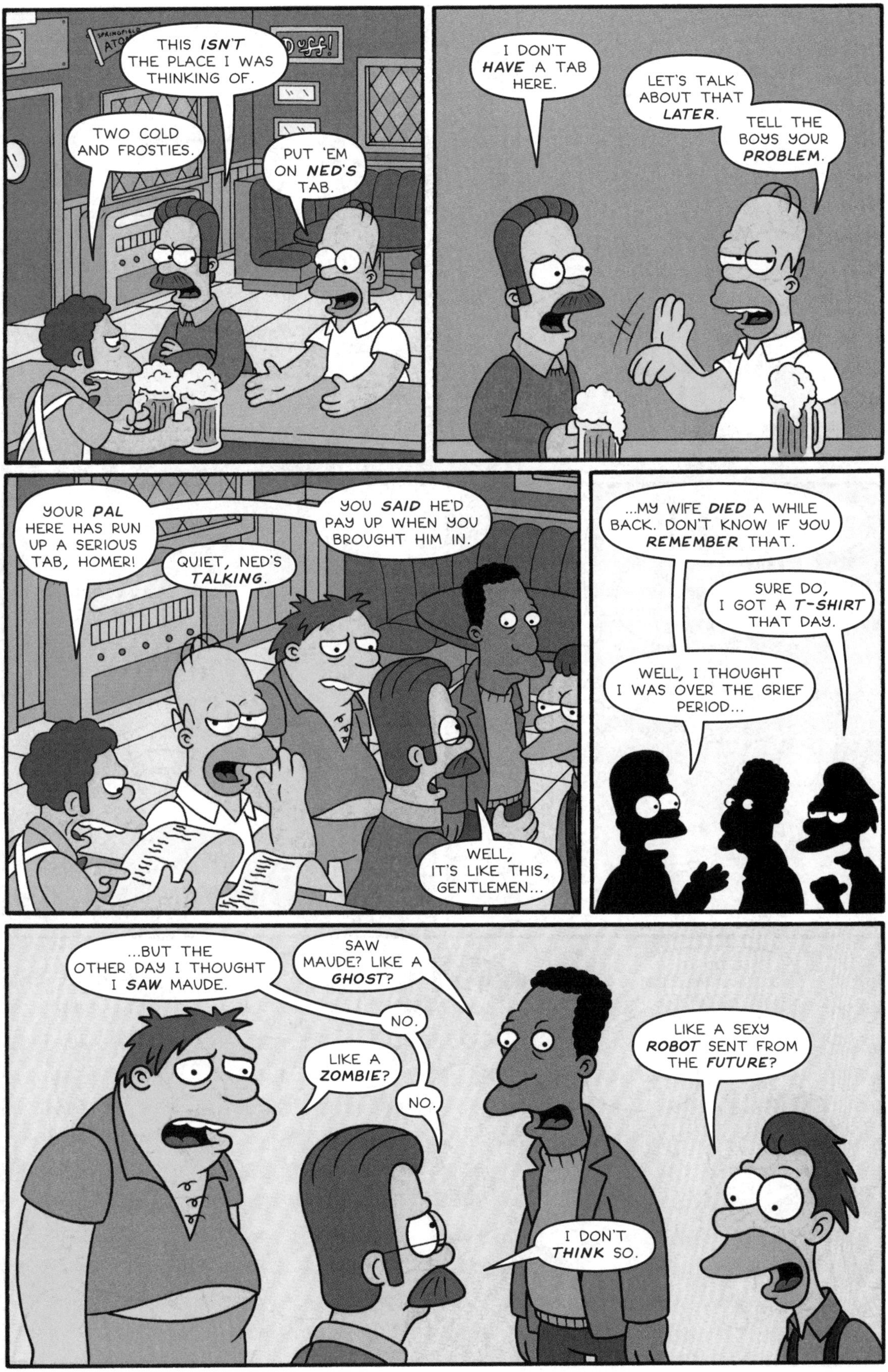
TWO COLD AND FROSTIES.
THIS ISN'T THE PLACE I WAS THINKING OF.
PUT 'EM ON NED'S TAB.
I DON'T HAVE A TAB HERE.
LET'S TALK ABOUT THAT LATER.
TELL THE BOYS YOUR PROBLEM.
YOUR PAL HERE HAS RUN UP A SERIOUS TAB, HOMER!
YOU SAID HE'D PAY UP WHEN YOU BROUGHT HIM IN.
QUIET, NED'S TALKING.
WELL, IT'S LIKE THIS, GENTLEMEN...
...MY WIFE DIED A WHILE BACK. DON'T KNOW IF YOU REMEMBER THAT.
SURE DO, I GOT A T-SHIRT THAT DAY.
WELL, I THOUGHT I WAS OVER THE GRIEF PERIOD...
...BUT THE OTHER DAY I THOUGHT I SAW MAUDE.
SAW MAUDE? LIKE A GHOST?
NO.
LIKE A ZOMBIE?
NO.
LIKE A SEXY ROBOT SENT FROM THE FUTURE?
I DON'T THINK SO.

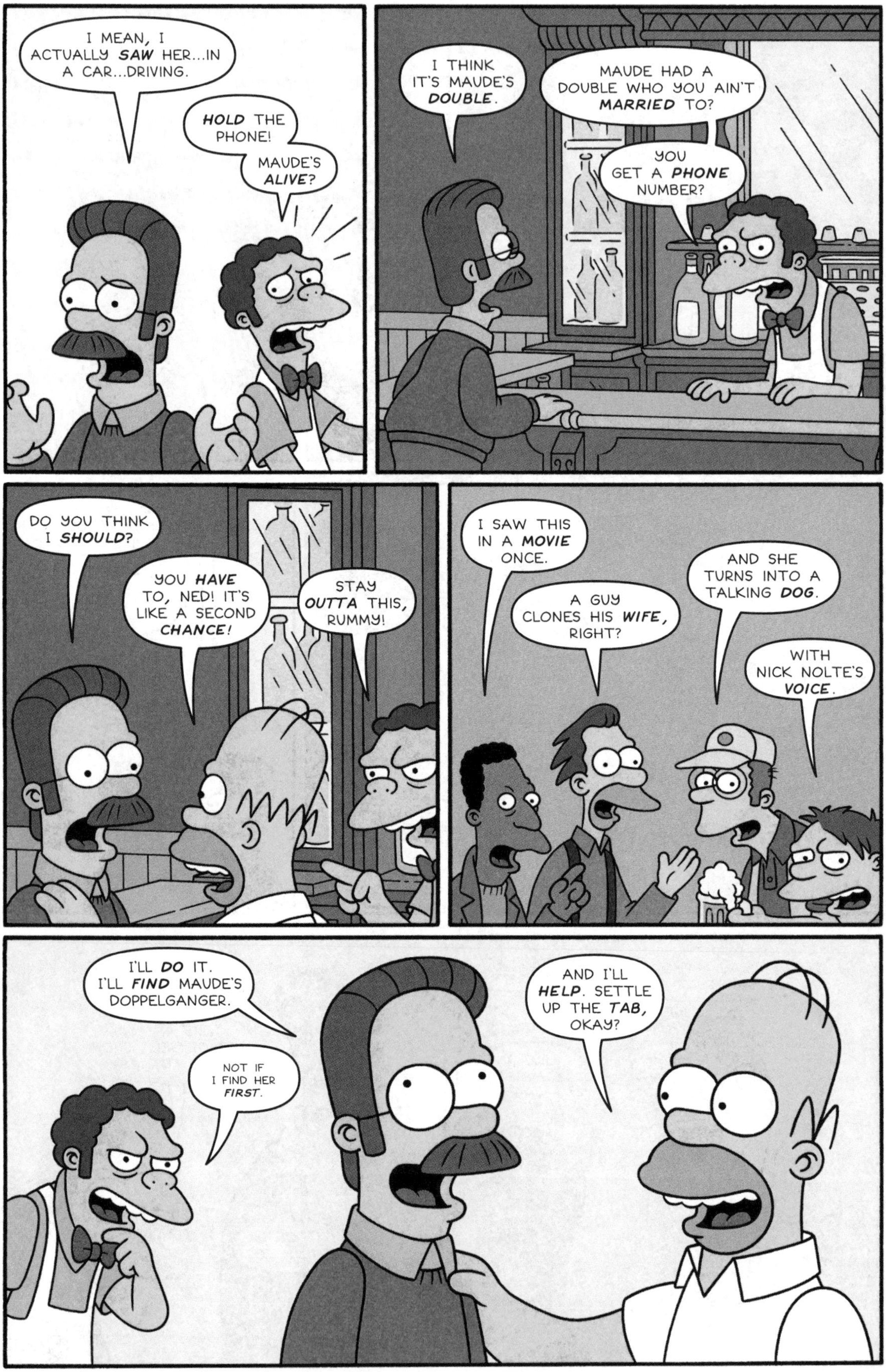
I MEAN, I ACTUALLY SAW HER...IN A CAR...DRIVING.
HOLD THE PHONE!
MAUDE'S ALIVE?
I THINK IT'S MAUDE'S DOUBLE.
MAUDE HAD A DOUBLE WHO YOU AIN'T MARRIED TO?
YOU GET A PHONE NUMBER?
DO YOU THINK I SHOULD?
YOU HAVE TO, NED! IT'S LIKE A SECOND CHANCE!
STAY OUTTA THIS, RUMMY!
I SAW THIS IN A MOVIE ONCE.
A GUY CLONES HIS WIFE, RIGHT?
AND SHE TURNS INTO A TALKING DOG.
WITH NICK NOLTE'S VOICE.
I'LL DO IT. I'LL FIND MAUDE'S DOPPELGANGER.
NOT IF I FIND HER FIRST.
AND I'LL HELP. SETTLE UP THE TAB, OKAY?

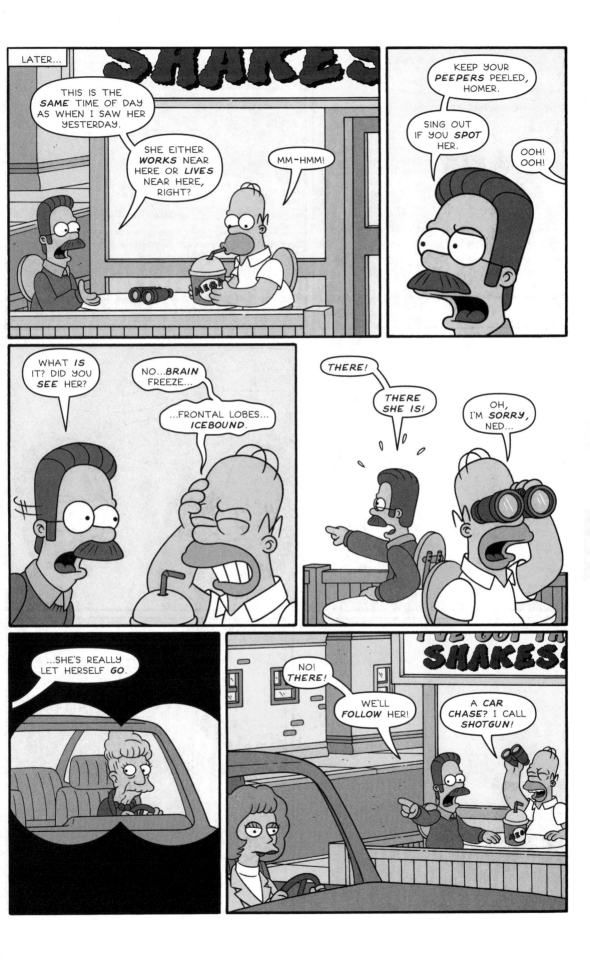

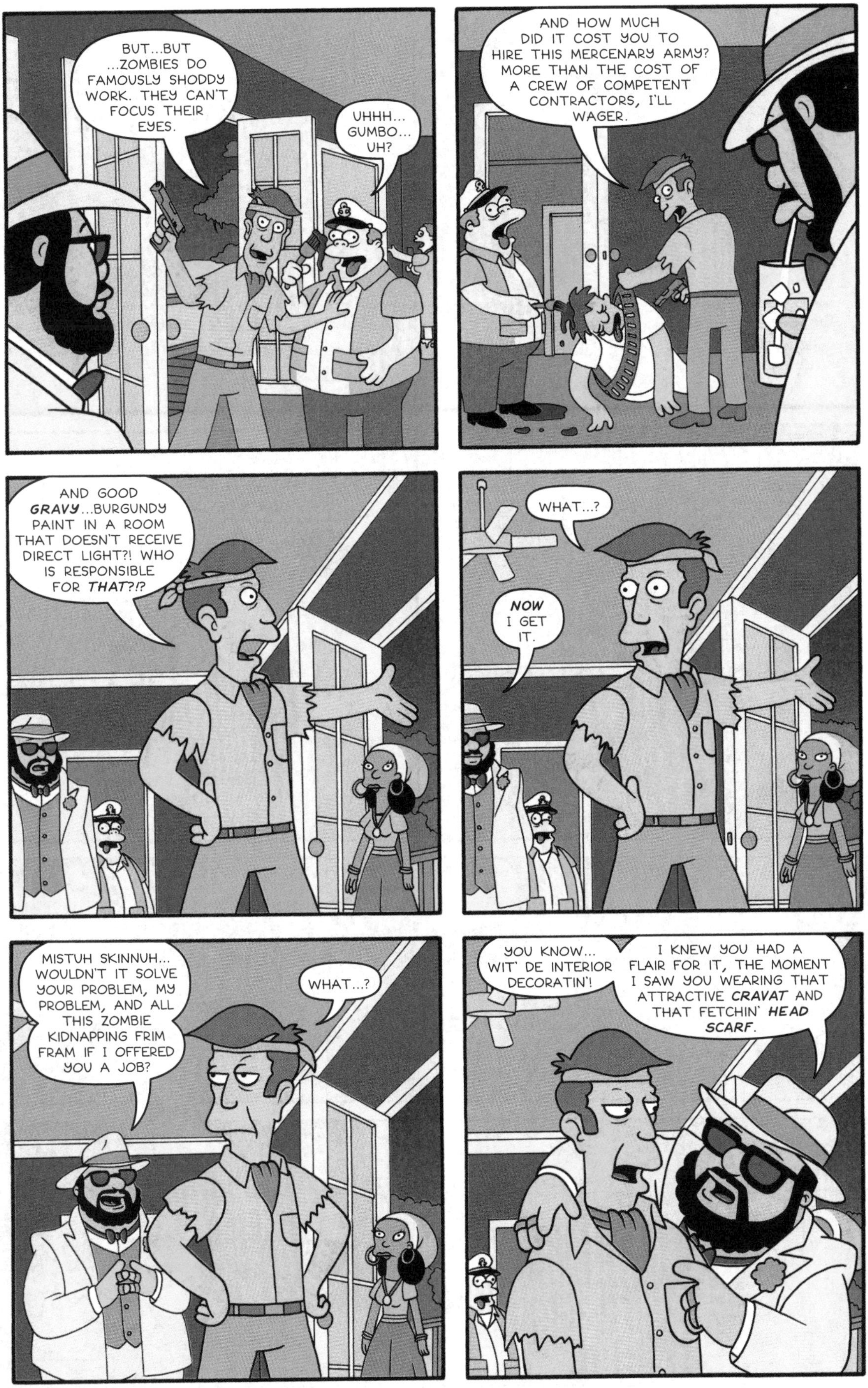

BUT...BUT ...ZOMBIES DO FAMOUSLY SHODDY WORK. THEY CAN'T FOCUS THEIR EYES.
UHHH... GUMBO... UH?
AND HOW MUCH DID IT COST YOU TO HIRE THIS MERCENARY ARMY? MORE THAN THE COST OF A CREW OF COMPETENT CONTRACTORS, I'LL WAGER.
AND GOOD GRAVY...BURGUNDY PAINT IN A ROOM THAT DOESN'T RECEIVE DIRECT LIGHT?! WHO IS RESPONSIBLE FOR THAT?!?
WHAT...?
NOW I GET IT.
MISTUH SKINNUH... WOULDN'T IT SOLVE YOUR PROBLEM, MY PROBLEM, AND ALL THIS ZOMBIE KIDNAPPING FRIM FRAM IF I OFFERED YOU A JOB?
WHAT...?
YOU KNOW... WIT' DE INTERIOR DECORATIN'!
I KNEW YOU HAD A FLAIR FOR IT, THE MOMENT I SAW YOU WEARING THAT ATTRACTIVE CRAVAT AND THAT FETCHIN' HEAD SCARF.

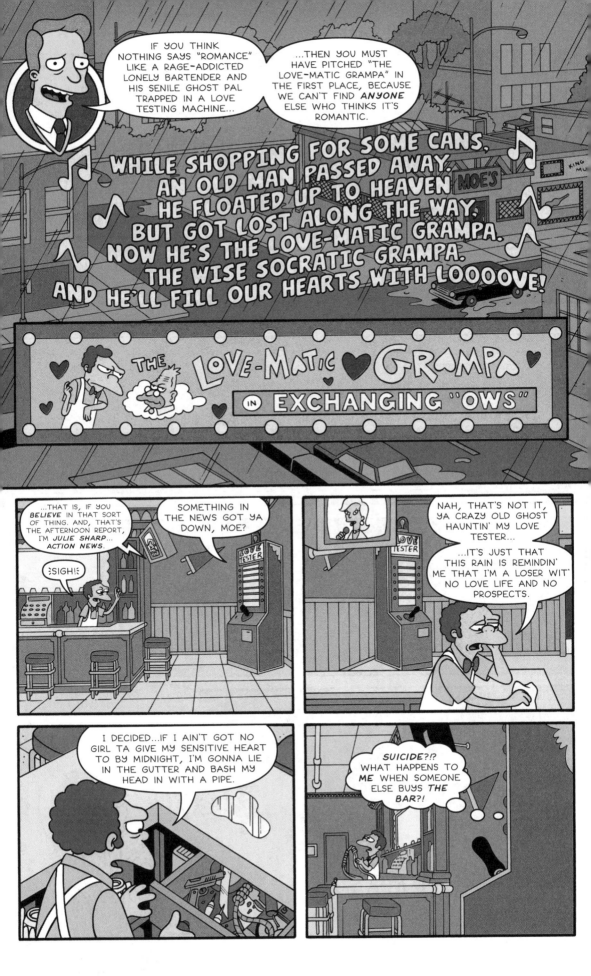

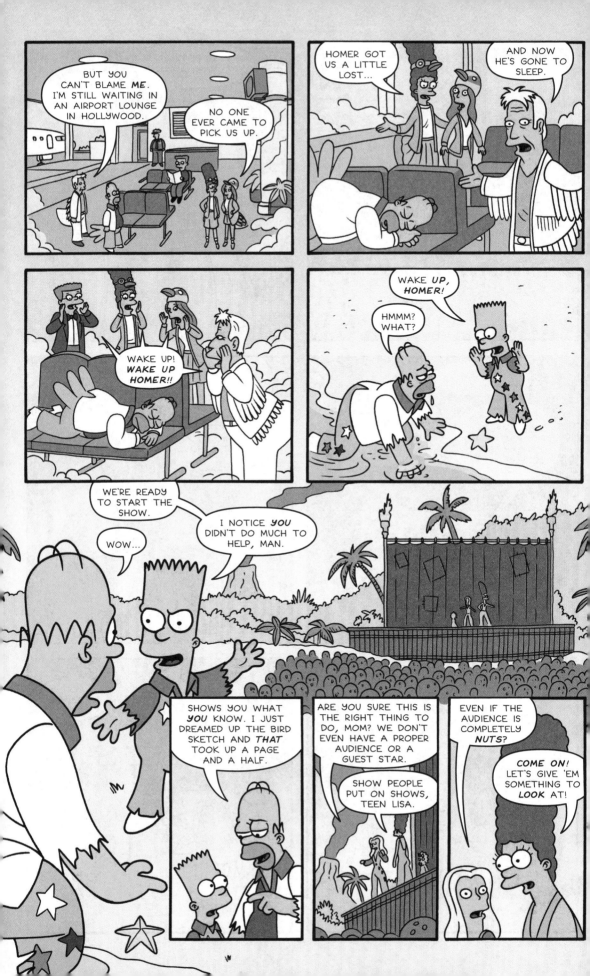

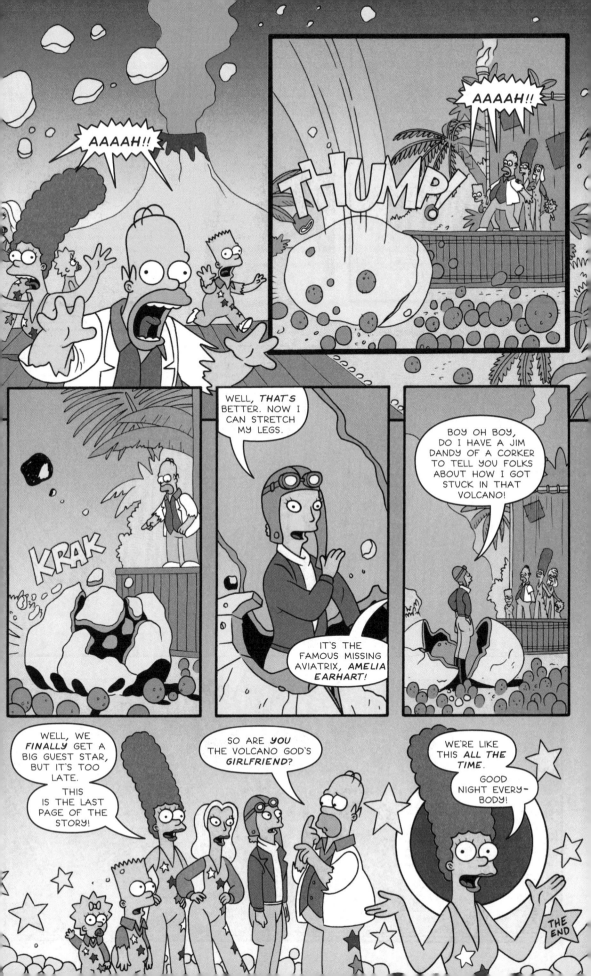

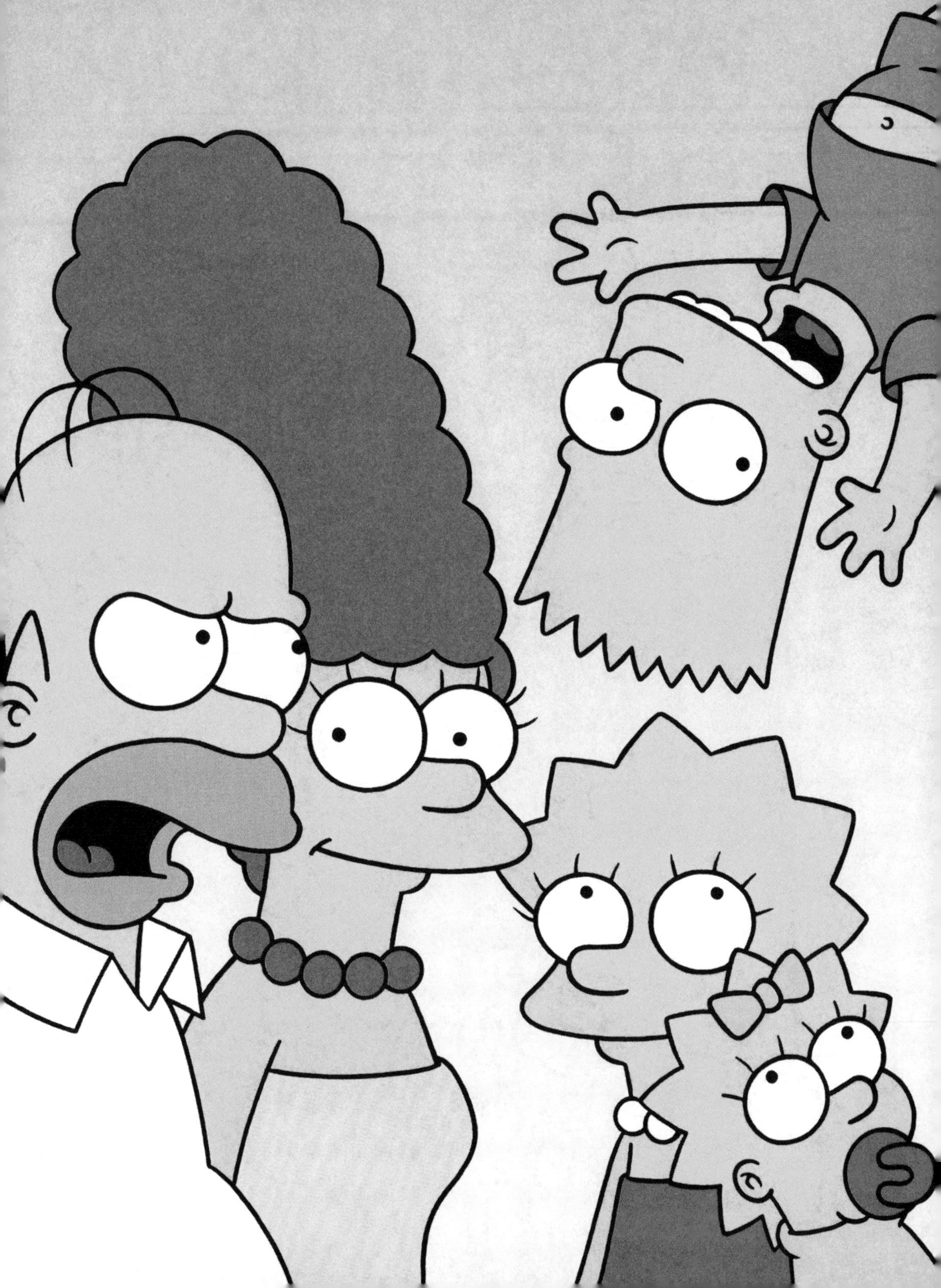

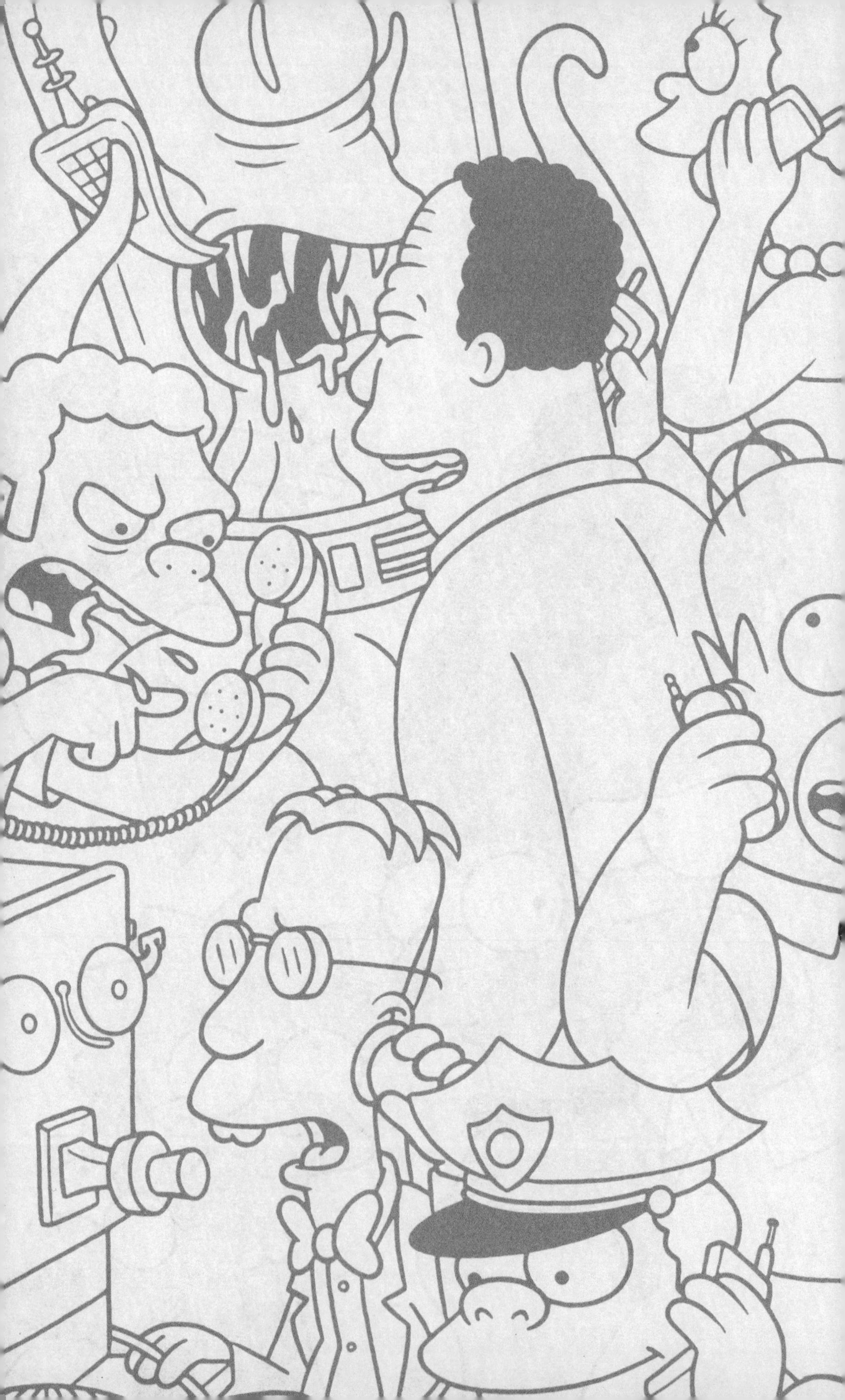